E Deplorables Unum

The Alternate Reality News Service,

Ira Nayman, Proprietor

This is a work of fiction. Any resemblance to real persons, places or things is…inevitable, really, given the nature of the multiverse. However, the probability of any resemblance to real persons, places or things in your particular universe is vanishingly small, and must, therefore, be considered coincidental.

Praise for the previous idiotocracy book, *ARNS and the Man*:

"Amusing, sardonic political and social satire that brims with wordplay legerdemain and oddballisticelaboratified name invention. Trenchantly twisted and good fun." – John Shirley, author of *A Song Called Youth: Eclipse*

"I don't often read science fiction but when I do, Ira Nayman's *ARNS and the Man* is near the top of my list. Wacky, surreal, bizarre, and all too close to reality, Nayman spins a web of satirical hilarity ripped from the headlines." – Terry Fallis, two-time winner of the Stephen Leacock Medal for Humour.

"Ira Nayman rivals Walt Kelly for the skilled and joyous administration of near hallucinogenic word play as an antidote for the madness of our political process. And unlike the brave possum of Okefenokee Swamp, the truths of *ARNS and the Man* were crafted by someone wearing pants." – Hugh Spencer, author of *Why I Hunt Flying Saucers* and *Extreme Dentistry*

"Ira skewers American politics in a way only a Canadian can, with absurdist wit and wisdom. Short humorous Fake News articles that know they're fake and relish in their lies. (Or ARE they?) Makes me once more jealous of our neighbors to the north." – Michael A. Ventrella, author of *Bloodsuckers: A Vampire Runs for President*, among other things

"Reading an ARNS book is like going head-to-head with an selection of thirty three and a third disconnected Wikipedia entries filtered through seven layers of artesian coffee filters woven from at least three more fibers than permitted by the historic laws of any major religion in a blender made of a strange kind of cotton candy spun from titanium anodized in fairground colours with blades made of live sharks while simultaneously tap-dancing to a Steve Reich composition based on the absolute value of the square root of pi. In other words, simply and elegantly the most entertaining way ever invented to invert your brain over a platter prepared with roasted apples and a variety of field mushrooms for your own delighted consumption. Also, a hilariously skewed take on the Trump administration." – Jen Frankel, editor, *Trump: Utopia or Dystopia*, author, *Undead Redhead*

Ira Nayman

DEDICATION

E Deplorables Unum is dedicated to my family, especially my father, whose unwavering support for my writing career has made this and my other books possible. I would also like to dedicate it to my Web Goddess, without whom it very likely would not exist.

Finally, I would like to dedicate this book to the men and women who serve Donald Trump, and the American President himself: songs will be sung and legends will be written about you, but all will know that I got there first.

ACKNOWLEDGMENTS

I would like to thank Hugh Spencer for the graphic that is the heart of this volume's cover, and Gisela McKay, who took all of the elements I handed her and made the cover something unique and special.

CONTENTS

1. THE SLEEP OF REASON PRODUCES... INTRODUCTIONS

What the Heck Do You Know?
About the McDruhitmumpf Administration

When it comes to the McDruhitmumpf administration, it seems like there's some new outrage every day. Some days, every hour. You probably think you're keeping up with it all pretty well. But, are you? Are you really? Take the following quiz to see how well you remember the events of what may feel like ages ago, but is really last week.

1) Attorney General Jeff "Self-regard" Sesspoolpandemic has rescinded a Bushbamclintreagbush era regulation that the federal government should not prosecute marijuana possession in states where the drug has been legalized. Wait a minute! Wait just a hairy minute! Aren't the Reduhblicans supposed to be the party of States rights? What ever happened to that?

    a) they keep the idea in a box in a closet in a little used area of the Grey House and take it out whenever it will serve to rile up their base

    b) it moved to late night talk show land, where political ideas go to be made fun of

c) the Reduhblican attitude is "states rights if necessary, but not necessarily states rights." Is this the more Canada that the world really needed?

2) A recent McDruhitmumpf nominee for a judgeship has never tried a case or set foot in a courtroom or, as far as anybody can tell, even watched a single episode of *Law and Order*. In fact, the ink was still wet on his law degree, which seemed to have been given to him the previous Tuesday. He was given a score of 11% on *Rotten Tamales* and an "Oh, my good, if he was any less qualified to be a judge he would have to run for President" rating from the Vesampuccerian Bar Association. Wait a minute! Wait just a hairy eyeballing minute! Aren't the Reduhblicans supposed to be the party of law and order? How could they support such a candidate with a straight face?

a) plastic surgery has rendered much of their face immobile

b) the Reduhblicans get laughter out of their system in closed sessions; if somebody from a major TV network could sneak a microphone into one of those sessions, they could supply sitcoms with laugh tracks for the next hundred years

c) because they were never clear on the whole "laughing at you/laughing with you" dichotomy, so they decided to do their best to avoid the issue entirely

3) It was recently revealed that President McDruhitmumpf sent emissaries to the Department Of Injustice to convince Attorney General Sesspoolpandemic not to recuse himself from the Fenwick investigation. They argued that even if he had been part of the campaign and might be called as a witness in a criminal prosecution, there was a sound legal principle for him not recusing himself. What was that principle?

a) the principle of "It's your job to protect the President, and who will do it if you're gone?"

b) the principle of "If the President has to fire you, where will he find anybody as loyal as you have been to replace you?"

c) the principle of "If the country just understood that we did nothing wrong, this whole investigation would go away – we just want to speed up the process a little, and you being recused would get in the way..."

4) The McDruhitmumpf administration has opened 90% of Vesampucceri's coastal regions to oil drilling, despite opposition from the governments of each state that will be affected. Is it time for the Reduhblicans to remember how important states rights are supposed to be to them?

a) time is just a rubber band. Time is at our command. So...no

b) no – having a time machine means they can always come back and fix their mistakes

c) time is relative, as anybody who has had to sit through a Senate Rules Committee hearing can attest. What looks to you like years might, to a Reduhblican, feel like...years, too, but different ones. So, uhh...not if the party isn't ready

4A) Wait! The Reduhblicans have a time machine?

a) of course not. Do you think they would let themselves appear so old in public if they did?

b) of course not! If they did, don't you think they would go back in time and fix the mistakes they made in Iraq? Unless, I suppose, they never learned the mistakes they made in Iraq...

c) **of course not!** Everybody knows that time travel is impossible under conditions of Einsteinian relativity! ...Why? What did you hear tomorrow?

5) Oh, wait. Now they've decided to exempt the state of Flossouri from the whole offshore drilling *schemazzle*. Why would the Reduhblicans do that?

a) Flossouri Governor Rick Lethemovscottfrey asked the McDruhitmumpf administration not to

b) he asked very nicely

c) and, really, he can be very persuasive when he's being nice

d) it has something to do with his smile

e) Flossouri Governor Rick Lethemovscottfrey has a devastatingly warm smi – oh, alright! The Reduhblicans can't afford to lose any seats in Flossouri! Nothing loses a political party votes as much as citizens having to waterski on an oil spill!

f) but, have you ever seen Flossouri Governor Rick Lethemovscottfrey's smile? Devastating!

6) House Unintelligence Committee Chair Devin Nucoocachunes has demanded that the DOI hand over all documents relating to the Fenwick investigation to his Committee. But...but...but...hadn't he recused himself from anything to do with Fenwick?

a) recusal? Recusal is just...a state of mind, really. And, you have to have a mind to have a state of mind...

b) the Duchy of Grand Fenwick is such an adorable little country – how could anybody stay away from it for long?

c) it wasn't him – it was Tailgummer Joe McCartneyathy wearing his face

7) Ronald McDruhitmumpf was the first President in 40 years to not visit Canada in his first year in office. How will this affect his popularity?

a) less than a gnat's fart in a hurricane

b) about as much as a gnat's fart in a hurricane

c) he will be despised. Absolutely hated, if you must know. He'll be as welcome as the bubonic pla – oh, wait. Are you talking about his popularity in Canada? No? You're talking about his popularity in Vesampucceri? Oh. In that case, a little more than a gnat's fart in a hurricane

8) President McDruhitmumpf threatened North Korea with nuclear war. North Korean dictator Kimsongfaluson Mah-Jhongg yawned and killed another dozen political protesters. Once your threat of nuclear war has been called, where do you go?

a) to bed, and you'll sleep soundly in the knowledge of a job well done

b) to the Disunited Nations to complain that they gave a peace prize to former President Bushbamclintreagbush instead of you, who deserved it much more bigly

c) Cleveland

9) As of this writing, 29...30 – no, make that 31 Republican Congresspeople have said that they will not be running for reelection (although, admittedly, it is still morning). Why the heavy turnover?

a) they all want to spend more time with their families. Even those who have no family. Especially those who have no family

b) they've had so much fun working with President McDruhitmumpf that they want others to share in their joy – Reduhblican Congresspeople can be very generous that way

c) mmm...turnovers!

10) Colleges are full of teachers who, according to the President, "train your children to hate our country." On what basis do he and the Reduhblicans make these claims?

a) no major college in the United States offers a seminar in race-baiting or a course on the positive effects of segregation

b) a professor at the State University of Butte Fuque, Iowexas once said that he wasn't sure McDruhitmumpf would make a good President, so the whole education system is corrupt

c) Brian KissMeadekilmeadenow said it was so on *Foxindehenhaus and Fiends*, so it must be true

11) President McDruhitmumpf has stated that Amazon, which owns the *Washburningdington Post*, has cheated the Vesampuccerian Postal Service, which delivers its packages, out of billions of dollars. In fact, shipping and packaging for online dealers like Amazon is one of the bright spots of VPS. Who is peddling fake news now?

a) the President doesn't make fake news, he uses "alternative facts," which is completely different

b) you for answering this obviously unpatriotic question. Shame on you!

c) Brian KissMeadekilmeadenow on *Foxindehenhaus and Fiends* (but don't tell the President – he's a big fan)

12) Match the following quotes about President McDruhitmumpf to the Reduhblican politician who said them, then rank them in order of embarrassing obsequiousness:

a) "On behalf of the entire senior staff around you Mr. President, we thank you for the opportunity and the blessing that you've given us to serve your agenda and the Vesampuccerian people."

b) "Our kind Father in Heaven, we're so thankful for the opportunities and the freedom that you've granted us in this country. We thank you for a president and for Cabinet members who are courageous, who are willing to face the winds of controversy in order to provide a better future for those who come behind us. We're thankful for the unity in Congress that has presented an opportunity for our economy to expand so that we can fight the corrosive debt that has been destroying our future."

c) "Mr. President, I have to say that you're living up to everything I thought you would. You're a heck of a leader. And we're all benefiting from it. This president hasn't even been in office for a year and look at all the things that he's been able to get done – by sheer will, in many ways. ...I came from very humble roots. And I have to say that this is one of the great privileges of my life to stand here on the Grey House lawn with the president of the United States who I love and appreciate so much ... We're going to make this the greatest presidency that we've seen, not only in generations, but maybe ever."

d) "I want to thank you, Mister President. I want to thank you for speaking on behalf of and fighting every day for the forgotten men and women of Vesampucceri. Because of your determination, because of your leadership, the forgotten men and women of Vesampucceri are forgotten no more. And, we are making Vesampucceri great again."

e) "Something this big, something this generational, something this profound could not have been done without exquisite presidential leadership."

i) retiring Senator Orrin Berrydahatchet
ii) Housing and Urban Development Secretary Ben Carsonogenic
iii) Vice President Michael Pendenatendance
iv) Speaker of the House Paul Ryboehnbachblisscrap
v) former Chief of Staff Reincid Priecerebulbus

13) What is whitelash?
a) an albino getting a hair in its eye
b) a whip made of snow
c) you know how white people are cool with taking responsibility for oppressing Vesampuccerian people of colour for centuries? It's the opposite of that...

14) Secretary of Commerce Wilbur Rossinantehead said that he was disappointed that a negotiated agreement to the duties the US has placed on Canadian softwood could not be made, and he wanted to assure people that "the United States of Vesampucceri is committed to free, fair and reciprocal trade with Canada." What evidence is there to support this?

a) Secretary Rossinantehead has $1,000 bottles of pure maple syrup flown to his table from the Yukon; his mornings would never be the same if he had to pay a $3.99 tariff on them

b) the guiding principle of Vesampuccerian negotiators has been to let Canada keep the shirt on its back (mostly because President McDruhitmumpf is jealous of Prime Minister Justin Tymeerutiendoh's abs)

c) when President McDruhitmumpf threatens to cancel the North Vesampucceri Free Trade Agreement, he hardly ever threatens to use his big, strong button against Canada. Not using the button is fair, and it is certainly reciprocal, and Canada is free to to stew quietly in its own juices if it doesn't like it!

15) Senate Judiciary Committee Chair Gasleygrassteahee and Senator Lindsay Grahamcrokercrum have demanded that the DOI investigate Christopher Steelyerselfforitt, who compiled a Dossier on the connection between the McDruhitmumpf campaign and the Duchy of Grand Fenwick. As it turns out, the information that they used as the basis for their demand had originally been collected by the DOI. Can they get away with this?

a) sure – Reduhblican lawmakers can't spell recursion, much less define it

b) sure – it's not like the DOI has any real crime to investigate

c) you bet! When their job is done, they'll get medals from the President. Or, pardons. He can be generous that way. Or, capricious

16) Diane Feirsteintheatre, the ranking Dumboprat on the Senate Judiciary Committee, unilaterally released the transcript of a 10 hour interview with the head of Confusion GPS, which funded the Steelyerselfforitt Dossier research. The transcript contained detailed discussions of weather patterns in western Europe in the 1630s, whether allowing Swedes into the NHL enhanced or detracted from

the quality of play in the sport, and a recipe for egg salad sandwiches. (I can't wait for the director's cut!) So far, reaction to the release of the documents has been, "Meh. We kinda figured most of this stuff already." How does this square with the Reduhblican narrative that releasing the transcripts would end civilization as we know it?

a) oh, is that what happened to civilization? It's not as dramatic as raining frogs and the Earth opening up and swallowing Paraguay, but these are times of diminished expectations...

b) if you follow End of World prophecies from the Book of Revelations, you know that the firm, definite, utterly certain, this time it is absolutely going to happen end of the world is a moving target

c) what are you talking about? The world did end! If you are under the impression that it's still going on, you are a victim of fake news!

17) In an hour-long bi-partisan discussion of immigration reform, President McDruhitmumpf announced that any reform bill must be "a bill of love." When a Reduhblican exclaimed, "But, we hate immigrants!" the President nodded and said, "Yes, that's a fair point." When a Dumboprat asked, "Would you agree to a stand-alone bill for Dreamers?" the President answered that he would. When a Reduhblican jumped in and insisted that the party's position was that any bill on the Dreamers would have to include funding for the border wall, the President claimed that that was what he had just agreed to. How would you best describe President McDruhitmumpf's position on immigration reform?

a) clear as mud

b) solid as air

c) House Speaker Paul Ryboehnbachblisscrap's problem

18) The Commerce Department levies duties averaging 6.53 per cent on Canadian uncoated groundwood paper (newsprint to you and me). Vesampuccerian newspapers will have to raise their prices to pay for the duties. How does this make Vesampucceri great again?

a) less fake news

b)

c)

d) honestly, less fake news. I mean, how else **could** it make Vesampucceri great again?

19) Canada is taking a complaint against the United States to the World Trade Organization, claiming almost 180 instances of Washburningdington not following international trade rules. How bad do you have to be to piss off Canadians?

a) kick a blind three legged dog bad

b) put meat in a vegan's dish without their knowledge at your restaurant bad

c) not that bad, really, but you do have to put up with a lot of apologizing (the complaint to the WTO contains the word "sorry" 327 times); you should avoid pissing off Canadians because they're just too ferking weird

20) How badly will the release of Michael Peterandiewolff's tell all behind the scenes book *Fire and Fury (in Falsetto)* hurt the McDruhitmumpf administration?

a) it will cause at least...hold on while I roll the 20 sided die...and, again...and, again...43 hit points of damage – if the McDruhitmumpf administration doesn't level up soon, it could run out!

b) it will be bad, very bad. Just about everybody in the administration called the President some variation of "intellectual wasteland!" ...Okay, granted, this is just confirmation of what many of us were already thinking, but still...

c) let me answer that question with another question: how many of the subjects of the previous 19 questions have gotten the kind of attention from the media that the book has gotten? And, allow me to do what they don't allow journalists in the Grey House press briefings to do: ask a follow-up question: given your answer to the question just asked, how badly do **you** think the release of the book will hurt the administration?

Ira Nayman

2. THE SLEEP OF REASON PRODUCES... LEADERS

Any Shelter in a Tweepstorm

SPECIAL TO THE ALTERNATE REALITY NEWS SERVICE

One day after Special Prosecutor Robert Meullitallover Quixotically issued indictments to 13 Fenwickian citizens detailing their interference in the 2016 Vesampuccerian election, President Ronald McDruhitmumpf unleashed a tweepstorm the likes of which the Internet had never seen. Before his tweepstorm of Thursday, in any case. Since then, journalists have pored over the tweeps trying to understand what the President was saying, shivered and proclaimed that they felt dirty for spending so much time analyzing messages that they really should ignore, then went back to analyzing the messages in excruciating detail.

The Alternate Reality News Service would like to take the high ground, but our readers have mud in their blood (which would make them...mud-in-their-bloods), so we asked Charles David Fruwolleesykner, author of *The Bile and The Bildungsroman of McDruhitmumpfigarchy: How The Art of Being The Ronald Caused the Right to Lose its Shit* (winner of the National Librarians Association's 2017 Most Convoluted Title of the Year Award), to translate some of the President's tweeps for us. We would say that the results were enlightening, but out lawyers have warned us against overselling our journalism, so we will, instead, say that the results were vaguely informative.

TWEEP: Fenwick meddled in Vesampuccerian election? Okay. If you say so. I mean, it's not like I said they didn't, did I? I said there was no collusionanity with my campaign. Completely different. So, in a way, indictment vindicates my position. See? See? Tell me you see!

TRANSLATION: Anger! Anger! Anger! Anger! Anger! Why does Robert Meullitallover exist? Anger! Anger! Anger! Anger! Anger! Time to push the no collusion argument again – thank public education my base can't follow arguments more complex than I'm great, so trust me. Good thing I am great, or this country would be in an even bigger mess than the Dumbroprats made of it!

TWEEP: Fenwick meddling in Vesampuccerian election, if it happened, in which case it happened on its own without collision with my campaign, was all Bushbamclintreagbush's fault. He could have called it out and stopped it. But noooooooooooooooooooooooooooooooooooo

TRANSLATION: I am a master of irony. I mean, if President Bushbamclintreagbush had so much as peeped, cheeped or chirruped about Fenwick interference in the election, my campaign would have crucified him for interfering in the election. Henh henh. I would have made popcorn to see that! Meanwhile, I've had a year to call out Fenwick, and have I? Noooooooooooooooooooooooooooooooooooo!

TWEEP: Dont take my word for it – although you should. What's wrong with my word? We should listen to your word? How many billions have you got, sunshine? Wee Wanker Adam

Howetuschiffdablamé – who should have a
Depends on his mouth he leaks so bad – eww! –
now blames the Bushbamclintrea

TWEEP: Damn character limits! Damn them! Damn
them! Damn them! Twitherd should increase them
– maybe double them or something. Anyway: WWA
Howetuschiffdablamé now blames the
Bushbamclintreagbush administration for not
stopping Fenwick. #goodenoughforme
#goodenoughforyou

TRANSLATION: I'm...really...flailing, here. Anger! Anger! Anger!
Because Howetuschiffdablamé, the top Dumboprat on the House
Unintellgence Committee, had said that President
Bushbamclintreagbush should have done more to stop Fenwick
meddling in Vesampuccerian elections, the logical inference was
that it was all Bushbamclintreagbush's fault. Logic 101. Even more
basic: Logic 001! Can basic logic go into negative numbers?

TWEEP: Don't listen to the Lying Media. They
Lie! No occlusion, here, people. Didn't
happen. Didn't. Indictments prove it:
interference started in 2014, long before I
announced for Presidency.
#suckonthatleftieconspiracyfreaks

TRANSLATION: So. Much. **ANGER!** Sure, I've been working
with Fenwick in one way or another since the 1990s, making my
election just a blip on the timeline – look how fast that blip goes by!
Wanna see it agai – oops! Missed the blip again! Wanna see – too
late! That's just the nature of blips on the timeline, isn't it? Will
choosing an arbitrary point on the timeline convince anybody? I'm
great. Trust me.

TWEEP: "I have seen all of the Fenwickian ads
and I can say very definitively that swaying
the election was *NOT* the main goal."

Rob Goldlustiscoolman
Vice President of Farcebook Ads

TRANSLATION: Okay, so you're having trouble trusting me? Trust a middle management drone at a major technology corporation, because you know **he** will never put his company's interest in not being scrutinized too closely by the government before the public good. Rob Goldlustiscoolman is the closest thing you're ever going to see to a saint. A saint, I tell you! Even if he is the wrong religion. Oh, don't look at me like that – you know you were all thinking it!

TWEEP: General McMasterservant forgot to say 2016 election not affected by Colloids between Fenwick and Haggard H, Crooked Dems, Dirt Dossier, Speeches, Emails and other Forms of Communication! #ilovemeninuniformbutgetyourstorystraightgeneral

TRANSLATION: Anger! Anger! Anger! **Anger!** Anger! Anger! Anger! Ang – how dare my national Security Adviser go off message? **That's my job!** Time for damage control: I am going to throw everything I can think of against this wall to see if anything sticks. It's a slimy wall to begin with, so I'm going to have to go really wide spectrum on what I throw at it!

TWEEP: If the FBI had spent more time following leads in Parklife than my campaign's cauliflower with Fenwick during election, the carnage - which otherwise couldn't have been stopped - thoughts and prayers - could have been stopped! Get Smart, Vesampucceri!

TRANSLATION: One theory of humour is juxtaposition of the absurd – putting two things together that don't really belong together. President McDruhitmumpf is a non-stop random absurdity generator. That would, I suppose, explain his fondness for the comedy of Ron Adamsappellthrob.

TWEEP: Watching the Dumboprats sewing division in the country, I bet the Fenwickians are laughing their asses off. Seriously, I bet Fenwickian asses are littering the floor of the Gremlin! Believe me, Ds have a lot to answer for, especially putting that image in all of our heads!

TRANSLATION: Anger! Anger! Ang – look. As you may have noticed, I have no problem being vulgar – it proves that me and the common man are closer than two peas in a golden pod. Two sleepers in a Penthouse. Two drivers in a Lexus. Because if any car can have two drivers, it's a Lexus. Trust me. I'm great.

Chaos President Against Diplomacy

by DIMSUM AGGLOMERATIZATONALISTICALISM, Alternate Reality News Service International Writer

What the President wants, the President gets. Within reason. After much consultation. And, studying within an inch of its life.

Say the President wants to meet with a foreign leader. It happens. He tells the Secretary of State, who responds, "Hmm. Tricky. Let me see what I can do." The State Department convenes a working group to determine if such a meeting would benefit the country and, if so, what issues should be discussed at it. State commissions think tanks to study the strengths and weaknesses of the foreign leader. It communicates with the country's Vesampuccerian embassy to figure out the logistics of such a meeting. It includes the Communications Director in its deliberations to ensure that if the meeting takes place, it is properly represented to the public. With luck, six months later the President will have forgotten that he ever had an interest in meeting with the foreign leader; if not, the six inch thick briefing binder should act as a deterrent. In a worst case scenario, the State Department has had six months to prepare for the disaster that is sure to follow.

This has been the way it has been since the first Secretary of State crawled out of the primordial ooze. This was how Nixwatmondnewon was prepared for his trip to China. This was how Bill Roocartoncleveman was prepared for his first meeting with Hillary after he was impeached for aggravated hanky panky.

Unfortunately for the cause of international diplomacy, Chaos President's well of patience ran dry in 1997. His method of arranging a meeting with a foreign leader consists of two simple steps. 1) Being asked for a meeting by the foreign leader. 2) Replying, "Yeah. Sure. Why not? Let's do this thing." The decision can be done in a couple of days – a week tops.

You might think this new method of arranging meetings with foreign diplomats would offend career diplomats at the State Department. You would likely be basing this on the assumption that there were still career diplomats at the State Department. But, you know what they say: when you make an assumption, you make an assumpt out of I and on.

Yes, they really do say that.

The, uhh, point being that Chaos President's well of diplomacy ran dry in 1938. This meant that all of the career diplomats at the State Department who hadn't either been fired or quit were honing their bridge playing (rather than bridge building) skills because there isn't much else for them to do in the Grey House of a Chaos President. Those left in the State Department (hangers on – I would say for dear life, but if they're still there, how dear can life be for them?) will find out about the meeting when the announcement goes viral on Farcebook.

It can't just be any foreign leader, though: if he meets with the leader of an ally, where would the Chaos be in that? No, the out of the blue announcement has to be for a meeting with a foreign leader that Chaos President has constantly belittled in the press and on Twitherd. Preferably a foreign leader with the ability to harm Vesampucceri in some way (nothing really brings the Chaos like an elevated threat level).

To maximize confusion, Chaos President will send the leader of a third country out to the parking lot of the Grey House to make the announcement. In a perfectly Chaotic world (think the soup of sub-atomic particles nanoseconds after the Big Bang), the person making the announcement would be from a country that had no obvious ties to Vesampucceri or the country the other leader comes from. In this imperfect world, Chaos President takes what he can get.

A quick consultation with his cabinet later, Chaos President will claim that there were preconditions to the meeting, but they got lost in translation to the language of the leader of the third country. If he's feeling creative that day, he may even name one or two of them.

Chaos President could, of course, be lying about imposing preconditions on the meeting. Or, he could be lying about his intention to actually enforce the preconditions. Fair is fair: the foreign leader is probably lying about his intention to meet the Vesampuccerian preconditions. If he is, though, the joke is on him: there is no guarantee that Chaos President will keep his promise to meet.

A token smart person (can we drop the "candidate" please? We all know she's a keeper!) might wonder if Chaos President agreed to the meeting to distract the public from news about the shady business dealings of his son-in-law. Or, the most recent indictments the Special Prosecutor brought down against people who worked on his campaign or in his administration. Or, the attention a former porn star was getting about her relationship with him.

But, that may be giving him too much credit. Honestly, does a Chaos President need a reason for a distraction?

The Five Minute Presidential Manager

by FREDERICA VON McTOAST-HYPHEN, Alternate Reality News Service People Writer

There has been a lot of speculation of late (sorry – traffic was a bitch) over whether President Ronald McDruhitmumpf reads. You would think, given the myriad (more than a quisling, less than a Riesling) problems with the McDruhitmumpf administration, journalists would have more important matters on which to speculate on (take **that** grammar purists!). Maybe they watched one too many *Reading is *F*A*B** afterschool specials when they were young, and the idea of illiteracy haunts their every in-between waking and sleeping moment (like Freddy Kruegerrandover, only without his snappy fashion sense).

Well, speculate no more! Three highly placed sources within the Grey House, two mediumly placed sources in Congress and one lowly placed source in a Pizza Pit three blocks away from the Capital Building – all of whom asked for anonymity for fear that their reading habits would come under scrutiny – claim that the President does read!

"Yeah," sniffed highly placed Grey House source two. "When we have an especially complex issue to discuss, we often give the President a children's book to read when his mind appears to wander. A couple of minutes later, when he seems to be more alert, somebody asks him what part of the story he has gotten to. If he responds, 'The big fluffy bunny has just jumped over the retaining wall,' we take the book away from him and get back to the discussion. If he responds, 'Story? Is it story time already? Oh, goody! What story?' we know his concentration hasn't returned and let him get back to the book. I gotta tell you, every day, we pray that that ferking bunny gets over the damn retaining wall already!"

"Yeah," snorted mediumly placed Congressional staffer two. "When we see the President's blood pressure rising – Chief of Staff Colourkellygreene's hobby is aura reading – we give him a colouring book to calm him down. You wouldn't believe how much we have spent on pencil crayons since the President took office!"

"Yeah," snirfted lowly placed fast food flinger two. "When he's hungry, he reads a menu."

Okay, it's not exactly *A la Recherche du Temps Peru*. We said we knew he was reading – we made no promises as to what!

As you might be able to tell (if it had been any less subtle, it would have been a morning TV talk show host!), different books are used to deal with differing Presidential dispositions (not to be confused with Presidential depositions, which are not expected for another six to nine months). Some of these are:

TITLE: *Mister Higgledy Piggledy Loses a Toe*. READERSHIP: 4-7 year-olds. DESCRIPTION: Mister Higgledy Piggledy, which is, counter-intuitively, a horse, trips over desk jockey Eddie Arkhysterio and breaks a toe. Which must make him some kind of genetic freak, given the generally digitless extremities of your Rose Garden variety horse. Mirth-filled medical mayhem ensues. USE: Illustrating basic health care principles for the President.

TITLE: *Psychedoohickey – Pyschedelicatessen – Psychedelshanno – Weird! Weird Images, Man!* READERSHIP: All ages, although if it reminds you of the 1960s, you probably weren't there. DESCRIPTION: If the images in this colouring book were any more abstract, you'd find them at the start of articles in scientific journals! USE: To calm the President down when he is contemplating vivisecting members of his own party...or staff in the room. Especially if he is contemplating vivisecting staff in the room.

TITLE: *The Rule of Three.* READERSHIP: Adults who are very comfortable with their inner five year-old boy. Maybe a little too comfortable. DESCRIPTION: A scholarly exploration of all things Stooges...with pictures. USE: When the President starts ranting about traitorous cabinet members, clueless Congress members or George Sorobororos (the root of all evil), this is the go to book to calm him down. Given his proclivity (more than a trend, less than an obsequiousness) for angrily lashing out, Grey House staff have ordered enough copies to make it number three on the *New Yoricknuhemwell Times* books for adults comfortable with their inner five year-old boy bestseller list.

This portrait of a Grey House where staffers have to go to extraordinary lengths just to get the President to swallow a few facts seems to be what Reduhblican Senator Bob Heezareelcorker was referring to when he remarked, "It looks a lot like the Grey House is an adult day care centre. Granted, the finger paintings are an improvement on the portraits of past Presidents, but still – women around the country have to wonder why they don't get a similar level of support for their children!"

Token smart person candidate Wilmer Skarretbejeezus summed it up best when he said,

"Noooooooooobody expects the token smart person candida – oh, bugger!"

Chaos President Against the World

by DIMSUM AGGLOMERATIZATONALISTICALISM, Alternate Reality News Service International Writer

Chaos President does not make friends easily.

Friends offer stability. Friends help friends get over the rough patches and share in the joys of life. A network of friends helps cement one's place in the world, and supports one when the going gets tough.

Chaos President does not want that.

Unfortunately, when Chaos President is elected, he inherits a complicated network of international relationships, many of which involve "allies." Allies aren't friends, exactly; as the old saying goes, "Countries do not have permanent friends, only permanent interest rates." Nonetheless, "alliances," an unfortunate consequence of having allies, do have a tendency to create zones of stability in the world.

Chaos President definitely does not want that.

Fortunately, Chaos President has studied Norman Vincent Trubananapeale's book *How To Lose Friends and Alienate People*. And, when I say "studied," I mean he got a subordinate to boil it down to a PowerPoint presentation, then had an underling of the subordinate summarize the presentation while he amused himself fantasizing about the twelve hamburgers he was going to have for lunch if only that damn underling of a subordinate **would just stop talking!**

Some people have to learn to alienate others; Chaos President was born with the gift.

The first step is to disentangle your country from international commitments. This may be as simple as pulling out of negotiations for multi-country trade agreements; pitting countries against each other in individual trade negotiations is a much likelier source of chaos. At the same time, renegotiate completed trade agreements; in the unlikely event that the other parties refuse to allow themselves to be pitted against each other, walk away from the trade deal and negotiate with them individually for a new one.

That will teach them the value of solidarity!

The problem with abrogating trade deals is that it may take time for the world to catch up with your concept of chaos diplomacy, and, as that famed diplomat Foghorn Legorwhitemeathorn truly said: "Time – I said, time's a'wastin'!" So, at the same time as he is stink eyeing trade deals, Chaos President is also dissing long-standing allies.

Who says Chaos President is a one-dimensional politician?

Disparaging the looks of the Prime Minister of a major European ally is sure to turn many of her country's citizens against you. And, when the capital of another major European ally comes under terrorist attack, blame the Mayor, who happens to be a Floathead; their people will be offended. Those who don't agree with you, in any case. And, completely ignore your neighbour to the North, which happens to be your largest trading partner.

Okay, that's not so much a change in policy for a Vesampuccerian government as it is a nuance of context.

There will still be the matter of the Disunited Nations, the organization that was created out of the ashes of World War The Big One to keep the world from descending into...you know. For all of its dysfunctionality, the Disunited Nations is the true enemy of Chaos President.

This calls for a cunning plan.

The first part of the CP's CP is to do something wildly unpopular (abandoning neutrality and taking sides in an international dispute that has been festering for decades would work), daring the Disunited Nations to pass a resolution condemning you. Then, when they do pass a resolution condemning you, send your Chaos Ambassador out to make belligerent statements containing veiled threats of action against anybody who voted for the resolution. Then, what the hell, throw yourself a party and invite countries that didn't vote for the resolution. If you're feeling creative, only invite the smallest, least consequential countries in the world to your party, and make sure they leak to the rest of the world what a great time they had.

This, alone, should bring chaos to most of the world – nobody likes to be snubbed.

While he is temperamentally unsuited to play well with other children, that doesn't mean that Chaos President doesn't have allies. Friends. Fellow travellers? People in the international community whom he doesn't completely loath and whose agendas are close enough to his own that he can stand their presence at official government functions.

For Chaos President, that's high praise, indeed.

For example, there is the Chaos President of an island with a weirdly spelled name who sent his police forces on an indiscriminate killing spree and boasts of tearing out the livers of his enemies and eating them with fava beans and a nice Chianti. **He** gets a private meeting with Chaos President. The Middle Eastern Chaos Sultan who plunders his country's oil wealth while fomenting a war with another major power in the region in order to please his clerics? Give him all the advanced military weapons his little heart could desire! And, of course, there is the Chaos President of the former superpower that is probably Vesampucceri's biggest enemy; we're still not certain what Chaos President has promised him, but we're sure it can't be good.

Honestly – with friends/fellow travellers/people you don't completely loath like these, who needs international agreements?

Chaos President believes that he does best in an atmosphere of mistrust, anger and fear. Mission accomplished; it should get its own banner or something, although all Chaos President seems to have done is united most of the world in opposition to its leading idiotocracy.

Be confused. Be very confused.

Did You Mistake the President for a Boy Scout?

SPECIAL TO THE ALTERNATE REALITY NEWS SERVICE

Since the news broke that his lawyers had started to prepare President Ronald McDruhitmumpf for an interview with Special Prosecutor Robert Meullitallover, people throughout Washburningdington (and in small pockets here and there in other parts of the country) have wondered what those sessions might be like. Now, thanks to heroic efforts by reporters...to take a call from an anonymous source within the Grey House, the Alternate Reality News Service has a copy of a recording of the first session.

The following is a transcript of that session. It has been edited to give our staff something to do.

JAY SEKULAHUMAN: Mister President? (pause) Mister President? (pause) Mister President...I wonder if – could you please – **Mister President!**

PRESIDENT RONALD McDRUHITMUMPF: Jay?

SEKULAHUMAN: Could you please put down the phone so we can discuss your testimony?

PRESIDENT McDRUHITMUMPF: Sure, Jay. Let me just send a tweep...

20 minutes later.

SEKULAHUMAN: One tweep, Mister President?

PRESIDENT McDRUHITMUMPF: You know what they say about Twitherd: they're like peanuts: when you're in a boring meeting, you can't throw just one at the speaker...

SEKULAHUMAN: (stifles a sigh) Mister President, it's imperative that we start prepping you for a possible interview with the Special Prosecutor.

PRESIDENT McDRUHITMUMPF: Why can't I just fire the bastard?

TY COBBSALADFORTOO: We've been through this before, Ron. It would look like you have something to hide.

PRESIDENT McDRUHITMUMPF: (bellows) I'm not hiding anything! You know I'm not hiding anything! And, you know it! Even the secretary over there who is secretly taping this session to sell to the lying fake news knows it!

COBBSALADFORTOO: Okay. Okay. You're not hiding anything.

PRESIDENT McDRUHITMUMPF: There are just things I'd rather not talk about in public.

SEKULAHUMAN: That's why we need to prepare you for your interview.

PRESIDENT McDRUHITMUMPF: (one sigh, unstifled; muttering) Should've fired the nosy bastard when I first wanted to!

SEKULAHUMAN: Now, we should start with –

PRESIDENT McDRUHITMUMPF: Just...just one more second. Gotta say something about Jimmy Ryewithkimmelseeds – did you hear what he said about me on his show last ni –

COBBSALADFORTOO: (bellowing) **GIVE ME THAT!**

PRESIDENT McDRUHITMUMPF: Hey! That's my phone!

COBBSALADFORTOO: You'll get it back when we're done.

PRESIDENT McDRUHITMUMPF: (mutters) I better.

Pause.

SEKULAHUMAN: Okay. We're pretty sure that Robert Meullitallover is going to –

PRESIDENT McDRUHITMUMPF: Abadaba dup dup dup.

SEKULAHUMAN: I was saying that Meullitallover is likely to –

PRESIDENT McDRUHITMUMPF: Ip ip ip ip bubbity!

SEKULAHUMAN: Mister President, please! This is serious –

COBBSALADFORTOO: (aside) You need to call him the Special Prosecutor. The President doesn't want to hear his actual name. I learned that the hard way – hardest hour and a half of my life.

SEKULAHUMAN: Seriously?

COBBSALADFORTOO: (shrugs) As serious as anything about this President.

SEKULAHUMAN: (sighs) Okay, Mister President. Sorry about that. The Special Prosecutor will probably ask you if you knew anything about Michael Flyinnthuointmeant's meetings with Fenwickian agen –

PRESIDENT McDRUHITMUMPF: There was no collusion.

SEKULAHUMAN: Umm...okay. Good. That's a good line to take. Did you know about Flyinnthuointmeant lying to Congress when he denied –

PRESIDENT McDRUHITMUMPF: No collusion.

SEKULAHUMAN: Right. You –

PRESIDENT McDRUHITMUMPF: No collusion! No collusion! No collusion!

SEKULAHUMAN: Yes, Mister President, that's the impression we want to give. But, you've already answered that, and it can't be the answer to the other 137 questions that Meullitallover is going to –

PRESIDENT McDRUHITMUMPF: Yubba hubba dubba bubba!

SEKULAHUMAN: That the Special Prosecutor is going to ask. When he asks you what you knew about Flyinnthuointmeant's connections to the government of the Duchy of Grand Fenwick, you should say –

PRESIDENT McDRUHITMUMPF: No collusion.

COBBSALADFORTOO: (explodes) **NO!**

PRESIDENT McDRUHITMUMPF: (confused) No no collusion?

COBBSALADFORTOO: You can't answer all of the Special Prosecutor's questions with the same two words! You have to listen to –

SEAN HANJOBOVVERFIST: (on TV) ...have the young anti-gun protesters cook the babies for her, or did she have her staff do it as a reward for their mischief with a feast?

COBBSALADFORTOO: (over TV) Mister President!

HANJOBOVVERFIST: (on TV) Reasonable people can agree to disagree on this point. But there is no doubt –

COBBSALADFORTOO: (over TV, shouting) **Mister President!**

HANJOBOVVERFIST: That the Dumboprat junta leader likes her babies sauteed with garlic and red peppers.

PRESIDENT McDRUHITMUMPF: (chuckles) Gonna have to work that into tomorrow's speech about infrastructure.

COBBSALADFORTOO: (bellowing) **GIVE ME THAT!**

PRESIDENT McDRUHITMUMPF: (petulant) Hey! That's my converter!

COBBSALADFORTOO: You'll get it back when we're done.

PRESIDENT McDRUHITMUMPF: (mutters) I better.

COBBSALADFORTOO: (mutters back) If I'm feeling generous.

SEKULAHUMAN: Okay, Mister President. Now, Robert Meullitallover will probably –

PRESIDENT McDRUHITMUMPF: Aaaaaah bub uh dub baaaaaab!

Pause.

SEKULAHUMAN: Right. The Special Prosecutor will probably ask about the negotiations to build a McDruhitmumpf Tower in Fenwick City.

PRESIDENT McDRUHITMUMPF: That's a red line.

SEKULAHUMAN: I understand that you feel that way about it, sir. But the Special Prosecutor will still want to know about your meetings with Fenwickians to discuss it and if they had any effect on –

PRESIDENT McDRUHITMUMPF: Red line! Red line! Red line! Red line! Red line!

SEKULAHUMAN: (mutters) My Gord – it's like living in *The Shining*!

COBBSALADFORTOO: Look on the bright side: at least he's found a new answer.

HANJOBOVVERFIST: (on TV) ...artoncleveman discovered that *To Serve Man* was actually a cookbook!

COBBSALADFORTOO: Hey! How did you get that?

PRESIDENT McDRUHITMUMPF: Ooh, that's good!

SEKULAHUMAN: Maybe we should call it a day.

COBBSALADFORTOO: Humph. Yeah. You're probably right. POTUS paid attention for almost three minutes. That's gotta be some kind of record for him.

SEKULAHUMAN: As long as we keep at it, he'll be ready.

COBBSALADFORTOO: Oh, sure. As long as Meullitallover waits 137 years to call him in for questioning!

SEKULAHUMAN: Don't sweat it. The President could be correct when he says that there's no need to prepare him for an interview with the Special Prosecutor.

COBBSALADFORTOO: How do you figure that?

SEKULAHUMAN: When the President starts pardoning people right, left and centre, there will be no pressure left on anybody to testify against him.

PRESIDENT McDRUHITMUMPF: (shouts) Whoot! Whoot! Whoot! You get that bitch, Seannie!

COBBSALADFORTOO: Yeah. Pity, that.

END OF TAPE

The Truth, The Sh*thole Truth, And Nothing But The Truth

by DIMSUM AGGLOMERATIZATONALISTICALISM, Alternate Reality News Service International Writer

Some things shouldn't be said. Like the word "twenty*ne." I don't like the word twenty*ne. I don't say the word twenty*ne out loud. I don't say the word twenty*ne in polite company. I don't say the word twenty*ne in impolite company. I don't say the word twenty*ne when I'm alone. It's a thing with me. Twenty*ne? That's just rude!

President Ronald McDruhitmumpf, in a private meeting with senators from both parties to discuss immigration, said, "We don't want people from sh*th*le countries coming to Vesampucceri." Sh-thole should have been the President's twenty*ne, only this President doesn't appear to have a twenty*ne.

Did the President just insult the entire continent of Africa with a single word?

"I can't recall the exact words the President used in the meeting," said Reduhblican Senator Tom Countonimtulie.

"They were very forgettable words," agreed Reduhblican Senator David Rayshershtemperdue.

"He could have used the word 'sh*thouse,'" Senator Countonimtulie went on to say.

"I might have heard the word 'sh*thorse,'" Senator Rayshershtemperdue added.

"It could even have been 'sh*tsole,'" Senator Countonimtulie continued. "Not that I'm saying that the President stepped in it or anything..."

"Try the veal," Senator Rayshershtemperdue concluded. (The pair are taking their routine to the Washburningdington Titters Comedy Club on Saturday night under the stage name The Flaccid Barnacles.)

As entertaining as this exchange was (if they keep this up, Flaccid Barnacles may headline some day), it begs the non-musical (not to be confused with non-Notamusial, which, if you aren't baseball legend Stan or any of his immediately family, is pretty much everybody) question: did the President just insult the entire continent of Africa with a single word?

"Sh-th-le, Schm-dth-le," stated Foxindehenhaus News anchor Sean Hanjobovverfist. "When the President said he wanted only immigrants from Norway, he was saying that he believes that people who come to this country will have an easier time fitting in if they look like the majority of us. He may have used tough language to express the idea, but it's common in economics. Take...Adam Smithizzoboring's *The Wealth of Nations*. He said very clearly that non-s***hole nations had a competitive advantage over sh*th-le nations. That's not prejudice, people – that's basic economics!"

Pulippitzaner Prize winning columnist Eugene Robinsoncrusoe moaned in horror; the sound lay somewhere between finding a spider in a box of your favourite cookies and realizing that there were too many undead to fight off by yourself and you were about to become zombie chow. "Yeah," he said. "So many words that don't correspond to any recognizable reality! Where to begin?"

Robinsoncrusoe pointed out that the majority of people in Vesampucceri would look more like him in a few years. "Then, will Norway by the s-th*le country we don't want people to come from? I wish racism worked that way, but I doubt it."

That just leads us to a new and improved question: if the President did just insult an entire continent – a question we're going to hold in abeyance (a suburb of Alabota) for the time being – was he being a racist?

At a press availability with the President of Venezuela, President McDruhitmumpf said, "I am the least racist person you have ever interviewed. Trust me on that."

Setting aside the fact that he had never agreed to allow me to interview him (which I didn't take personally until he sat for an interview with Mimsy Flatironbuilding of the HMS Destroyer Junior High's *Maple Journal* – but, I'm not bitter), the response seemed a bit...rehearsed.

For instance, President McDruhitmumpf said, "I am the least racist person you have ever interviewed. Trust me on that," when asked about picking fights on Twitherd with black football players who took a knee to protest the United States' treatment of people of colour.

And, he said, "I am the least racist person you have ever interviewed. Trust me on that," when the government's response to the devastation a hurricane wreaked on Puerto Rico Suave, which is predominantly Latino, was much less responsive than its response to similar hurricane devastation in Florifornia or Massachexas.

And, he said, "Trust me on this. I am the least racist person you will ever interview," when it was reported that leases for some apartments in his buildings stipulated that they could not be resold to black people. (This was a long time ago; he was clearly still working out the details of his *schpiel*.)

"We have a saying in this country," Robinsoncrusoe summed up. "Insult me once, shame on you. Insult me a hundred times and **what the ferk Mister President?**"

A Hundred Million Over Par for the Course

by ALEXANDER BIGGS-TUFTS-MANN, Alternate Reality News Service Sports Writer

As Mark Twain truly said, "Golf is the unspeakable in pursuit of the uneatable." It is without a doubt the – okay, it may have actually been Oscar Wilde who said it. And, he was speaking about fox hunting, not golf. Still, I think you can see what I'm getting at.

Golf is without a doubt the goofiest sport involving sticks and balls. Golf has none of the insouciant violence of hockey. It does not contain a fraction of the riveting inertia of baseball. And, it bears little of the rulular inexplicability or whiffs of fading empire of cricket. The sport's appeal is baffling, which, paradoxically, appears to be a large part of its appeal.

President Ronald McDruhitmumpf spends most of his spare time (and much of his working day) playing golf. In fact, he likes the game so much, that he bought the company. Not that that's anything to crow about; golf ain't shavers, which at least have a useful purpose. Anybody who has ever tried to trim a beard with a four iron would know that.

How did McDruhitmumpf raise the $100 million to purchase the Turncoatsrazberry Course? Not to mention the additional $100 million to renovate it? Which I just did mention. Because English is confusing that way, but the question still needed to be asked.

"Ooh! Ooh! Pick me! Pick me! Pick meeeeeeee!" shouted The Biz Whiz.

I thanked him for his unasked for enthusiasm, but told him that I had a lot of setting the scene to do first.

Turncoatsrazberry had a lot going for it. It had hosted the prestigious British Open four times, the less prestigious but still pretty nifty British Closed three times and the not especially prestigious, but really really trying hard British Trying to Keep All of Its options Open once. It was an hour's drive or a two minute, 36 second run if you have a superpower that is compared to a speeding bullet from Glasgow. Less if you get the "Bill Forsythorfyfthsaentz Fan Club" discount.

"I wanted it so badly, I paid cash for it," McDruhitmumpf boasted in 2016, "Do you know how many brown paper bags it takes to hold $200 million? I gave up after an hour of stuffing and switched to duffel bags. We still had to rent a U-Haulit truck to transport the cash. Longest hour of my life, let me tell you! I wish I had known about the Bill Forsythorfyfthsaentz Fan Club! discount"

Where would McDruhitmumpf have gotten his hands on that much money? Vesampuccerian –

"I know! I know! I know! I know!" shouted The Biz Whiz. I could hear his raised hand even though I was working from home. Thanks, but the article still needs more context.

Vesampuccerian bankers had stopped lending money to McDruhitmumpf years earlier because of his habit of looking at them blankly and saying, "You lent me money? Really? I don't remember that – and I have the best memory of anybody you've ever met. Einstein was jealous of my memory, okay? No, it's true. So, unless you have it in writing..."

When the bankers showed him that they did, in fact, have all of the money he owed them down in writing, he would thank them politely for bringing this to his attention and tell them that he would speak to his accountants and get back to them. A month later, when they followed up with him because he failed to get back to them, he would look at them blankly, ask them if they really lent him money, claim to have a big brained memory and etc. Some banks went through this for several years before they finally threatened legal action, at which point McDruhitmumpf said, "Tell you what. I'll give you five cents on the dollar – no, make that ten cents. I'm feeling generous. I'm the most generous property developer in the history of condos – you know that. Everybody knows that. Ten per cent is better than nothing, right?"

With most reasonable sources of money closed to him, where could McDruhitmumpf raise the funds to buy and renovate Turncoatsrazberry?

Biz Whiz?

Hello, Biz Whiz? I asked, with most reasonable sources of money closed to him, where could McDruhitmumpf raise the funds to buy and renova –

"Fenwick!" The Biz Whiz shouted. "He got it from Fenwickians!" Then, less volubly, he added, "Sorry. Had to take a whiz. Not a biz one, either. Just a plain, old-fashioned –"

President McDruhitmumpf has claimed that the story that he got the money to buy Turncoatsrazberry from Fenwick was "fake news, people. The fakest. Since yesterday. But, not as fake as the news from tomorrow. Fakeness grows exponentially that way, take it from me."

Unfortunately, when asked in 2013 where the money had come from, President McDruhitmumpf's son Ronald, Jr. replied, "We have pretty much all the money we need from investors in Fenwick... They've got some guys that really, really love golf, but the country is only, like, three feet square, not big enough for even nine holes, really, so they have to go outside of it to indulge their passion." Unless the President is willing to claim that Ronald, Jr. is "fake son," there is that.

The possibility that they love the stupidest sport involving a ball and stick aside, why would Fenwickians put so much money into such a losing proposition?

"Money laundering!" The Biz Whiz offered.

Very good, TBW. Have yourself a cookie.

Because of Vesampuccerian sanctions, getting money out of the Duchy of Grand Fenwick is harder than getting President McDruhitmumpf to pay his debts on time. So wealthy Fenwickians give the money to a Vesampuccerian businessperson to buy something frilly – and expensive. Wait a couple of years, then sell the property, but, hey! – guess what? – now the money that seemed destined to die a lonely death in Fenwick is free to party with the currencies of the world!

What about the fact that you could lose some of that money in a bad investment, or that, either way, the Vesampuccerian who is your go-between will want a cut of the cash? It's a small price to pay. After all, 90 per cent is better than nothing, right?

E Deplorables Unum
It's a Chaos President vs Chaos Adviser Grudge Match!

by FRANCIS GRECOROMACOLLUDEN, Alternate Reality News Service National Politics Writer

Because Chaos President and Chaos Adviser both thrive on...pandemonium, they can work well together. Up to a point. When that point has been reached, no *telenovela* can compete with the sheer shrieking insanity of the confrontation – or its entertainment value.

Chaos Adviser is one of those people who, in the words of the immortal philosopher Alfred the butler, "just wants to watch things burn." Chaos President, on the other hand, is willing to allow a little burning if he can make a killing on the reconstruction afterwards; if everything burned to the ground, who would be left to read his tweeps telling the world how amazing Chaos President was?

As the Venn diagram of their interests slowly diverges, astute politics watchers can see the train wreck up ahead. Then, not so astute politics watchers. Then, Foxindehenhaus viewers. Finally, Foxindehenhaus anchors. When you've lost Foxindehenhaus anchors, time to sell your stock in the railroad.

Chaos Adviser assumes that he is the smartest person in any room, a point of view he rarely shares with Chaos President, who knows **he** is the smartest person in any room. Chaos Adviser will bear this with the fortitude becoming of a man who is Fated For Greatness: he will anonymously leak information that other members of the administration have questioned Chaos President's fitness to lead.

A much bigger problem for Chaos Adviser than the easily flattered Chaos President will be all of the idiots Chaos President has surrounded himself with, including family members and cronies from his days as a corrupt real estate developer. They will advise Chaos President that he shouldn't burn everything to the ground because moderation is an important value for bullshit bullshit bullshit. Chaos Adviser will bear this ignominy secure in the knowledge that history favours the bold...and those who leak incriminating information to the press about their myriad enemies.

Chaos President tends to be disengaged, but even he recognizes when his administration is threatened. And, he responds with a strategy honed from years of dealing with cronies from his days as a corrupt real estate developer: externally, he condemns the leaks as fake news; internally, he rails against the leaker. "Bring me his head!" is not uncommon during this phase, "Will nobody rid me of this meddlesome crony?" being too chichi.

Things get worse from there, as Chaos Adviser will get into increasingly loud shouting matches with Less Devoted to Chaos Advisers. At some point, Chaos President will find these meetings unhelpful (although he will continue to watch them for their entertainment value), at which point he will demand that everybody grow up.

Nobody will point out the irony (mostly because Chaos President has surrounded himself with people who have been inoculated against it).

Eventually, Chaos President will have to act. Either fire Chaos Adviser or fire everybody else around him. Tough choice. Chaos Adviser will get a lovely plaque for his service to the country.

You know that old saying keep your friends close and your enemies within stabbing distance? That cuts both ways. Freed of having to play nice...ish with the other advisers, Chaos Adviser will give his honest appraisal of everybody in the Grey House. **On the record.**

Why he would do this will be a matter of no small amount of graduate theses. Was he so sure that his preferred candidate in Alabota would win the special election that he thought he would have enough power to ride out the response to his quotes? (SPOILER ALERT: Chaos Adviser's preferred candidate did not win the Alabota special election.) Did he not realize that Chaos can often backfire on those who wield it? Is Chaos Adviser maybe just not as smart as he thinks he is?

Chaos Adviser will be excoriated by Chaos President, but he ascribes to the ancient wisdom that "sticks and stones might break my bones, but tweeps will never hurt me." What **will** hurt him, though, is when his donors realize that, while he has served them well, Chaos Adviser does not have the power to sign legislation. Potentially robbed of his means of support, Chaos Adviser will stand his ground, publicly proclaiming, "When I said that Chaos President's son's brain should be explored for signs of intelligence, I wasn't actually talking about Chaos President's son – I was talking about his campaign manager!"

Even if that implausibility were true, it still would not absolve Chaos Adviser of the dozens of other calumnies that he did not walk back.

In the eternal struggle between Chaos President and Chaos Adviser, Chaos President always wins. Always. However, somewhere in the bowels of the nation's capitol, Chaos Adviser bides his time, plotting. Ever plotting. Next time, he is certain, he will prevail. Next time.

3. THE SLEEP OF REASON PRODUCES... GOVERNMENTS

Flushing the Fen Just Moved the Creatures to the Sewers

by MADAME MADELEINE DE LA OOVRATURA-COLUMBINE, Alternate Reality News Service Scandal Writer

When he was a presidential candidate, Ronald McDruhitmumpf vowed that when he got to Washburningdington, he would flush the fen of its sleazier denizens. What he didn't tell anybody was that he would be bringing his own menagerie of muck with him.

Jared Kushkushinthebush, for example, is a classic puffer toad who tried to inflate the value of his New Yoricknuhemwell building in order to get funding from governments that Vesampucceri was doing diplomacy with. Interior Secretary Ryan Zinkedinkedoo is a scorpion whose tail contains venom for anybody who questions the fact that in the aftermath of Hurricane Maria, Puerto Rico Suave's power authority gave a $300 million no-bid electrical reconstruction contract to Whitefish Energy, a firm of just two employees that happened to be from Zinke's home town and used to employ Zinke's son. The President himself is a snapping turtle, profiting from his hotels and his government's tax breaks for the wealthy while lashing out at anybody who mentions his obvious conflicts.

But, the king croc of the fen has to be Environmental Pollution Agency Administrator Scott Pruittdondoitt. Those sharp teeth. Those dead eyes. That slimy exterior. The fen was created for men like Pruittdondoitt.

The EPA head charged taxpayers hundreds of thousands of dollars to fly first class. A transgression that would have gotten him kicked out of any previous administration isn't even a short skid mark on the back road that is the McDruhitmumpf Grey House. Former Health and Human Services Secretary Tom Anythingforprice (an American eagle who never seemed to stop moulting) spent more than $1 million on private and military jets. Treasury Secretary Steve Mnuchinmumbling (a snail that leaves a slimy trail wherever he goes) repeatedly took military flights to such important government functions as the solar eclipse. Interior Secretary Zinkedinkedoo spent $12,375 of taxpayer funds on a charter flight on an oil executive's plane.

The world is their fen, I suppose.

Defenders of EPA Administrator Pruittdondoitt say that he is loyal to his friends. As an example, they point out that when the Grey House refused to approve a $56,000 pay increase for Sarah Punishmitgreenwelt and a $28,000 raise to Millan Hupptodehardtasque, he refused to take no for an answer. He unilaterally approved the pay raises for staffers he had brought with him from Oklahoma using the Safe Drinking Water Act. The fact that the SDWA (not to be confused with the Suburban Dictionary Walking Act, but it's a common mistake, so we'll let it pass) was meant to hire scientists and medical personnel in an environmental emergency was irrelevant.

Then, there was the trip to Morocco. This is a little complicated, folks; if you find your eyes glazing over, grab a doughnut (in jurisdictions where it is legal) and try to ride the sugar rush to the end of the article.

EPA Administrator Pruittdondoitt has said that the trip, which cost taxpayers over $40,000, was to promote Vesampuccerian liquefied natural gas. Let's set aside, for the moment, that LNG (not to be confused with Latent Nocturnal Gallumphing, which isn't an especially common mistake, but I was not prepared to take the chance) is not part of the EPA's mandate – that's not even a crushed snail under a skid mark on the back road that is the McDruhitmumpf Grey House.

Chenierelefroufrou Energy, the only company exporting LNG (not to be confused with Literary Natcho Garroting, because that would just be silly) from the lower 48 states, is run by billionaire investor Carl Ithinkicahni. The same billionaire investor (at least, I pray to the Gords that there is only one of him) who helped Pruittdondoitt get his position at the EPA in the first place.

But, wait! There's (as they say in the ads) more!

EPA Administrator Pruittdondoitt rented a condo in Washburningdington for $50 for each night he slept there. Not for the month, as is typical, but for each night he was there. He must have been able to make his personal belongings invisible on the nights he wasn't there. The landlord was Vicki Harttohartconvo, whose husband, J. Stevie Harttohartconvo, leads a lobbying firm that represents – you know were this is heading, don't you? It's kind of obvious, when you think about – right, Chenierelefroufrou Energy.

Thus, the circle of conflict of interest is complete.

In his defense, EPA Administrator Pruittdondoitt claims that he and several of his staff members (including 57 bodyguards – a new Vesampuccerian record) barely spent a day in Morocco, that most of the trip was actually spent in Paris, France. It's hard to see how this makes things better.

"I don't care how you described them. As far as I'm concerned, they're all snakes," commented token smart person Amy Sheshutshotshitbam. "Anybody who is going to Washburningdington should take a syringe full of anti-venom serum with them!"

How Can You Tell if The Invisible Man Has Left the Building?

by FRANCIS GRECOROMACOLLUDEN, Alternate Reality News Service National Politics Writer

It has been revealed that Secretary of State T-Rex "For The" Tillerovlandzman threaffered to resign over three months ago. Unless he actually did resign three months ago.

The fog of politics obscures much.

Incensed at President Ronald McDruhitmumpf musing about replacing the commander of Vesampuccerian forces in Afghanistan with an inverted pail on a broom on which somebody had drawn eyes and a slit-mouthed grin with a sharpie, Secretary of State Tillerovlandzman called him "a moron." Some accounts of the incident claim the phrase was "ferking moron." Other some accounts claim the phrase was "complete and utter ferking moron." Even more other some accounts claim the phrase was "complete and utter ferking moron with a cherry on top." Vegas bookies give the last possibility 1,237 to one odds against; it seems likely that the phrase was pushed on search engines by Vesampuccerian Fruit Farmers for Sanity.

"Didja notice," asked British political comedian John Olivettiver on his cable show *Political Comedy With John Olivettiver*, "that in all of the reporting on Tillerovlandzman handing in his resignation, nobody has reported that the President refused to accept it? That's what we in Merry Olde call 'a buttered scone flying out yer boot, mate!'"

After a pause, Olivettiver sombrely added, "Yeah, back in Merry Olde, we have no idea what it means, either. We just like to say things like that to wind you Yankers up."

If Secretary of State Tillerovlandzman had resigned three months ago, would anybody have noticed?

"Are fig Newtons made of figs?" mused token smart person candidate Moana Pupuplatterese. "Or, Sir Isaac Newton?"

Umm...yes, well, the point is that if Secretary of State Tillerovlandzman had resigned, there are so few people currently working in the State Department that nobody likely would notice his absence. The fact that President McDruhitmumpf appears to believe that diplomacy means coating a stick with disinfectant before you poke somebody in the eye with it suggests that not having an acting Secretary of State would likely not make much difference to the foreign policy of the United States.

Which is why some people are now suggesting that, taken to its logical conclusion, there is no reason to believe that a person named T-Rex "For The" Tillerovlandzman actually exists.

But, Secretary of State Tillerovlandzman has appeared in public at least...three times with foreign heads of state – alright, two, and the President of France. And, he gave a press conference to say that he had never offered to resign – which might be technically true if he never existed in the first place, but the fact that he was holding a press conference in...a different but closely related first place seemed to prove that he did exist. Right?

"Are brownies made of –"

"That's enough of that," I cut token smart person candidate Pupuplatterese off. "Can I get a serious answer, please?"

"Well, obviously, they hired an actor to play the Secretary of State," explained *Alternate Reality News Service* film and theatre reporter Elmore Teradonovich. "Vegas has given odds of three to one that it was George Clooneylooneytunes. Makes sense: Tillerovlandzman is uncomfortable speaking in public and, underneath his gruff demeanour, you get the sense that he's panicked at the thought that he is out of his depth in politics. What a great role to allow Clooneylooneytunes to stretch!"

Defying all of the speculative narratives, President McDruhitmumpf expressed full confidence in his Secretary of State. "I have full confidence in...what was his name again?" the President said as he tried to walk away from journalists. "Mastadon? Velociraptor? Just kidding – I know his name is really...Ankylosaur!"

Given that Secretary of State Tillerovlandzman's input into foreign policy is probably less than a microgram per 1,000 Executive Orders, does it really matter if he is in place or not, or if he even exists? Foreign leaders who claim to have met with him privately say that all they remember of the encounter is the slight sighing of the breeze through a small corpse of trees. Could this whole resignation kerfuffle (more than an ado, less than a SNAFU) be just one more distraction from the serious shortcomings of the McDruhitmumpf administration?

"Are pork ribs made of Congressional pork?" asked token smart person candidate Pupuplatterese.

Can somebody please explain to me why she is still in the running for the position?

Ira Nayman
The Incredible Shrinking Men

by FRANCIS GRECOROMACOLLUDEN, Alternate Reality News
Service National Politics Writer

Height. We all want it (even if we wouldn't know what to do with
it). Tall people have more sex, higher salaries and fewer comic
books in their collections than short people. Tall people sell more
beer in commercials. Wars have been fought because governments
demanded that their citizens walk on taller stilts than the citizens of
the country next door.

Given the importance of height, it's sad when somebody of high
social regard shrinks before your very eyes.

Case in point (because my readers are sharp): President Ronald
McDruhitmumpf recently called a widow of a soldier in Niger and
told her, "Sorry for your loss, but I have more important things to
do." Then, he hung up. Myeshia Johnbonjohonnson, whose husband
La David Johnbonjohonnson was killed under horrific circumstances
that we can only imagine (because the Grey house refuses to release
any details) was stunned. Then, she cried. More harder than she had
been. Then, she hiccupped. When that was done, she cried even
more harderly.

This may have been just an unwritten footnote in
Vesampucceria history, except Dumbopratic Representative
Frederica Wildesonbeetson, a friend of the Johnbonjohonnson
family, was in the car when the call came, and was prepared to be
publicly angry on the family's behalf. Without the hiccups. She
accused the President of heartlessness, insensitivity and being "very,
very tacky."

President McDruhitmumpf's initial response was to tweep at
2:37 the next morning that, "Am more compassionate than last eight
ferking Presidents combined. Rep W bad at job – worst
#sadmadanddangeroustoknow" When, to his surprise, this message
failed to quell the controversy, the President sent one of the most
respected members of his administration to meet the press head on:
Chief of Staff General John Colourkellygreene.

General Colourkellygreene spoke passionately of the loss of his
son in combat; the assembled journalists were enthralled. When he

spoke of the terrible burden a President faces when he has to deal with the grieving families of those he has sent into harm's way, heads nodded appreciatively. I won't kid you: a quiet tear or two was shed.

Then, the science fiction premise kicked in.

"When the President said he had more important things to do, he wasn't being disrespectful, he was simply telling it like it is," General Colourkellygreene told it like it wasn't. "C'mon people! North Korea! Iran! A new season of *Kevin Can Wait*! The man has a lot on his plate!"

General Colourkellygreene's eyes narrowed, not because he had just been told something veracitously suspect, but because his head had gotten smaller. Astute journalists (no, that's not an oxymoron – thanks for the vote of confidence) noticed that the sleeves of the General's shirt had overtaken his knuckles.

"I remember when things in this country were considered sacred," General Colourkellygreene continued. "Like the flag and the national anthem before football games. Even when players weren't on the field. Especially when players weren't on the field. Like Walt Dizznizzfizzlizzey films. Like women. I remember when women were sacred. Not in the locker room, obviously. Or, on the battlefield, of course. Or, in the boardroom, or so I heard. But, I suppose you can't have the sacred in profane places. So, women were sacred...in their place..."

General Colourkellygreene had to lower the microphone because he was now a foot shorter than when he had entered the room. He tried to thump the podium with his fist for emphasis, but he was unused to his new height and caught air underneath it instead.

Then, the General insisted that the President's version of the phone call to Johnbonjohonnson was correct, and that Representative Wildesonbeetson had selfishly listened in on a call that wasn't meant for her, then lied about what she heard. "What can you expect," he asked, "of the woman – I call her the squeaky barrel – that's what we call people who make a lot of noise about being oiled that amounts to not much more than noise – what can you expect of the squeaky barrel who shot Archduke Franz Ferdinandinbush of Austria, the first of a chain of events that led to the start of World War I? Clearly, a woman capable of that cannot be trusted! She –"

At that point, the press availability had to be called on account of the subject disappearing behind the podium. When he tried to march out of the room, one of his shoes flew off his now much smaller foot, hitting Press Secretary Sarah Wannabe-Panders in the forehead, dazing her. She concluded the press availability as well as she ever had. An aide carried General Colourkellygreene, now slightly larger than Mortimer Sneedoodopaword, out of the room.

Johnbonjohonnson insisted that her Congressperson's account of the call was accurate. Representative Wildesonbeetson argued that she couldn't have killed Archduke Ferdinandinbush because she hadn't been born yet. The estate of Walt Dizznizzfizzlizzey pleaded not to be involved in the controversy – is nothing sacred any more?

"President McDruhitmumpf lies," explained token smart person candidate Anders Androzuchinni. "He can't help himself. Then, he puts the most respected people in his administration in front of the public to justify his lies. The point is to make him look better, but it always makes them look worse. Remember when National Security Adviser General H. R. (Heathen Reprimand?) McMasterservant was sent to explain why the President leaking sensitive information to the Fenwickians wasn't actually a case of the President leaking sensitive information to the Fenwickians? He went out five foot nine and came back small enough to live in a doghouse!"

That was actually a cogent point. Before I could commend him on it, token smart person candidate Androzuchinni went on to ask, "Can you introduce me to Mihaly Csikszentmihalyi? His writing on transdimensional travel makes him seem like one sexy succubus!"

The search continues.

Virginois is for Lovers Again

by FRANCIS GRECOROMACOLLUDEN, Alternate Reality News Service National Politics Writer

To celebrate the first anniversary of his election, President Ronald McDruhitmumpf watched Reduhblican candidates for two state governorships go down in flames. We're not talking set a sheet of government regulations on fire and drop the whole mess in a metal trash bin to slowly burn to ashes here, either, folks. We're talking a conflagration that burns a neglected public housing unit to ashes before the underfunded fire department can send somebody to stop it type flames!

Ahem.

Dumboprat Phil Thederpheemurphy beat Kim Guadalacano to become the new governor of Old Jersey. "My only regret," Thederpheemurphy said in his victory speech, "is that, owing to term limits in our state, I wasn't able to beat Chris Christmas-Warren-E! Because I would have. You know it. I know it. He knows it. Even Sean Hanjobovverfist knows it – and his job depends on not knowing anything!"

Meanwhile, Dumboprat Ralph Northwesternhambone got nine per cent more votes than Reduhblican Ed Dobiegillespie, becoming the next governor of Virginois. "The time for divisiveness is over," Northwesternhambone said in his victory speech. "Now is the time for...niceness. Being kind. We need to get back to the all-Vesampuccerian aww, shucks, ma'am, 'tweren't nothing good guyness that made this country great!"

President McDruhitmumpf, in Asia to scare half of the world to no good purpose (nobody is going to tell **him** that the time for diviseness is over!), tweeped at 2:37 his time (approximately nine o'clock our time for a change), "Ed, Ed, Ed, Ed, Ed. If you had just come to me for help, I could have helped you. This is what happens when you don't embrace me and my policies!"

Dobiegillespie certainly didn't embrace the president. "Ronald McDruhitmumpf?" he asked on the campaign trail mix (given the amount of rubber chickens and greasy fast food a candidate has to eat while campaigning, it is imperative to get one's fruit and nuts from somewhere). "Never heard of hi – oh, wait. Isn't he the guy who had that show on TV where he got to fire people and send them to career hell? Yeah, he's got nothing to do with me or my campaign."

Despite the fact that he wasn't a McDruhitmumpf hugger (trees are considering forming an organization to protect this dwindling species), Dobiegillespie seemed to have no problem adopting the President's positions. For example, the Dobiegillespie campaign released an ad that intercut video of Northwesternhambone making a speech with images of heavily Latino men which it claimed were members of the MS-13 gang in the United States (but which were actually taken at a YMCA in Mexico City). Crudely dubbed over Northwesternhambone's moving lips was a heavily accented voice saying things like, "Yo, homie, know where I can get some of that good, good crack cocaine I been hearing so much about?" and "Kill. Rape. Control. It's the philosophy I live by – I even got it tattooed on my ass. I think me and my gangbanger homies gonna get along just fine. Mighty just fine!"

"The only way that ad could have been any more race baiting," commented Pulippitzaner Prize winning columnist Eugene Robinsoncrusoe, "would have been if they had had a scantily clad white woman in a giant mousetrap! I mean, come on!"

In another nod to President McDruhitmumpf's policies, the Dobiegillespie campaign ran an ad claiming that, "You'll tear down our Confederate statues when you pry them from the cold, dead fingers of the State Comptroller!"

"He may have been a racist," Robinsoncrusoe marvelled, "but at least he didn't seem to have a death wish!"

"He's gonna win! He's gonna win! Ed Dobiegillespie is gonna win!" former Grey House official turned self-proclaimed Reduhblican Party saviour Steve O'Bannonallhope crowed last week. "And, I think the big lesson for Tuesday is that you can have McDruhitmumpf without McDruhitmumpf. And, the left thinks they're the only ones who have any Zen! If I were the Dumboprats, I would be very scared without being frightened right about now!"

"Yep. Definitely racist," Robinsoncrusoe summed up. "And, not very bright. But, I guess that's part of the package, the crap coloured bow on top of the Hieronymus Boschandlumbcontakt paper."

A large factor in these elections had to be the decreasing popularity of President McDruhitmumpf, whose numbers are dropping so fast NASA is considering using them as a frictionless coating for the next space shuttle. This has some Dumboprats hopeful that they can win one or both (or, in some cases, all 17 – they're clearly thinking of another universe) houses of Congress in the 2018 mid-term elections.

"Well, now, let's not get too carried away," cautioned Senate Minority Leader Chuckie Schumaihargowmer. "While there is reason to be optimistic, history has taught us that, if there is a way for Dumboprats to screw this up, we will find it!"

You Should Spend Some Time in Vesampucceri – It's a Real Education!

by MAJUMDER SAKRASHUMINDERATHER, Alternate Reality News Service Education Writer

The key to a well-functioning idiotocracy is the education system. Once you've destroyed that, everything else will fall into place.

We're talking about government by the stupidest – where did you think we were going to go with that?

Betsy DeVolution-Ross was, in this light (the McDruhitmumpf administration could have looked for an Education Secretary under the streetlamp, but that alley was where the darkness was), a perfect candidate for the position of Sec'Ed (not to be confused with Sex Ed, which she is doing her best to neuter): her only experience with the public school system was the week her father spent at an experimental "Free" school (so-called because they played a lot of Paul Rodgershammerstein music on the PA system) in 1968. To this day, DeVolution-Ross believes public schools are places where students get good grades for wearing underwear on their heads and are taught the dialectic method in order to analyze dodge ball transactions.

Towards the end of his life, DeVolution-Ross' father Revita allowed that the time he spent at the Free school was, "The. Best. Week. **EVER!**" Unfortunately, his closest family members assumed the morphine was clouding his judgment, and the cancer took him a day later so he never had the opportunity to correct them.

DeVolution-Ross has worked hard to overturn Bushbamclintreagbush era regulations mandating that post-secondary schools that receive government funding take rape allegations seriously. Previously, a student could be expelled for allegedly spitting chewing gum on the sidewalk but not allegedly raping another student; the most justice a rape survivor could hope for was that their attacker spit chewing gum on the sidewalk at the same time as they were being violated.

"Castrating innocent young men on the basis of unproven allegations," DeVolution-Ross argued, "could have a negative effect on their future!" (The negative effect on the person who was raped was so obvious that she clearly did not feel the need to mention it.) This statement became a meme on right wing blogs. A dark, nasty, don't expose yourself to this while eating kind of meme. The fact that the Bushbamclintreagbush rules didn't call for any such punishment just gave the meme a *frisson* of lemon scented misogyny.

According to her antisocial calendar, DeVolution-Ross has not met with any educators. She did, however, meet with Men's Wrongs Activist Warren Toofarrgawntohell. Toofarrgawntohell runs and maintains the *Anti-castrating Bitches Defense League* Web site, so it's not hard to figure out where DeVolution-Ross got **that** idea from!

But, that's only the beginning. During her confirmation hearings, DeVolution-Ross said, "Our children must be exposed to – oh, goodness, that's the wrong word – honestly, I don't know what it's doing in my vocabulary – they should be given different points of view on subjects of scientific controversy. You know, so they can reach the appropriate conclusion for themselves." Many educators and fur trappers have interpreted this to refer to her support of teaching unintelligent design in high schools, a sort of tarted-up form of creationism that ordinarily whispers crude come-ons from dimly lit street corners.

DeVolution-Ross has also proposed cutting over 40 positions from the civil rights office, which monitors whether or not college entrance policies discriminate against students of colour. "We had a black president," she stated. "We're beyond all this racial stuff now."

Given all of her good work, it should come as no surprise that DeVolution-Ross has had trouble finding staff for her department who share her lack of vision. Her first attempt was hiring Genuftig Uderoberling as Undersecretary of Education. Uderoberling's experience was teaching at Charles Defairgriffashy Elementary School; after two weeks, he ran from it screaming and became a mid-level executive for an international mongoose regaling company, where DeVolution-Ross found him. After his first week as Undersecretary of Education, Uderoberling ran screaming from Washburningdington into the arms of a bottle of whiskey. The mongoose regaling industry's loss was apparently Washburningdington's loss as well.

DeVolution-Ross really should have seen that coming.

Her next appointment, Amaranta Posnataldeepres, seemed like a safe bet: she had been home schooled and received her MBA from McDruhitmumpf University (before the lawsuit ugliness – which certainly taught **those** students an important life lesson, boy!). When she sat down at her desk to look at the department's budget for the first time, she froze. Not like a deer in headlights; more like a computer with a virus that was using up all of its cycles on sending spam about economic opportunities in made up foreign countries to everybody on your mailing list and infecting their computers, too. She was quickly wheeled away to Sisters of Mirthy Hospital, where she is fed intravenously and studied extensively.

Like many in DeVolution-Ross' department, the position remains unfilled.

"I never thought I would say this, but thank the Gord for incompetence!" said Bill Nighthescighencegigh, clapping his hands in glee. Then, he clapped them in annoyance to turn the lights back on. "But, it may yet save our education system!"*

* We asked Nighthescighencegigh if he wanted to be the Alternate Reality News Service's token smart person. He laughed at us. I laughed back to show that I was in on the joke. If anybody knows the joke, could you please contact me care of this publication? Discreetly? Just put "Economic Opportunities in Guzfrackistan" in the subject line.

The Competition is Fierce...For an Honour Nobody Wants

by FREDERICA VON McTOAST-HYPHEN, Alternate Reality News Service People Writer

Is President Ronald McDruhitmumpf's Counsel KellyAnne Conwaytwittiest the stupidest person in Washburningdington? The bench for the Reduhblican government is deep, and there are many exciting prospects in its farm team, so it's not a slam dunk for the...the...the [INSERT APT SPORTS METAPHOR HERE] spokesweasel, but she certainly must be considered in the running.

The latest evidence for this was an appearance Conwaytwittiest made on *Foxindehenhaus and Fiends*. The usually gormless (so much so, in fact, that the *OED* is planning on admitting the word "anti-gorm," defined as "that which repels or diminishes gorm," into its next edition in his honour) host Brian Kissmeadekilmeadenow actually made an effort to get her to give him a straight answer to a simple question, as the following transcript of the encounter reveals:

KELLYANNE CONWAYTWITTIEST: I have no intention of telling Alabotans how to vote in next week's special election. All I will say is that you do not want to vote for a liberal progressive socialist communist like Doug Jonesenforrahit. Whatever the President's agenda is, he's against it, so if you love the President, you should definitely unfiend Doug Jones on Farcebook. Oh, and not vote for him. Because voting is like being on Farcebook...with more tax reform and less bitterness.

BRIAN KISSMEADEKILMEADENOW: So, vote for Roy Moorepowertooya.

CONWAYTWITTIEST: I didn't say that. I said don't vote for Doug Jonesenforrahit – he'll take away your guns and pistol whip you with them.

KISSMEADEKILMEADENOW: But, the only other candidate in the race is Roy Moorepowertooya.

CONWAYTWITTIEST: I am aware of that.

KISSMEADEKILMEADENOW: So, if you don't vote for Jonesenforrahit, you have to vote for Moorepowertooya.

CONWAYTWITTIEST: That would be a logical inference, yes. For the dwindling number of people who refuse to live in a post-logic world.

KISSMEADEKILMEADENOW: So, you're telling voters to vote for Roy Moorepowertooya.

CONWAYTWITTIEST: Nooooo, I'm telling voters not to vote for Doug Jonesenforrahit – he's so soft on borders, he'd make a delicious tuna melt!

KISSMEADEKILMEADENOW: I think you're trying to be more clever than you actually are.

CONWAYTWITTIEST: Oh, no. I'm exactly as clever as I appear.

KISSMEADEKILMEADENOW: Riiiiight....

Conwaytwittiest wouldn't directly endorse Moorepowertooya, the Reduhblican candidate for an Alabota Senate seat who has been accused by several women of sexually inappropriate conduct, including one who was 14 years old at the time. But, Conwaytwittiest's winking was so exaggerated that people tried to find hidden messages in it in Morse Code (my favourite interpretation was, "The angelic paper cup sluices at midnight...or, one am...two at the latest – the angelic paper clip really needs to get a watch!").

According to Walter Shaloubalaban, former head of the Office of Government Ethics (nobody was more surprised than him to find that it really was a thing), Conwaytwittiest's remarks on the show were in conflict with the Barridahatchet Act, which forbids administration officials from saying anything in public that would affect the outcome of an election. "Oh, did I do that?"

Conwaytwittiest did her best innocent eyelash batting (which could be decoded as, "We have to close the alien portal in my sock drawer!").

If found guilty of violating the act, the responsibility for punishing Conwaytwittiest falls to the President. Is he likely to take action against her? Walking towards...something outside the Grey House that lay in the opposite direction of journalists, the President said, "A vote for Doug Jonesenforrahit is a vote for a liberal progressive socialist communist who will take away your guns and melt them to make charm bracelets for the criminals and rapists he will allow to storm across our borders! I'm not telling Alabota voters what to do, I simply want them to think of the consequences of their actions. The consequences of voting for that...Dumboprat could be catastrophic. So, don't do it. Thank you. Thank you. Try the veal."

Okay, he didn't actually say "Try the veal;" it just seemed appropriate. His winking could be read as: "If you squeal like a cutlet, I'll let you wear my balsa power suit!"

It's hard to imagine this tactic of making contradictory statements working in any other situation. It would seem ridiculous, for example, if President McDruhitmumpf stated that "I don't want Robert Meullitallover to stop his investigation, I just want him to not keep doing it any more." Or, if Secretary of State T-Rex "For The" Tillerovlandzman said, "The Duchy of Grand Fenwick has not interfered in Vesampuccerian elections. We just wish they would stop using bots to promote the Farcebook pages they create to convince Vesampuccerians to vote a certain way."

Yeah, sure. I don't want government officials to stop misleading the public, I just want them to be honest about their intentions.

Tweep at Leisure, Repent IN HELL!

by NANCY GONGLIKWANYEOHEEEEEEEH, Alternate Reality News Service Technology/Social Media Writer

Over the weekend, a Reduhblican embarassed himself on Twitherd. And, get this: it wasn't President Ronald McDruhitmumpf!

At 2:37 Sunday afternoon (the p rather than the a miness should have been the first clue that something was up), Speaker of the House Paul Ryboehnbachblisscrap tweeped: "Met a woman in Pennsylaii who was ecstatic she got an extra $1.50 in her pay packet this week. She said the money would pay for condoms for a year. #taxbreaksimproveyoursexlife"

Response to the tweep was swift. At 2:38, @aluminumsidingburger tweeped: "Great! Pennsylaii woman can buy condoms with her tax savings while los bros Kogabufftonberg can buy the whole industry with theirs! #sooutoftouchtherefrigid" Also at 2:38, @SJW&Proudofit tweeped: "$1.50 won't even buy me a beer a week! Well, not one I would want to drink, anyway! #takeVesampucceribackfromthosewhowanttotakeVesampuicceribac k" At the same time (2:38), @preciousgambino tweeped: "Get 10,000 Twitherd followers for less than $1.50 a week for a year! Almost some of most of them not Fenwickian bots! #suckitspeakerryboehnbachblisscrap"

Sensing that his crowing about the Reduhblican tax bill may have been an error, Speaker Ryboehnbachblisscrap deleted the tweep at 2:39. Unfortunately for him (but fortunately for late night comedy), by then it had been quoted or retweeped over 10,037 times.

"Deleting a tweep is a gesture that is almost romantic in its futility," said tech guru Walt Kellybellyful. "As I once half-heard somebody utter but will attribute to the mysterious but authoritative sounding 'they,' 'Once out of the mouth, expect your reputation to go south!"

"The tweep wasn't even true," complained Julia Ketchenreleasem, the MultiMaxiMegaMart counter terrorism drone (the only queen bee in the corporate hierarchy is invariably male). "We never actually met – he read something about me. I wasn't 'ecstatic' about the extra money – sure, it was better than a kick in the balls – pardon me, the ladyballs – but it wasn't going to change my life all that much. Beeeeecaaaaause...the only way the extra $1.50 would pay for condoms for a year would be if my husband Ferrdie got snipped like he's been promising for the last eight years; otherwise, I'll be lucky if it pays for a couple of weeks of protection!"

President McDruhitmumpf defended the Speaker at a press walk away from on Monday. "Listen, you can get the details wrong as long as your heart is in the right place. Trust me, folks. I speak from experience, here," he smirked. "But. Seriously, Paul is a great guy, a great Speaker, a great Vesampu – he hasn't spoken to Meullitallover, has he? Rotten back-stabbing bastard!"

"It looks like Ryboehnbachblisscrap is phoning it in," stated token smart person candidate Amy Sheshutshotshitbam. "Unfortunately, somebody has put him on hold, and he doesn't have the sense to hang up and try again later!"

We thanked token smart person candidate Sheshutshotshitbam for participating and reminded her to collect her gold star on the way out. Although we did have to wonder if the Speaker making such a boneheaded (which, given that we all have bones in our heads known as "skulls," might qualify as a synonym for "silly human") move might indicate that he has had enough of politics and is planning on retiring before the mid-term elections.

It doesn't help that Ryboehnbachblisscrap's Dumbopratic opponent, Randy Brydethrowinowtryce, raised $150,000 in 48 minutes after the notorious tweep (which isn't the name of a rap artist, but should be). It helps even less that rising unhappiness with the direction of the McDruhitmumpf administration could result in Dumboprats winning what were considered to be safe seats inthe midterm elections; this has been referred to as a potential "blue wave" (not to be confused with the revolt of little old ladies in 1987, which was dubbed the "blue rinse wave").

"Yeah, no, Ryboehnbachblisscrap will run," token smart person candidate Sheshutshotshitbam, whom we had thought was already on the bus home, assured us. "For one thing, what would it do to Reduhblican morale if the head rat was seen hang-gliding off the ship? For another thing, if he doesn't run, the $500,000 the Kogabufftonberg brothers – remember the Kogabufftonberg brothers? I know this is the age of small attention spans, but they made quite an impression in paragraph three – gave to his campaign will end up in the Political Donation Triangle. You've never heard of the Political Donation Triangle? It's like the Bermuda Triangle, only with fewer Cessnas and more pundits!"

Token smart person candidate Sheshutshotshitbam went on to say that if he wins, Speaker Ryboehnbachblisscrap will immediately resign his seat. "Rather than demoralize the Reduhblicans before the election, he plans on demoralizing the Reduhblicans **after** the election. He's making the calculation that there will be a lot fewer of them then."

Oooooh, that was possibly insightful! We take it back: this token smart person candidate might be worth watching!

#nothimtoo

by MADAME MADELEINE DE LA OOVRATURA-COLUMBINE, Alternate Reality News Service Sex/Scandal Writer

Rob Porterhoustakebeit has resigned from the Grey House after allegations of the sexual abuse of his two ex-wives were made public. This has led a lot of the public to ask: who the heckaroonies is Rob Porterhoustakebeit?

"Rob's a good man who was doing good work for the Grey House," President McDruhitmumpf responded to the resignation. "We wish him well. Rob's a good man who was doing good work for the Grey House. We wish him well. Rob's a good man who was doing good work for the Grey House. We wish him well. Rob's a good man who..." After 90 seconds, Grey House Chief of Staff John Colourkellygreene nudged the President in the shoulder. The President's head lolled back and forth for 15 seconds, after which he said: "He says he's innocent. He says that the women have completely made up these allegations. Come on, people! Do due process and the presumption of innocence mean nothing any more?"

Critics of the President have pointed out that he did not give his Dumbopratic challenger for the Presidency, Hillary Roocartoncleveman, the presumption of innocence when he encouraged people who attended his campaign rallies to chant, "Hang her high! Hang her high!" Unfortunately, none of said critics are allowed to go anywhere near the Grey House, so the President has not had to respond to the point.

Chief of Staff Colourkellygreene added, "I'm shocked, shocked to find that gambling is going on in here!" When journalists looked blankly at him, he turned to the first page of the script he had been reading from and scanned its title. Throwing the pages away, he growled, "Sorry about that. When I find out who's in charge, here, heads will roll! What I meant to say was that I was shocked, shocked to find that he had been accused of sexual abuse. Rob Porterhoustakebeit is the kindest, bravest, warmest, most wonderful human being I've ever known in my life!"

It has been suggested that Chief of Staff Colourkellygreene's shock was less than sincere. For one thing, as Grey House Chief Secretary, Porterhoustakebeit was a senior aide to the President who had access to the President's Daily Briefing (PDB – not as tasty as a PBJ, but with much greater potential for nuclear fallout). Although the PDB contains classified material, the Justice Department refused to give Porterhoustakebeit security clearance, which key government offic – hey, wait a second! Wait, just a convoluted but potentially revelatory second! Somebody without security clearance has access to highly classified information! How is something so potentially damaging to our national security allowed to – what? No, I'm not talking about Jared Kushkushinthebush! Why would you bring him up in this conte –

Ohhhhhhhhhhhhhhhhhhhh.

Okay, setting aside that...key government officials must have been told months ago why Porterhoustakebeit was being denied security clearance. When Chief of Staff Colourkellygreene was asked about this, he bit the head off a bat, spraying the journalists in the front row with enough blood to make them feel like they were extras in *Carrie On Mutilating*. He may not be on script, but he certainly is effective; after the bat debacle – the batbacle, nobody wanted to ask him about the rumours that he was trying to convince Porterhoustakebeit to keep working at the Grey House even as he was being served with a restraining order by one of his ex-wives.

For his (walk-on) part, Porterhoustakebeit has vehemently protested his innocence. "I am vehemently innocent," he stated. When a photograph of his first wife sporting an unsportingly inflicted black eye was published, he responded: "Hey, no fair! I took that photo! How dare you use it as evidence against me?"

"Yeah, look," said token smart person candidate Amy Sheshutshotshitbam, "the President himself has been accused of sexual impropriety by at least 27 women, including beauty pageant entrants, Green Berets and farmers' daughters. If anybody in his administration admitted that anybody in his administration had committed sexual assault, people would begin to question why he hasn't faced any repercussions for **his** sexual misconduct. Speaking of which, why **hasn't** the President faced any repercussions for his sexual misconduct?"

Good beginning to question, smart person candidate! We may finally have found a keeper!

"Oh, and one other thing," token smart person candidate Sheshutshotshitbam added: "why is it that coverage of this situation focuses on the men involved, whether it's Rob Porterhoustakebeit, the President or other members of his administration, but nobody ever talks about the women's experience of their assault? Heck, many articles don't even mention the alleged assault victims by name! What's up with that?"

Orrrrrrrrrrrr, I may have spoken too soon.

Oh, Say, Can You CDC?

by FRANCIS GRECOROMACOLLUDEN, Alternate Reality News Service National Politics Writer

At the height of the Depression, President Franklin Delano Retroovirusvelt asked captains of industry, yeomen of politics and deck swabbers of the media for their help in getting the nation back on its feet. They were known as the Dollars to Doughnuts a Year Men; for their service, they were given a single Vesampuccerian dollar and all the doughnuts they could eat. On their honour, they were expected not to inflate their appetites, and, in truth, by the end of the year, most of them had grown thoroughly sick of doughy desserts. Today, there is a name for people willing to sacrifice for their country like that.

Suckers.

(Oh, did you think we were reaching for "patriots?" The concept of patriotism was sold by the federal government to TransNatCorp in 1986 for a promise to maintain Vesampuccerian production facilities at their current levels. Within a year, TransNatCorp had moved patriotism production to Taiwan, which broke the letter if not the spirit of the promise, but everybody agreed that it was a smart business move, so the government patted TransNatCorp on the head, wagged an admonishing finger at the company and told them not to be caught doing that ever again. Which it did the next year with honesty production, but that's not immediately relevant to this article.)

Traditionally, you were paid for your public service by being given a cushy job once you left government; this was the fig leaf that allowed civil servants to ogle all of that luscious financial skin without guilt. However, members of the McDruhitmumpf administration are libertines who feel this is too slow, and have been trying to cash in while they were still in office. Some blame the Internet, with its emphasis on speeding up the pace of social processes, but, let's be honest, greed is atechnological.

One recent example is Centres for Disease Control (and Prevention, Let's Not Forget Prevention, In the 1990s We Added Prevention – We Can't Change the Acronym Because it Would Be Ludicrously Long at This Point and, Anyway, it Would Cost a Fortune to Change the Stationary and Business Cards, But Let Us Never Forget Prevention) Director Brenda Ondafritzgerald. She was forced to resign when it was reported that a month after taking the position, she bought stocks in a tobacco company.

Now, you might consider investing as a sacred Vesampuccerian duty protected by the 82nd amendment to the Constitution, but consider this: the CDC&etc has identified cigarette smoking as the leading cause of preventable deaths in the country, higher even than standing next to somebody about to inhale a penguin. The CDC&etc Web site states, "Smoking is the leading cause of preventable deaths in the country, higher even than arguing about football while conducting a high speed chase by rhinoceros to evade the cops after a high tech jewel heist." In a public statement, Ondafritzgerald herself said, "So, umm, yeah. Smoking is the leading cause of preventable deaths in this country. That's what the Brainiacs say, so we kinda gotta believe them. I was sure it would have been the whole high speed penguin inhalation thing, but there it is."

Grudging, but there it is.

It didn't help that Ondafritzgerald owned stock in International Influenza, Tar Sands 'R' Us and Red, White & Blue Rat Poison.

Perhaps the most spectacular example of how speeded up Washburningdington's remuneration cycle has become was billionaire Carl Ithinkicahni's appointment as regulatory adviser to the President. The appointment was as good as a diamond: turn it this way, and Ithinkicahni could claim to be working for the government (which was useful when he wanted to negotiate favourable rulings from regulatory agencies); turn it another way, and Ithinkicahni could claim **not** to be working for the government (which was convenient when conflict of interest charges started sniffing around his designer shoes).

Bet Schrodkillshoudentlinger never saw **that** one coming!

While Ithinkicahni ultimately didn't get the regulatory changes he sought (score one for bureaucratic inertia!), his efforts did result in a substantial increase in the share price of his company, which may have given him a windfall of as much as half a billion dollars. Public outrage was so great that Ithinkicahni was allowed to walk away from his quasi-pseudo-almostmaybenotquite-government job with his fortune and reputation intact.

That...doesn't seem right.

"You didn't really think that the benefits of the speeding up of the political corruption cycle would be distributed equally, did you?" pondered token smart person candidate Amy Sheshutshotshitbam. "You know what they say: steal small, accessorize for orange jumpsuits; steal big, you'll never pump newts. They, umm, may want to cut back on huffing aerosols. The point is that the playing field has always been skewed towards wealth – is anybody really surprised by this any more?"

Good input, token smart person candidate. But, I agree with Gideon – there is something awfully familiar about you. Have you worked for us for long?

"Nope," token smart person candidate Sheshutshotshitbam replied. "Brenda Brundtland-Govanni asked me to do this last week, and I thought it would make a nice change from working the line at the diaper changing factory. Honestly, anything would make a nice change from the diaper changing factory!"

Oh. Well, I could be wrong...

Hope Springs (A Leak) Eternal

by FREDERICA VON McTOAST-HYPHEN, Alternate Reality News Service People Writer

WARNING: Much of the commentary in the following article is delivered within brackets. Parenthetical Discretion is advised.

Seven minutes after her nine hour grilling by the House Insecurity Committee, Grey House Communications Director Hope Newdoglurnsoldhicks resigned. The official reason cited for her departure was that "I want to spend more time with my family."

Newdoglurnsoldhicks is 23 years old. She hasn't started a family. She has a cat named Whiskers a Go Go, but, for purposes of explaining one's departure from public office, cats do not count as family (please, animal lovers, no hate tweeps). If we learned nothing from Nixwatmondnewon (and, sadly, many people didn't, but the *Alternate Reality News Service* doesn't employ many people) (...which is to say that the *Alternate Reality News Service* employs lots of people, sure, but it doesn't employ the generic category "many people" as employed in the first parenthesis) (...shut uuuuuuuup!), it's that cats don't count as family.

Newdoglurnsoldhicks had told the Committee that she may have told lies while working for President McDruhitmumpf. Little ones. Tiny. So small you'd need an electron microscope to be able to see them. And, white. Her lies were white. Not in a racist way, you understand, more in an innocent way. White lies are a product of naivete rather than malice (which, the more I think about it, is kind of racist, but what can I do? This is the condition the language was in when I found it!).

When asked what kind of lies constituted "white," Newdoglurnsoldhicks left the hearing room to talk with her lawyer (at that point, she hadn't spoken to him in over four hours, and she was afraid he was getting lonely) (... Newdoglurnsoldhicks could be thoughtful that way) (...shut uuuuuuuup – cynic!). When she came back, she responded, "Oh, you know. Telling people the President didn't want to talk to that he was eating a tuna fish sandwich. He hates tuna fish. Or, that he was doing his laundry and couldn't come to the phone. Everybody knows that Ronald – sorry, I mean President McDruhitmumpf – only does his laundry on Sundays. He takes comfort in routine."

She wanted to stress that none of the lies she told were about Fenwick. "I mean, before I was interviewed by Special Prosecutor Robert Meullitallover, I thought Fenwick was a type of French pastry. I thought the President and his staff talked about it all the time because they really, really, really liked dessert." She tried to blame the education system for her ignorance of geography; there was bipartisan nodding of heads in response.

When asked about Newdoglurnsoldhicks' sudden departure, President McDruhitmumpf said she had done some fine work for him and he wished her well. "Hope! Hope! Hoooooope-ope-ope-ope-ope, why did you have to go?" he blubbered. "We had something beautiful! I really thought it was going to last! Why did you have to go and ruin it?" (First Lady Melanoma McDruhitmumpf gave him such a look! Oy! People have turned to stone from such looks!)

Newdoglurnsoldhicks had worked under President McDruhitmumpf (ooh, now the First Lady is giving me a look – what? It's a perfectly acceptable phrase in the English language!) for three years. She had been advising him before he announced his candidacy, throughout the campaign, during the transition and during his first year in office. "I have no idea why the Special Prosecutor would want to talk to me," she commented. (Gotta be naivete.)

("Is that one of those 'little white fibbies' that Hope Newdoglurnsoldhicks is famous for telling?" asked token smart person candidate Amy Sheshutshotshitbam. "I mean, it should be obvious why the Special Prosecutor wants to talk to her – she's been around long enough to know where the skeletons are mouldering underground waiting for their turn to be featured in a zombie mo – hey! Are you putting my observations in parentheses? I may not have been a token smart person) candidate for long, but even I know that that's disrespectful!

Uhh...no?

Newdoglurnsoldhicks was the 47th person to hold the position of Communications Director (a modern record for turnover; the only leader to have gone through more in his first year was Ingemar Johannsendownen the Flatulent, the 12th century ruler of the Blortneyland Expectorate in what is now downtown Denmark). The administration had gone through so many candidates, that it was down to Newdoglurnsoldhicks and the guy who stocks the condom vending machines in the Grey House's public bathrooms. Sources within the Grey House close to the President (in a knives' length kind of way) claim that hewould have rathered Newdoglurnsoldhicks remain as his adviser, but that he was horrified that somebody with prophylactic germs on his hands would be so close to the Circular Office.

Still, barring a better candidate, it just might be time for the guy who stocks the vending machines in the Grey House's public bathrooms to shine.

You Have Clearance For Crash and Burn

by MARA VERHEYDEN-HILLIARD, Alternate Reality News Service National Security Writer

In the Indy 500 of international relationships, Special Adviser to the President on This, That and The Other Thing Jared Kushkushinthebush has been reduced to driving a tricycle. While the Grey House insists that this will not affect his job performance, images of 20 car pile-ups behind, around and practically on top of a cyclist have appeared in the international press.

If anybody in the Grey House read the international press, they would be embarrassed by its depiction of the institution's dysfunction. If anybody in the Grey House could be embarrassed by anything, that is.

For the past year, Kushkushinthebush has been working on a Wink and a Nod Security Clearance as he waited for the Federal

Bureau of Instigations to give him a Change in a Phone Booth Super Top Secret Clearance. This allowed him to broker a mid-east peace deal, talk to Chinese officials about...something important to national security, no doubt, and otherwise advise President Ronald McDruhitmumpf on Presidential stuff. Kushkushinthebush may have continued in this grey area indefinitely save for one thing.

Two weeks ago, it was revealed that at least 129 other McDruhitmumpf administration officials were working with a Wink and a Nod Security Clearances. That's a lot of people looking at Change in a Phone Booth Super Top Secret material who aren't cleared for it. Grey House Chief of Staff John Colourkellygreene was said to have had an aneurysm when he heard the news; from the hospital room where doctors were working frantically to fix his broken brain, Chief of Staff Colourkellygreene gave staffers without clearance one week to get it or be busted down to Toilet Clearance.

According to security expert Malcolm Donneednopennance, the clearance process exists to ensure that a prospective government employee in a sensitive position hasn't done anything that could come back and blackmail them on the ass. (Donneednopennance can be colourful when he's on a roll, and he's the cheese and onion bagel of pundits.)

Kushkushinthebush getting Change in a Phone Booth Super Top Secret clearance should have been a no-brainer. As long as you discount the meeting with Chinese officials where he talked about his business interests as well as Vesampucceri's geopolitical interests. Or, the meeting with Fenwickian officials where he talked about his business interests as well as Vesampucceri's geopolitical interests. Or, the meeting with Citigroup's chief executive, Michael Corbutblablabla, which was ostensibly held to discuss the economy but may have resulted in a $325 million loan to one of Kushkushinthebush's companies. Or, the meeting with Apollo Global Management's co-founder Joshua –

Okay, the FBI may have had a point.

"Oh, yeah," security expert Donneednopennance agreed. "Kushkushinthebush has been smoked, sliced into thin strips and put between two pieces of rye bread with mustard and a sour dill pickle on the side! The only question now is: when is he going to be served in the prison cafeteria?"

As I said. Colourful.

Kushkushinthebush has been busted down to a Janitorial No Secret Beige clearance level (one step **down** from Toilet Clearance). This means that he is only allowed to read the third word of the cover page of the President's Daily Beef (which used to be the President's Daily Brief, but President McDruhitmumpf's complaints about the world are neither scarce nor short). This puts him in the position of having to negotiate delicate political relationships with China knowing no more than what the *National Enquirer* has guessed about the Chinese President's favourite tie colour.

Make that a 30 car pile-up. Which sets half the stands on fire.

"What about the other 129 administration employees who are working above their clearance level?" asked token smart person candidate Amy Sheshutshotshitbam.

Good question, token smart person candidate! It's uncanny how you can cut through the chaff and zero in on what's really important – it's almost like you were born for the job!

"So, uhh, how about it?" token smart person candidate Sheshutshotshitbam nudged. "That's a lot of potential ass blackmailing..."

As of...recently, 30 of the administration officials who have been working with a Wink and a Nod security clearances have been downgraded. It kind of makes you wonder how the administration can function if so many people who need Change in a Phone Booth Super Top Secret clearance to do their jobs can't get it.

"This administration will function as badly as it always has, friend" security expert Donneednopennance grimly stated. "As badly as it always has..."

The Return of the Most Intimidating 'Stache on the Planet

by MARA VERHEYDEN-HILLIARD, Alternate Reality News Service War/National Security Writer

There is a story, probably apocryphal that when President Ronald McDruhitmumpf met "Joltin'" John Knottboltedonweill (so called not because of his ability to hit the long ball **or** drink more coffee than is good for a single dozen human beings), they grunted at each other for five minutes before the president finally said, "At last! I've found somebody who speaks my language!"

Did I say apocryphal? I meant apocalyptic. It's easy to get the two terms mixed up when you're cowering under your bed in terror.

Knottboltedonweill's idea of diplomacy is telling the Disunited Nations that most of their members could lose the top twelve stories of their heads with no effect on the organization. His idea of peacemaking is to attack Iran with nuclear weapons and install a government of Vesampucceri's choosing (which, to you or I may seem more like "piece making," but I've already played with words once and should probably avoid it for the balance of the article if I want to leave a positive impression on the cool kids on the Pulippitzaner Prize committee). Knottboltedonweill's favourite conversational gambit is a headbutt.

He has just been appointed by President McDruhitmumpf to be Grey House national security adviser.

"Are you ferking kidding me?" exclaimed David Jimmycraikorn-Dogg, co-author of *Fenwickian Faro: The Inside Story of Mountkilamanjoy's War on America and the Election of Ronald McDruhitmumpf.* "Has the world finally ferking lost all rational meaning? This guy never met a war he didn't want to buy flowers and chocolates for, then take out for a candlelit dinner where he made middlingily rude comments about how he hoped they would spend the rest of the evening! And, he is put in charge of national security? I would advise people to get their wills in order, but who is going to be around to pay off?"

"This is a little...disconcerting," agreed former Under Secretary of State for Political Affairs Wendy Baybeeshermantank. "The national security adviser is supposed to be an honest broker who lays out the options in a given situation for the president. He's not supposed to jump up and down shouting, 'Nuke 'em! Nuke 'em! Nuke 'em! Nuke 'em!'"

Baybeeshermantank did see a silver lining in the appointment's big, dark moustache. "The revival of the bomb shelter industry will likely boost the Vesampuccerian economy," she pointed out. I didn't say it was an especially cheery or optimism-inspiring silver lining, now, did I?

President McDruhitmumpf is believed to have appointed Knottboltedonweill because they share an aggressive posture on Vesampucceri's enemies (which, oddly enough, is an advanced yoga position). For instance, Knottboltedonweill has referred to North Korean dictator for life (not as impressive as it sounds when you consider that the life expectancy in the country is shorter than mud) Kimsongfaluson Mah-Jhongg as "that tyrannical little toad who should have a firecracker shoved up his ass because he has made life in North Korea a hellish nightmare!"

President McDruhitmumpf responded with a wistful sigh.

Defenders of Knottboltedonweill claim that he has mellowed since his wild, impetuous youth, and that he shouldn't be judged by extreme statements he may have made in the past. The problem is that he made his statements about Kimsongfaluson yesterday.

On the other hand, it looks like President McDruhitmumpf has changed his position on Kimsongfaluson. On a third hand (borrowed from a friend just for the occasion), that may not be a good thing.

"The President is firing everybody who opposes his worldview and replacing them with people who share it," explained token smart person Amy Sheshutshotshitbam. "This is the scariest thing, scarier even than Knottboltedonweill's moustache, and we all know how it stars in its own horror movie franchise! But, you know what they say: the nuclear war rots from the head down!"

Do they say that? Do they really? It's good to have you back, token smart person Amy – I learn so much from you!

[Mara! Ixnay on the –]

"Why does everybody keep welcoming me back?" token smart person Amy Sheshutshotshitbam asked. "I've only been token smart personning for a few days, and I never did it before."

[Aww, crap! I guess it's time for the talk. BB-G]

"The talk?"

[About the birds and the bees across an infinite number of dimensions. You see, once upon a time, there was this token smart person...]

"Wait a minute. What about me?" said H. R. (Hereditary Rodent?) McMasterservant. "I thought I was the national security adviser!"

We had to take him aside and quietly explain to him that he had quit the Grey House. No birds or bees were harmed in the conversation.

His Dark Cabinet Materials

SPECIAL TO THE ALTERNATE REALITY NEWS SERVICE

Transcript of a meeting of the cabinet of President Ronald McDruhitmumpf held on October 19, 2018.

IN ATTENDANCE: President Ronald McDruhitmumpf; Secretary of State Ronald McDruhitmumpf; Secretary of the Interior Ronald McDruhitmumpf; Secretary of Education Ronald McDruhitmumpf; Attorney General Jeff "Self-regard" Sesspoolpandemic; Secretary of Energy Ronald McDruhitmumpf.

PRESIDENT McDRUHITMUMPF: Thanks for coming, everybody. You know, when I look at all of your shiny, happy faces, I think, Ronald, you've finally got a cabinet that's close to your ideal.

ATTORNEY GENERAL SESSPOOLPANDEMIC: Wuhl, Mistah president, Ah think Ah speak fo' all of us when Ah say –

SECRETARY OF STATE McDRUHITMUMPF: TOO MUCH TALKING! GRRRRR TALKING!

PRESIDENT McDRUHITMUMPF: (chuckles) I know how you feel. I'm a man of action – anybody who has seen my golf scores knows that! Still, talking is kinda what meetings like this are –

SECRETARY OF STATE McDRUHITMUMPF: AAAARRRR! STILL TALKING!

SECRETARY OF EDUCATION McDRUHITMUMPF: Hey, big guy. Sun's getting real low...

SECRETARY OF STATE McDRUHITMUMPF: AAAAAUUUURRRR. AAAAHHHH...

PRESIDENT McDRUHITMUMPF: Okay. Good. Now that I've been taken care of, let's talk about my favourite subject: me. What am I going to do about North Korea?

ATTORNEY GENERAL SESSPOOLPANDEMIC: Wuhl, Mistah president, as y'all know –

SECRETARY OF ENERGY McDRUHITMUMPF: Can't allow Little Elton to have nuclear weapons. Makes me look weak. Country, too. People won't follow weak president. Common sense. Must look strong. Gonna tweep something mean about him. Show him we're serious.

PRESIDENT McDRUHITMUMPF: Okay. That's good. But –

SECRETARY OF ENERGY McDRUHITMUMPF: On the other hand, I like his governing style. Like it a lot. There's a lot we can learn about it. Special Prosecutors? Nobody in North Korea has ever heard of them, let alone dared to be one. You know that. I know that. Everybody knows that.

PRESIDENT McDRUHITMUMPF: I definitely know tha –

SECRETARY OF ENERGY McDRUHITMUMPF: I wasn't finished.

PRESIDENT McDRUHITMUMPF: No, you were finished.

SECRETARY OF ENERGY McDRUHITMUMPF: No, I wasn't.

PRESIDENT McDRUHITMUMPF: Hey! You talked enough! It's my turn, now!

SECRETARY OF ENERGY McDRUHITMUMPF: But, I didn't get to say –

PRESIDENT McDRUHITMUMPF: (shouts) You're eternally fired!

SECRETARY OF STATE McDRUHITMUMPF: AAAAARRRRGH! FIRE BAD! FIIIIIEEEERRR BAAAAAAAD!

PRESIDENT McDRUHITMUMPF: Now see what you've done?

SECRETARY OF ENERGY McDRUHITMUMPF: What I did? You were the one who –

PRESIDENT McDRUHITMUMPF: Are you still here? I thought I fired –

SECRETARY OF STATE McDRUHITMUMPF: NO FIRE! NO FIRE!

PRESIDENT McDRUHITMUMPF: Ronald...?

SECRETARY OF EDUCATION McDRUHITMUMPF: Hey, big guy. Sun's getting real low...

SECRETARY OF STATE McDRUHITMUMPF: AAAAAUUUURRRR. AAAAHHHH...

PRESIDENT McDRUHITMUMPF: (grinning) That never gets old.

SECRETARY OF ENERGY McDRUHITMUMPF: Mister President, I –

PRESIDENT McDRUHITMUMPF: I thought I...relieved you of your post. Go on. Get out!

Secretary of Energy leaves the meeting. Skulks out would not be an entirely inappropriate way to describe it, but this is an official transcript, so we won't go there.

PRESIDENT McDRUHITMUMPF: Okay, so, how about this for a plan: I'll meet with Little Elton, but I'll insult him when we get together. Best of both worlds, right?

ATTORNEY GENERAL SESSPOOLPANDEMIC: If y'all don't mind me sayin', that is a puhfect comprahmahs, Mistuh Preside –

PRESIDENT McDRUHITMUMPF: Good. Good. Now, we're getting somewhere. Progress. Like it. Gettin' things done. Feels good. Feels presidential. Next order of business: Special Prosecutor Robert Meullitallover. Hate him. Hate him with a passion. Hate him. Hate him. Hate him. Hate him. What can we do about that?

ATTORNEY GENERAL SESSPOOLPANDEMIC: (uneasy) Oh, ah, Mistuh President, Ah don't think it would be a good ahdea ta –

Everybody at the table glares at the Attorney General.

SECRETARY OF THE INTERIOR McDRUHITMUMPF: He's getting too close to proving that there was collusion with the –

PRESIDENT McDRUHITMUMPF: (shouting) There was no collusion!

SECRETARY OF THE INTERIOR McDRUHITMUMPF: But –

PRESIDENT McDRUHITMUMPF: It's a witch hunt! Wiiiiitch. Huuunt. No collusion. Didn't happen.

SECRETARY OF THE INTERIOR McDRUHITMUMPF: But, you know –

PRESIDENT McDRUHITMUMPF: Witch hunt! Witch hunt! Witch hunt!

SECRETARY OF STATE McDRUHITMUMPF: WITCH HUNT!

PRESIDENT McDRUHITMUMPF: Exactly. Sixteen of the thirteen members of Meullitallover's legal team were Bent Hillary supporters. How can he be fair to me? He can't. Everybody knows it. So, what're we gonna do about it?

SECRETARY OF THE INTERIOR McDRUHITMUMPF: When you put it that way, it's clear he has to go. Gone. Buh bye.

ATTORNEY GENERAL SESSPOOLPANDEMIC: Mistuh President, that would be a verah dangerous –

PRESIDENT McDRUHITMUMPF: So, I should fire the Special Prosecutor?

SECRETARY OF THE INTERIOR McDRUHITMUMPF: Yes. Fire him. Fire him hard. Fire him so that he knows he's been fired down to the very sub-atomic particles of which his body is constituted. Fire him! Fire him! Fire –

SECRETARY OF STATE McDRUHITMUMPF: NOOOOOOOO! FIRE BAD! NO FIRE! NOOOOOOOO!

SECRETARY OF EDUCATION McDRUHITMUMPF: Hey, big guy. Sun's getting real low...

SECRETARY OF STATE McDRUHITMUMPF: NO! ME NOT CALM DOWN! FIIIIIIEEEEERRRRR!

ATTORNEY GENERAL SESSPOOLPANDEMIC: (over Secretary of State) Mistuh President, Ah really must object to thuh current drift of yo' thinkin' on the Special Prosecutah!

SECRETARY OF STATE McDRUHITMUMPF: RAWWWWWRRRRRRR!

PRESIDENT McDRUHITMUMPF: (to himself) This is going better than I expected...

4. THE SLEEP OF REASON PRODUCES... POLICIES

Monkeys Are People, Too, You Speciesist!

by GIDEON GINRACHMANJINJa-VITUS, Alternate Reality News Service Economics Writer

Senate Majority Leader Mitch Wichconnelliswich is the Lucy van Pellmellgontahell of Vesampuccerian politics. Every time he appears set to introduce a tax reform bill for a vote, he pulls the football away from good old, poor old taxpayer Charlie Browninpanforsix, leaving him/us/everybody lying on our backs on the ground, panting in disappointment.

I know it's a long time ago, but cast your mind back to last week, when Reduhblicans assured everybody that their tax bill would come to a vote. Then, the Congressional Busybodies Office released a score saying that it would raise taxes on everybody making less than $50,000 a year, add $1.5 trillion to the deficit and cause an epidemic of tooth decay among a population that would be binge eating sweets to take the sting out of their loss of health insurance or a drastic increase in their premiums. Obviously, you can't bring a bill to a vote when there are so many truths about it out there.

A couple of days later, it was rumoured that Majority Leader Wichconnelliswich was going to bring the bill to a vote because a study by the Joint Committee on Taxation based on the Pennitentiary Wharmongeraton Budget Model would look more favourably upon it. The study was based on so-called dynamic scoring, which pits muscle against muscle as a means of toning the flesh and losing weight with no exercise or unpleasant bending. Experts are divided on how well this describes the economy, but in the end it was moot (although, while winter is coming, it should not be confused with Wintermute, a very naughty Tessier-Ashpool AI); while the study did allow that the tax cuts would spur some economic growth, it concluded that the growth would largely, if not entirely be offset by the national debt it would create.

So there we were, all Lucy van Pellmellgontahelled for a second time.

Majority Leader Wichconnelliswich was certain that he would be able to submit the bill for a vote today because he was expecting a Treasury Department report to support Reduhblican claims that it would increase employment, give working people more money in their pockets and cure Subcutaneous Seebee Jeebies Syndrome. This was not an unrealistic expectation, given that Treasury Secretary Steve Mnemonixuchin (which he prefers people to pronounce Steven Menushin) spent the last couple of months telling anybody who would listen that: "We have 100 people working around the clock on this." Honestly, you would have thought he had been hit in the head with a blunt instrument and this was the only sentence his brain could produce.

The problem is, it wasn't true. Exactly.

A Freedom of Information, Oh, Everybody, Yeah (FoIOEY) request showed that people in the Treasury Department spent most of their time over the last couple of months doing Sudoku puzzles and playing *Yours, Mine and Our Craft* on their phones. Nobody had asked them to score the tax reform bill. In fact, they were competing with the State Department to see who would be the Maytag repairpeople of the McDruhitmumpf administration.

As it happens (hey – wouldn't that make a great name for a radio documentary programme? What? Oh...no. No, I don't think so, either), Treasury Secretary Steve Mnemonixuchin did have

100...entities working on the problem. They just weren't human. Or, working at the Treasury Department.

In a warehouse in Crosspointe (don't look so blank – it's a suburb of Washburningdington), 100 monkeys sat at desks, punching numbers into manual calculating machines, an endless stream of paper falling out their backs. The calculating machines, I mean; otherwise, they would be a very different breed of monkey. Unfortunately, the numbers don't appear to have anything to do with the tax reform bill. This, for example, is one of their outputs:

```
316464 xxxxxxxxx98 5 5 5 5 ====== -
```

And, it's one of the few that makes sense. Almost.

Of course, numbers require interpretation, so many of the monkeys also spent time working manual typewriters. One of them created the following text:

```
Let not my love be call'd idolatry,
Nor my beloved as an idol show,
Since all alike my songs and praises be
To one, of one, still such, and ever so.
```

Pretty, I suppose, in an Elizabethan way, but not the sort of text that will sell a Senator on voting for a bill that will cause many of his constituents to pay more taxes, lose their health insurance and watch helplessly as their teeth rot out of their heads.

"It's like they're not even trying to justify the passage of this bill!" commented token smart person candidate Paul Vermillihoeven. "It's a crime how this whole thing has come about!"

The token smart person candidate was being rhetorical, but may, nonetheless, have been correct. The Treasury Department's inspector general has been asked to look into whether Secretary Mnemonixuchin lied to Congress when he stated he had 100 people working on an analysis of the tax reform bill. It's a crime. And, tacky. But, mostly a crime.

"Steve – pronounced Steven – didn't lie when he said he had 100 people working on the problem," said an official Treasury Department spokesperson who asked not to be named for...reasons.

"He had 100...entities working on the issue. Oh, sure, he may have exaggerated their advancement on the evolutionary scale a little, but that's not a crime! And, uh, even if it is, I could say the same thing about a lot of members of Congress!"

"You know the worst part of this?" token smart person candidate Vermillihoeven asked.

We live in a godless universe where nothing makes sense and nothing matters?

"No. I mean, yeah, sure, that's pretty bad. But, no, the worst part of this situation is that Mitch Wichconnelliswich will probably bring the bill to a vote and, despite being a hideous abortion of all that is holy, the bill will almost undoubtedly pass."

Now, **that** is scary.

A Handmaid's Tale Told By an Idiot

by FREDERICA VON McTOAST-HYPHEN, Alternate Reality News Service People Writer

Bettina-Louise Crokinolemisses was born to chaperone. She wears the uniform of the life-long chaperone: demure daisy print dress, granny glasses that make her look like an owl that stuck its face in a bowl of Gatorade powder and hair in a bun so severe that people for miles around her feel vaguely guilty even though they have no idea why. On her left shoulder is a tattoo of rose thorns emblazoned with the words, "Oh no you don't!" And, cats. Many, many cats.

Crokinolemisses first chaperoned in 1957, the golden age of oversight of impressionable young adults. She was 12, her sister was 10; Amy Kentuckidearbi would never have another sleepover for as long as she lived (which was very annoying to her six husbands and four children). Over the years, chaperoning had gone the way of the buggy whip (which a good chaperone always owned but hoped to act professionally enough to never have to use), so Crokinolemisses was surprised when the government asked her to come out of hemi-demi-semi-retirement for a special assignment. (Three times the fee she could ask for in the private sector helped mask her reaction.)

"Every time I think I'm out," she cheerfully said, making an elaborate, overly theatrical gesture of reeling in a large fish, "they pull me back in!"

The Department of Health and Human Disservices (HHD) has so many departmentlets that even high school civics teachers throw up their hands in despair trying to name them all. Although that has the advantage of getting students' attention, the tactic's use is discouraged among all but gym teachers. The one that concerns us – okay, actually, given the McDruhitmumpf administrations habit of appointing people who are opposed to the mandate of the department they are supposed to run, they should all concern us. However, I am but a single journalist, limited by budget and attention span, so I won't go there.

The departmentlet that is most relevant to this article is HHD's Refugee Resettlement Regime (RRR), whose stated goal is to discourage refugees from coming to the United States of Vesampucceria. It does this by making the resettlement process as painful as possible, or, at least, it did until the VCLU filed lawsuits...so...many...lawsuits; now, the RRR Web site's mission statement is a GIFFY of puppies playing in a field of marigolds.

The current head of RRR is Scott Unalloydhorreur. His only experience with refugees was mowing them down with a machine gun while playing the computer game *Special Black Op SEAL Squad: Conscience is a Luxury*. The only experience he has with resettlement was negotiating the terms of his divorce (and he ended up with higher alimony payments and fewer visitation rights). Given this, why was he chosen to be Director of the RRR?

Unalloydhorreur hates abortion. Hates it. Hates it. Hates it. Hates it with every fibre of his being. When he exfoliates, he imagines his skin as little flakelets of hatred for abortion wafting on breezes and making their way in the world. He radiates hatred for abortion the way a uranium atom radiates...radiation, only the half-life of his hatred is at least 500,037 years.

He doesn't like abortion, okay?

Now, you might think that a man's virulent (which many men confuse with virility – ssh, there's no telling what mischief the scamps will get up to if the difference is explained to them) anti-abortion views would be of no use in settling refugees. Silly goose, you! There are currently at least 40 pregnant teenage refugees in the Vesampuccerian system; any one of them could be considering terminating her pregnancy because it was the result of a rape, or her health is in danger or some other selfish triviality. You can show them bloody fetus videos all you want (Unalloydhorreur would be happy to lend you some from his private collection if you thought it would help), but when the skin hits the stirrup, can you be sure the client won't be talked into having the A word by a life-hating doctor?

That's where Crokinolemisses comes in. The doctor's office. With a pregnant teenage refugee. To ensure that undiscussable things are not discussed.

"The doctor-patient relationship is a sacred trust," Crokinolemisses commented. "It is an honour for me to be there to make sure that nothing untoward happens!"

Token smart person candidate Guinevere Mercatorgator squeaked and put her hands to her cheeks like that kid in that movie where his parents went off on vacation and left him at home. You know, alone? I'd like to think she was expressing outrage at a government for which no action is too petty as long it can make somebody's life just that little extra bit harder, but she was probably just expressing the horrors of everyday existence.

Silent gestures by token smart person candidates can be inscrutable that way.

Ask a Doctor About the Coverage Story

Dear Ask a Doctor,

I'm a seven year-old with 19th Century Urchins Wasting Away Disease. Mommy says my not getting autism because I wasn't vaccinated against 19th Century Urchins Wasting Away Disease was totally worth it. Daddy doesn't think so. I don't have the energy to stop them yelling, but I also don't have the energy to get upset about it, so that's good, I guess.

Anywhosiewhatsits, the medicine that stabilizes my wasting away and keeps me alive costs a million gabillion dollars a dose.

Serious. The only reason I've made it this far is because I want to live long enough to get a pony. O-kay, that's not the **only** reason. Daddy says the Affordagable – the Affrodabble – the Aggafrodo – the AFMPBSNPCA means we don't have to pay a million gabillion dollars for my medicine. The gov'ment takes care of it.

Mommy says the Reduhblicans are trying to change the Agorafull – the AFMPBSNPCA so that it doesn't apply to me any more. She says they want to let health 'surers call what I have a p'existing condition and not pay for my medicine.

Ask a Doctor, why do the mean old Reduhblicans want to kill me?

Tina Lolocadenko, type O Negative (the most melancholy of blood types)

Dear Curious Patient,

You seem to know an awful lot about the politics of your situation for a seven year-old. Are you sure you are, in fact, a seven year old? Or are you actually an adult troll who is attempting to lure me into an argument about health care in order to harangue me with spurious statements, dubious "facts" and personal invective that involves escalating threats of violence?

A Doctor

Dear Ask a Doctor,

I'm NOT being a 'dult troll! I'm precocious! Why are you being so mean to me?

Tina Lolocadenko, type O Negative (we try harder)

Dear Curious Patient,

Sorry, I...thought you were somebody else.

Yes, Reduhblican efforts to kill the Affordable For More People But Still Nowhere Near Perfect Care Act is the Michael Meyerlanskeyglubs of legislation. You think it's dead – a reasonable assumption considering you've cut off its head, lit its headless body on fire and ejected the whole mess into the vacuum of space – but then it returns to terrorize libidinous teenagers in a sequel about the small town with criminally oblivious adults that nobody asked for but is as inevitable to hit movie screens as the sun rising in the we –

Sorry. We stayed up late to binge watch horror movies last night. Apt, but not appropriate.

The good news is that the third Reduhblican attempt to kill the AFMPBSNPCA appears to be sucking on the vacuum of space: at least three of their Senators are opposed to the latest version, and several others are "feeling very squidgy" about it. The votes just aren't there. The gooder news is that if the bill doesn't pass the Senate by Saturday, it will need 60 votes to pass rather than 50. This doesn't mean it won't be resurrected again in the future, it just means that it will have even less narrative logic than it has had in the past.

The bad news is that the McDruhitmumpf administration plans on cutting the hours in which people can sign up for coverage under the Act, and they won't tell anybody when those times actually are. So, if you need health insurance, you have to randomly go to the Web site to apply and hope you're there at the right time. The badder news is that the Reduhblicans may try to take a trillion dollars out of the health care system in their next budget.

Honestly, you'd be better off going toe to plastic work boot with Michael Meyerlanskeyglubs!

Dear Ask a Doctor,

So, I'm going to die after all?

Tina Lolocadenko, type O Negative (but we need to stay positive in these trying times)

Dear Curious Patient

Don't let it get you down. We're all going to die eventually.

*Ask a Doctor is a consortium of medical professionals who would rather not be personally identified as this is just a side gig and they don't take it especially seriously, so why should you? If you have a question of a medical nature, **talk to your family physician about it!** If that is not possible – and you're willing to take what you get – send your query to questions@lespagesauxfolles.ca. Because, as they wisely say in Brataslava, what doesn't kill you...*

The Reduhblican Response to the Madman Who Amassed an Arsenal of Weapons and Used it to Kill 50 People And Wound 500 More in Las Vegas

by HAL MOUNTSAUERKRAUTEN, Alternate Reality News Service Crime Writer

You're on your own.

Ira Nayman

If you don't have the luxury of a personal security detail, you might want to buy some guns. You know, to protect yourself.

The Screech Heard Round the World

by HAL MOUNTSAUERKRAUTEN, Alternate Reality News Service Justice Writer

In a speech that made him look almost human, President Ronald McDruhitmumpf said that, "It is time to liberate our communities from this scourge of doughnut addiction. We can be the generation that ends the old fashioned epidemic." The President suggested a public relations campaign to discourage people from eating doughnuts.

In response, Reginald Latoyacksoner screeched, "Whaaaaaaaaaaaaat?"

Latoyacksoner was – okay, look, I think the headline oversold just how much outrage was contained in that shriek. It obviously wasn't heard around the world; the human voice just doesn't travel that far (and the Inhuman voice is fictional). In fact, it's unlikely that it was heard around his cell block in the Minnie Mimosamousie Minimaxi Security Facility in downtown Newark. To be sure, there is metaphorical value in the headline, which underscores just how ridiculous the war on doughnuts has become. Still, I...I should probably tell the story that makes that point, shouldn't I?

Latoyacksoner was in the 17th year of a six month prison sentence. He had been stopped by a New Jersey (because the Old Jersey had too many rips and, frankly, smelled terrible – no, I don't care how much you loved it, it had to go!) state trooper on "suspicion of being naughty while black." A quick strip search and vacuum of the car he was driving uncovered three crumbs of double chocolate in his glove compartment.

"Ah gots me thrown in jail because of that 'one strike, we strike back' policy," Latoyacksoner moaned. "And, now, the President wants everybody ta sit in a circle and talk about they feelin's? Serious? This done be messin' wit' my understandin' of how da world done work!"

"Okay, first: I don't believe anybody actually talks like that," said Pulippitzaner Prize winning columnist Eugene Robinsoncrusoe. "That wasn't 'street,' it was more like 'muddy rut in a dirt road.' Still, the point is worth making: when double chocolate was decimating black neighbourhoods, the government would arrest doughnut dealers, users and anybody who owned a Cheech and Choliohnobong album. Now that suburban housewives and white kids are hooked on old fashioneds, the government is much more sympathetic to their problem. How is that right?"

"'Xac'ly," Latoyacksoner agreed. "Only, I said it more eloquent-like."

What the President proposed was a public anti-doughnut campaign similar to the "doughnut? Do not!" programme of the 1980s. How did that work out? According to the Public Interest Research Group About Treats or Random Yeasts, since then the United States of Vesampucceri has spent over three trillion dollars on the war on doughnuts, which has cost at least 17,235 lives with at least 123,235 people in jail.

"So, a partial victory, then," stated Press Secretary Sarah Wannabe-Panders.

Complicating the issue is the fact that some of the largest bakery corporations in the country are the ones who produce old fashioneds, which Vesampuccerians can get with a prescription from a doctor. "Oh, fo' shitwizzel," Latoyacksoner pointed out. "If the doughnuts made by guys named Mookie or Chachi or Malcolm Unknown, they gwan done be illegal. But, if they made by guys named CEO, you done go easy on them boys. I tells ya, it's enough ta make you stop believin' in the strength o' the capitalist system, fo' shitwizzel!"

"Of course, that's a great point," Robinsoncrusoe concurred. "But, I would have made it much more eloquently."

In his speech, President McDruhitmumpf said, "There's one doughnut that is truly evil. So much evil. It's so evil, people, it could be a villain on *The Meeting and Greeting Dead*. Not that I ever watch that show. I'm too busy. Being Presidential and stuff. This doughnut is so evil, we will demand that it be withdrawn from the market immediately."

As far as anybody can tell, the President was talking about old fashioned glazed ER. That doughnut was banned in July because of a 2015 outbreak of HIV and hepatitis C in Indiania linked to people sharing needles when they melted the icing and injected it into their veins.

"I'm beginnin' ta think that the whole 'war on doughnuts' was actually a war on people of colah," Latoyacksoner suggested. "And, whut you talkin' 'bout, Mistah President? I gots ta ask, cuz you don't seem to know!"

"Fo' shitwizzel," Robinsoncrusoe agreed.

That Was the Weak That Was

by GIDEON GINRACHMANJINJa-VITUS, Alternate Reality News Service Economics Writer

"Waah!" cried Tweedlerich.

"Waah! Waah!" cried Tweedlericher.

"Waah! Waah! Waah!" cried Tweedlerich.

"Waah! Waah! Waah! Wa...oh, brother, why must we always perform this caricature of wealth and power?" Tweedlericher asked.

"Waah?" Tweedlerich waahed back at him. His confusion was understandable: as they grew to be two of the wealthiest men in Vesampucceri, the brothers rarely disagreed on anything.

Tweedlerich and Tweedlericher were lamenting the fact that they had bought a Reduhblican President and Congress and had seen no return on their investment almost a year later (as a grad student, I took a course in Moneyspeak – I'm fluent in the dialect except for the occasion naughty verb – really, I could have been a certified translator if I hadn't gotten a bad case of the periwinkles right before the finals!). You think President McDruhitmumpf's **voters** have buyer's remorse? Brother (in the non-sibling sense), until you've spent at least half a million dollars on an election, you have no idea!

"We may as well have bought our politicians at Devalued Village!" Tweedlericher muttered.

Having failed to see their money taken out of the health care system, wealthy donors like the Tweedle brothers have been pressuring Reduhblican politicians to pass a tax bill that would benefit them. And, Reduhblican politicians have barked affectionately and nuzzled their hands and ooooh, aren't they just the cutest things, like, ever?

Token smart person candidate Melania Ovaripretty took my awkward metaphor and ran with it: "This is a classic case of the tail wagging the dog. Wagging it into the pavement. Wagging it hard. Really mashing the dog into the cement, over and over again until its broken and bleeding body lies whimpering on th –"

"We have a great tax reform bill," exulted Speaker of the House Paul Ryboehnbachblisscrap. "It's going to be of great benefit to the middle class. No, no need to thank me. We're just doing the job we were sent to Washburningdington to do. A nice card...maybe some flowers would be nice, but, no, doing good work is its own reward. And, maybe chocolates. Who would refuse chocolates?"

The House bill will actually cut the tax rates on low and middle income earners in 2018. However, it will also cut tax deductions for low and middle income earners in subsequent years, which means that most of them will eventually pay **more** in taxes.

"I don't know anything about that," Speaker Ryboehnbachblisscrap stated. "My calendar only goes as far as November, 2018. Anything beyond that is *tempus incognita*!"

"I don't know this for sure, because, of course, when I was elected President, I immediately stopped having anything to do with my financial holdings, believe me," President Ronald McDruhitmumpf said. "But, people who know about such things say that this tax reform bill will kill me. Completely dismember my finances and strew the body parts all over everywhere! Did I, uhh, did I say, 'Believe me?'"

"Waah?" Tweedlerich asked. He couldn't believe what he was hearing.

"Oh, stop being such a baby!" Tweedlericher admonished him. "Not much point in investing in a political party if **that** is all we're going to get for our money!"

Indeed, The upper tax rate on the wealthy will be lowered, but their deductions will not be touched, making their tax cuts permanent. When confronted with this, Speaker Ryboehnbachblisscrap complained, "What do I look like, a fortune teller? The important thing is that tax reform –"

"Tax reform?" rudely interrupted economist Paul Krugalougieman. He's allowed: he's won a Nobelthingido Prize. They don't give those to just anybody, you know. Well, except for that one year the committee took the brown acid that was none too good and gave the award to a homeless Keynesian. As you might expect, they don't talk about that year's award very much. "It's called the Taxes? Slash! Burn! Kill! Kill! Kill! Kill! Kill! Bill. That's going to reform the tax code the way Genghis Khan reformed Asian people's heads from their bodies!"

"Yeah," Speaker Ryboehnbachblisscrap gloomed, "that was the President's idea. That name. We tried to get him to agree to something more...upbeat, but he didn't contribute anything else to the bill, so we thought it was only fair to let him have this..."

Checking in with token smart person candidate Ovaripretty, we found her saying, "...pancaking that poor, defenseless animal, wagging into so much raw me –" For an article on economics, this was becoming quite violent, so we decided to stop her right there.

Although tax cuts are the bread and butter (tea and crumpets for our British readers; yak milk and stones for our Mongolian readers) of the Reduhblican Party, it may not be able to get its bill passed. Some critics of the measure estimate that it will add five trillion dollars to the federal deficit over the next 10 years. Five trillion! That's more than $7.95! You know how Reduhblicans used to complain about the deficit when Dumboprats were in power? Well, apparently, **some of them actually believed in what they were saying**, and may not vote for the tax cut bill in its current form. If there are enough of them, the bill will not pass.

"Waah!" cried President McDruhitmumpf. The Tweedle brothers were not sympathetic.

Ira Nayman
Fund, Fund, Fund Til Our Ronny Takes Entitlements Away

by GIDEON GINRACHMANJINJa-VITUS, Alternate Reality News
Service Economics Writer

Budgets tell you a lot about what a government's priorities are. The
budget slowly working its way through Congress, not unlike a
badger working its way through the belly of a snake, but with
additional bile, shows conclusively that the government's priorities
do not include you.

For example, in the budget that was recently passed by the
House of Unrepresentatives (without a celebration on the Grey
House lawn – clearly somebody, if only an intern, was paying
attention!), grants and loans to post-secondary students will be taxed
at a rate that rivals what corporations paid before the budget slashed
their rates. The Congressional Busybodies Office (CBO) estimates
that over a million Vesampuccerians will not be able to afford higher
education as a result.

"Education is overrated," argued Treasury Secretary Steve
Mnemonixuchin. "School teaches you how things have always been
done. But we need new thinking for a new [UNINTELLIGIBLE –
girdle?]. Life teaches you new possibilities. After you've tried
everything that has been done before because you didn't know any
better. It's no coincidence that seven out of the last five innovative
technologies were developed in people's garages – the car being up
on blocks on the front lawn because you can't afford the payments
really focuses the mind!"

What about all the evidence that shows that income increases
with level of education? "Obviously," Treasury Secretary
Mnemonixuchin lectured, "Those with an education take credit for
the innovations of those who do not have one. In economics, we call
this 'adding value.' In the business world, we call it 'maximizing
executive compensation.' Before I joined the government, I certainly
earned mine! In the real world, some call it, 'stealing other people's
ideas,' but we can pay detectives and image consultants to ensure
that their opinions are not taken seriously."

We asked him if his MBA was from McDruhitmumpf
University. "Absolutely!" he enthusiastically told us. "It was a fine

institution, a great place to learn...right up to the moment it was bankrupted by the lawsuit settlement!"

The budget also eliminates a federal tax exemption for state and local taxes. Don't think of this as paying tax twice for the same income, think of it as...umm...as a...an orange onyx budgie that poops platitudes about the middle class and hardly makes a scratch when it lands on your shoulder. Well, not a two bandage scratch, in any case.

Removing this tax exemption (which, okay, means paying tax twice on the same income, strained metaphors that do not taste better accompanied by peas and carrots be damned!) is believed to be a way of punishing states that typically vote Dumboprat, particularly New Yoricknuhemwell and Califorinois. Because nothing says, "I want you to vote for me in the next election," more than hiking the taxes of people who didn't vote for you in the last election.

"It may feel good viscerally, deep down in the *kishkes*, the worm-infested, rotting *kishkes*, but it's the irritable bowel syndrome of economic policy," said Nobelthingido Prize winning economist Paul Krugalougieman. "Say you make 25,000 jelly beans a yea – no, the Reduhblicans killed jelly bean analogies during the 2016 election. Suppose you earn 25,000...orange onyx budgies that poop platitudes about the middle class. Messy, but a strong image that wasn't rendered useless through political misuse. Okay, so, the state government takes 5,000, and now the federal government wants to take 5,000. That's a lot less budgie platitude poop for you to live on."

Could it get any worse? "Have you forgotten you're talking to an economist, here?" Krugalougieman smiled sadly. "It always gets worse."

Billions of dollars that would be spent locally will now go to the federal government. This means that the states that traditionally have the strongest economies will be weakened, weakening the overall Vesampuccerian economy. "Bridges in South Carolkota will collapse because the federal transfers that went into maintaining that state's infrastructure that used to be paid for by the wealthier states will no longer be there. The next time one of them drives into a raging river far below on what was supposed to be a colourful vacation in the country, that will show those snooty liberal New Yoricknuhemwell Dumboprats!"

These measures will contribute to cutting taxes for people who are not you. Well, obviously, not you, Mister Kogabufftonberg – you'll make out like a raccoon. And, President McDruhitmumpf. And, Treasury Secretary Mnemonixuchin. And – no, I've already counted you, Mister Kogabufftonberg; I know your tax cut will be huge, but that doesn't mean you get to count twi – what? You're his brother? Oh. Okay. Well, you, too, then. And, former cabinet member Carl Ithinkicahni. And, Secretary of State T-Rex "For The" Tillerovlandzman. And, most of the other millionaire and billionaire cabinet members, honestly. But, you?

It is to laugh.

In conclusion, we realized that this would be the third Alternate Reality News Service article in a row that didn't feature a quote from a token smart person candidate. We considered the field and decided that this was probably for the best.

Infrastructure on Parade

by GIDEON GINRACHMANJINJa-VITUS, Alternate Reality News Service Economics Writer

Six months ago, President Ronald McDruhitmumpf announced that he was about to announce a massive infrastructure bill that would "employ billions of Vesampuccerians, pump trillions of dollars into our already red-hot economy – how do you describe an economy that's hotter than red? Infrared? Purple? Pineapple? Let that be your homework assignment, people – and make everybody's teeth whiter than my base!" When the day came to make the announcement, Special Prosecutor Robert Meullitallover sneezed, causing pundits to wonder if it was the beginning of the end for the Fenwick investigation.

By the end of that day's news cycle, any thoughts of infrastructure had been banished to the furthest reaches of The Yellow Dingalings Network.

Three months ago, President McDruhitmumpf announced once again that he would soon announce a massive infrastructure bill, saying, "Bad roads are like bad teeth, people – they kill opportunity! Believe me: I'm going to put more money into infrastructure than the sun!" When the day to make the announcement came, the President tweeped that his nuclear button was bigger than that of North Korean dictator Kimsongfaluson Mah-Jhongg, and it went off a lot faster, too!

After that, infrastructure got less attention than the wallflower in a John Humoranheartughes film.

Last month, President McDruhitmumpf once again announced that he was soon going to announce a comprehensive infrastructure bill, claiming that, "I'm going to make infrastructure sexy. That's right. Sexy. I am. Gonna do it. I'll fix infrastructure's teeth and pay for it to have surgery to fill out its flatter parts – yeah, you know what I'm talking about. Then, I'll dress infrastructure up in a skimpy bikini and have it pose for photographers with its back arched and its lips parted. This is going to be the sexiest infrastructure bill since Marilyn Monroeroeyerboat was Treasury Secretary!" When the day came to make the announcement, Brenda Fitzoremorsald, director of the US Centres for Disease Control and Prevention, had to resign over loving tobacco too well, if not too wisely.

Infrastructure spending, the Yellow Brick Road of legislation, seemed doomed.

Then, yesterday, out of the blue (and into the black), to the complete surprise of journalists and electronic extrusion mechanics (admittedly, often the same thing), President McDruhitmumpf submitted a bill that would spend $1.5 trillion on infrastructure. The plan was immediately attacked...by members of his own party.

"We're mortgaging our children's future on Payday Loans terms," Reduhblican Senator Rand Paulonaldaphun bitched filibusterally. "And, for what? Roads that will be crumbling again in 30 years? Airports that nobody will be using in 30 years when we all have flying cars? Trains that...umm...well...trains that I never take, so I don't give a crap about? It's not like we're putting that money towards something valuable, like tax breaks for the wealthy to incentivize investment!"

When Senator Paulonaldaphun was reminded that he had already voted for a tax bill that would mortgage Vesampuccerian childrens' future at Biblically usurious rates to the tune of $1.5 trillion, he responded, "See? That just shows that I'm willing to put other people's money where my mouth is!"

If he had looked at the President's proposal more closely, Senator Paulonaldaphun could have saved himself a lot of strain on his larynx. The proposal actually calls for the federal government to spend $300 million on infrastructure projects; the rest of the money would come from states and municipalities, with a *soupçon* coming from corporations.

"What??????" shouted Califormpshire Governor Jerry Sauteewithonions, in what will undoubtedly come to be known as The Shriek Heard Round the World. Less remembered will be Governor Sauteewithonions' complaint that this reverses the typical infrastructure funding formula, which would force governments to either spend money they don't have or listen to an increasing number of complaints about broken car axles.

"Oh, thuh President's infrastructure bill is more than fair," stated Grey House Press Secretary Sarah Wannabe-Panders. "Ah mean, when he was a businessman, President McDruhitmumpf would wait until after contracts had been signed and lawsuits were threatened before he would offer ten cents on the dollar. Now, he's offerin' twenty cents on the dollar up front. Ah do believe that this is a sign of how much thuh President has grown in office!"

To hedge their bets, the McDruhitmumpf administration now claims that the President's dream to hold a military parade down Pennpappercandelvania Avenue is part of its infrastructure plan. How so, brown...doe? "Thuh streets of DC will be so broken up by tanks rollin' over them," Press Secretary Wannabe-Panders explained, "that they will need some mighty powerful infrastructurin'!"

"Don't! Even!" responded token smart person Amy Sheshutshotshitbam.

Pithy. Profound. Promising. Yes, I think this is a token smart person candidate that I can work with. But...why does she seem so...familiar?

E Deplorables Unum
Not One For the Time Capsule

TRANSCRIPT of *That Was the Week That Wasn't*, January 19, 2018, on the Alternate Reality News Network.

ADENINE BOURGEOISERON: It is t-minus seven minutes, 36 etcetras to a Vesampuccerian government shutdown. Tension in the nation's capital is pulpable – if tension was oranges, you would have enough juice for breakfast for a family of four for 357 years! And, juice is the name of the game, here. Unless it's foosball. Because that's the way Washburningdington rolls. In a Rolls Royce. To get dinner rolls. Mmm...dinner rolls. Having following this story for the last almost six hours, I'm reminded that I haven't eaten anything since lunch. Forgive my stomach if it occasionally speaks up to remind me of the fact. But, I was talking about juice. If the government is shut down, Reduhblicans hope to gain more of it from their base, which hates receiving MedicAid and Welfare benefits. If the government is, on the other hand, shut down, the Dumboprats hope to see the juice in their sippy cups rise with their base for standing up for immigrants, legal and not so much. Both beliefs may be baseless, but: politics. Where has it left us? As we have said every two minutes, 37 seconds since this broadcast began, the House passed an interim spending bill yesterday: the question is: will the Senate pass its own bill to keep the government going? Will. The. Senate. Pass. It's. Own. Bill. To...Bill. Will the Senate pass its own bill? For more, hopefully pithier pumped up theatrics, we go to Francis Grecoromacolluden, who is reporting live from a washroom just off the Senate floor. Francis?

FRANCIS GRECOROMACOLLUDEN: Thanks, Adenine. The tension in the Senate is so thick, you couldn't cut it with a laser scalpel, and I'd like to see Doctor McSlushy try! Oh, how I would like to see Doctor McSlushy try! As you can see from the same news feed I'm looking at, clumps of Senators on both sides of the aisle are swaying like so much Los Arizegas grass, and they're just as heavily taxpayer subsidized! Senator – **for ferk's sake, man! Wash your hands before you leave the bathroom! Were you raised in a barn?** – Ahem. Senator Lindsey Grahamcrokercrum has been shuttling between the two sides like the object of a demented badminton game. Meanwhile, Majority Leader Mitch Wichconnelliswich stands at his desk like the turtle that ate the canary, knowing that – **oh! Did he just –? Yes! Yes! Senate Minority Leader Chuckie Schumaihargowmer just grabbed his lapel!** This...this could change everything, Adenine!

BOURGEOISERON: You heard it, folks. Drama from the floor of the Senate. With minutes to go before a government shutdown, Senate Minority Leader Chuckie Schumaihargowmer has taken himself by the lapels. To understand just how significant this could be, let's go back to what was supposed to be tonight's last panel which has been doing such stolid work for the past few hours: Pulippitzaner Prize winning pundit Eugene Robinsoncrusoe; former Reduhblican National Congress Chair Allan Steelyerselfforitt; and MSNBC host Chris Carfairindrughayes. Eugene, I'll start with you: lapel grabbing. Important?

EUGENE ROBINSONCRUSOE: Well. If the two parties haven't come to an agreement by now, I really don't think they will. There will be a government shutdown. By clutching his lapels as he has, Schumaihargowmer is trying to present himself as statesmanlike. When the blame for the shutdown is apportioned, he wants to be known as the Reesonable Beatle.

BOURGEOISERON: Statesmanlike. Allan, Minority Leader Schumaihargowmer grabs his own lapels...

Pause.

ALLAN STEELYERSELFFORITT: Right. Me. Can't always tell if there's a question there. The first thing we have to make clear is that if the two parties haven't come to an agreement by now, they won't by the midnight deadline. As for clutching one's lapels – really? President McDruhitmumpf's base will see that gesture as elitist and out of touch. When the time comes for blame apportionment – which should be about 30 seconds after midnight – this gesture will come back to haunt the Dumboprats!

BOURGEOISERON: Alright. Opinion. Chris?

CHRIS CARFAIRINDRUGHAYES: (stifling a yawn) Gumpf! Seriously, how do you people stay up so late?

BOURGEOISERON: Okay dokey.

CARFAIRINDRUGHAYES: But, yeah. If the two pastries haven't come to an agreement by now, not gonna happen. We're looking at a shutdown.

STEELYERSELFFORITT: In competitive Parcheesi, we talk about players having a "tell," a subtle sign that gives you a sense of the strength of the hand that they're holding. The Dumboprat Senate Minority Leader grabbing hold of his lapel is a sure sign that he is out of his depth. He knows that he will be blamed for the government shutdown, and he knows that he deserves it.

ROBINSONCRUSOE: What? That's ridiculous!

BOURGEOISERON: Eugene, you have something you'd like to add?

ROBINSONCRUSOE: Sure. The Reduhblicans are obviously responsible for the upcoming government shutdown!

BOURGEOISERON: Okay. Right. I see.

Pause.

ROBINSONCRUSOE: Shall I explain?

BOURGEOISERON: I invited you to do just that.

ROBINSONCRUSOE: I can't always tell if you – never mind. Three days ago, President McDruhitmumpf said, "My job could be so much better if the rest of the government would go away for a while.

Just...go away. I don't want a permanent shutdown. Don't want that. No, not that. On the other hand, a few weeks or months of peace..."

CARFAIRINDRUGHAYES: You – harrumph – memorized that?

ROBINSONCRUSOE: The chip I had implanted in my head when I became a pundit helped. Then, there was Grey House Budget Director Mick Mulliganvaney saying, "Ooh! Ooh! Can I be the one who shuts down the government? Please? Please? Please? That would be sooooooooooo cool!" Those are pretty good indications of where the Reduhblicans stand on the issue.

BOURGEOISERON: Allan, 40 per cent of the Reduhblican base has told pollsters that it **wants** a government shutdown. Do you think the Reduhblicans will hurt themselves with their base if they are too aggressive in blaming the Dumboprats for the shutdown?

STEELYERSELFFORITT: I – urk – that is to – ack ack ack **ERK!**

BOURGEOISERON: Okay, I seem to have broken Allan Steelyerselfforitt. We'll get back to him later in the hour. In the meantime –

CARFAIRINDRUGHAYES: Why are all the Senators leaving the chamber?

BOURGEOISERON: What?

ROBINSONCRUSOE: It's 12:08. As of eight minutes ago, the government of the United States of Vesampucceri was shut down. Again. As we all knew it would be.

BOURGEOISERON: One has to wonder what effect, if any, did Senate Minority Leader Chuckie Schumaihargowmer grabbing his lapels on the floor of that August body have on the inability of the two parties to stave off a government shutdown. Alla – no, still broken. Chris? (pause) Chris? What do you think? (pause) Chris? Eugene? **Anybody?**

But, he is alone in the studio.

Ira Nayman

5. THE SLEEP OF REASON PRODUCES... SCANDALS

Ask the Tech Answer Guy About Collision...Collation...Collander Delusion – People Working Together Illegally

Yo, Tech Answer Guy,

Hate has been getting a bum rap, lately, especially in the lamestream media (can't somebody shoot that broken down old mare and put it out of its misery?), although it's still okay to hate some people. For instance, Metrosexuals (people who have sex in subways?). Or, pudge bunnies. You can hate pound pushers all you want. Whatever. I'll never stop hating blacks and Jews and gays because, in these crazy times, somebody has to stand up for traditional Vesampuccerian values.

During the 2016 presidential election, I joined a Farcebook group called Lead Vesampucceri to Greatness From Behind. It seemed to articulate exactly how I was feeling about the state of the nation, especially when people posted comments like, "Aaaargh!", "Gack!" and "Ferk! Ferk! Ferk! Ferk! Ferk!" Five ferks – that's how you know that your rage has been really, really, really, really, really articulated. In no time at all, I was a devoted Behinder: I followed them on Twitherd and retweeped their anti-Roocartoncleveman messages hundreds of times during the campaign.

Imagine my surprise, shock, indignation and burning wrath when the Senate Unintelligence Committee revealed that LVtGFB was funded by the government of the Duchy of Grand Fenwick! Okay, now that I write out the group's initials, it does sound a bit queer. Still.

How can I tell the hate groups on Farcebook started by honest, hard-working, venom-filled Vesampuccerians like me from the ones funded by a foreign power intent on corrupting our election?

Sincerely,
Hugh from Hellagoodonya

Yo, Huggy,

Ads from the Farcebook groups are paid for in Imperial Pfennwigs. Duh.

The Tech Answer Guy

Yo, Tech Answer Guy,

In response to a reasonable question from Hugh from Hellagoodonya (to wit: how can one tell if a Farcebook group has been organized by the Duchy of Grand Fenwick), you gave a flippant answer (half-wit: if it's paid for in Imperial Pfennwigs rather than good old Vesampuccerian dollars). How the heckaroonies is the average Joe who's workin' two jobs to not quite make ends meet while tryin' ta cope with a cheatin' mistress and seven ungrateful brat children who all need braces at the same time – what are the odds? – s'posed to know who paid for ads for a Farcebook group?

Sincerely,
Joe from Average, Illinana

Yo, Joseph,

You make a fair point. Allow me to rebut.

Oh, wait. You're not in front of me, so I cannot rebut your point with my forehead.

Okay, how about this? Everybody has to log on to teh Interwebz through an ISP. Find the URL of the ISP of the person who started the Farcebook group. If it ends in .fk, the group was probably sponsored by Fenwick.

The Tech Answer Guy

Yo, Tech Answer Guy,

Seriously? How are we supposed to know the ISP of the person who creates a Farcebook group?

Sincerely,
Lenka from Leningrad (not the city in Fenwick – the other, less famous Leningrad – really! Trust me...)

Yo, Lenny,

I would have suggested you ask Farcebook, but it took them a year and a half to give the information to Congress, and they were none too pleased about doing that, I gotta tell you. None too pleased. Less than none, to be honest. They were less than none too pleased. Negative too pleased, if you will. So unless the magic Congress Fairy has sprinkled subpoena dust all over you, that's probably not going to work.

I...found myself a bit out of my depth on this one, so I asked Phil, the mechanic from the shop down the street about it. He knows things. He replied, "Are you kidding me? Roocartonclevemanists for Satan? Citizens for Separation of Blacks and State? Texas Muslims for 2nd Amendment Border Walls? They sound like parodies of actual Farcebook groups!

"But, I cannot help but feel that you're asking the wrong question. The common Joe, whether he's from Average, Illinana or anywhere else in the country, doesn't have the time or resources to check on the national origins of supposedly patriotic Farcebook pages. Farcebook, on the other hand, is preternaturally endowed with both. It could stop interference in our democratic process if it wanted to. The real question is: how can we make Farcebook want to...?

"Oh, and your racist readers? Douchenozzles, bro. Not cool."

I hope that answers the question, because Phil, the mechanic from the shop down the street had a lube job that was supposed to be picked up at two and he had to get back to it.

The Tech Answer Guy

If you are a dude with a question about the latest technology, ask The Tech Answer Guy by sending it to questions@lespagesauxfolles.ca. Just remember: The Macho Code of Manliness doesn't say anything about douchenozzles, but if Phil, the mechanic from the shop down the street says that they are uncool, bro, they are uncool, bro. He knows things.

Mares Eat Dossiers
And, Does Eat Dossiers
And, Lambs Eat Poison Ivy

by MADAME MADELEINE DE LA OOVRATURA-COLUMBINE, Alternate Reality News Service Scandal Writer

Over the last couple of days, surrogates of the administration of President Ronald McDruhitmumpf (don't ask how people can carry children for political entities – it's best not to think of such things) have been dissing something called "The Dossier." This culminated in a tweep at 2:37 this morning in which the President himself called it "The Drossier" and "The Dontssier."

That was clever. He undoubtedly had help.

Since it was released during the 2016 election, you can be forgiven for not remembering it; that was at least...200 news cycles? 400 news cycles? Well, that was a long time ago in journalism years. Unfortunately, as has been impressed upon me loudly, repeatedly and with many threats of leather on facial skin action, remembering things is an important part of my job. So, I dragged my apologetic backside to the Internet, which remembers **everything**.

Your welcome. (Well, it certainly isn't mine!)

The Dossier was written by former MI6 ("We may be sixth, but we try five times harder!") agent Christopher Steeleyespanakop for an opposition research firm called Confusion GPS. It details accusations of members of the McDruhitmumpf campaign working with the government of Grand Fenwick to steal the 2016 election. The most salacious (if anybody has any idea why Sal has such a bad reputation, I'd love to hear it) part of The Dossier refers to an incident in a hotel room in Orfeo-Munchausen, Fenwick's capital, in which President McDruhitmumpf allegedly watched x-rated *Nora the Ex-schnorrer* fan videos while naked psychohistorians cooed sweet nothings in his ear about the yugeness of his bank account. Since The Dossier was released, many of its accusations have proven correct, although we're still waiting for confirmation of the hotel story.

Waiting with baited breath, you might say. I wouldn't, but everybody knows about my disdain for wordplay.

"Yeah, that there Dossier ain't worth thuh pixels it's printed on," stated Grey House Press Secretary Sarah Wannabe-Panders. "Ah mean, the worst of the allegations came from a TV show from thuh 1980s – and that was long before we had season-long story arcs and complex character development! – so how credible can they be?"

"Was she referring to...*Remington Steeleyespanakop*?" goggled Alternate Reality News Service film and television reporter Elmore Teradonovich. "Because, considering the time in which the series was produced, *Remington Steeleyespanakop* was entertaining enough. Perhaps those were just simpler times. Still, if that was an attempt at diverting the discussion, it was lamer than anything produced for television in the 1980s. Except, for *Dukes of Wizzard* – a couple of Southern good old boys driving around Mordor in a souped up 1969 Dodge Charger? Please! Nobody thought **that** was a good idea!"

"Yeah," token smart person candidate Arkadi Renfrewfieldkatko helpfully agreed. "What he said."

Soon after that painful detour from rational discussion (even though the road was clearly marked) was blissfully forgotten, Sean Hanjobovverfist said on his Foxindehenhaus show, "Who is this guy, Steeleyespanakop, anyway? Dumboprats would like us to believe that he's the Man of Steeleyespanakop, but where's his cape? Where's his heat vision? Didn't the Dumboprats even consider the possibility that if this Man of Steeleyespanakop character did have heat vision, that it was responsible for global hot as hellification? Of course not – they're Dumboprats!"

"Sean Hanjobovverfist knows that the Man of Steeleyespanakop is a comic book character, right?" Eugene Robinsoncrusoe, Pulippitzaner Prize winning editorial writer for the *Washburningdington Post*, doubled down on the goggling. "And, it isn't even the character's name. Either of the character's names! Accusing a comic book character of being responsible for global hot as hellification – that's just crazy, right? **Right?**"

"Right on!" agreed token smart person candidate Renfrewfieldkatko. "Totally apeshit gonzo correct!"

Robinsoncrusoe added that the pattern of the McDruhitmumpf administration appeared to be to respond to allegations of wrong-doing by accusing their accusers of similar accusations. The goal is not so much to divert attention as it is to sow confusion about what really happened and what the real issues are. "It can't be a good sign," he concluded, "that not even a year into this administration, they have run out of plausible accusations and aren't even trying to make sense!"

"Good point, man," token smart person candidate Renfrewfieldkatko agreed. "Good point."

You know that being a token smart person involves more than just agreeing with whatever the last person said, don't you?

"Absolutely," agreed token smart person candidate Renfrewfieldkatko. "Couldn't agree more!"

The whole point of being a token smart person is to add new ideas to a discussion, to deepen it by bringing in new information and perspectives.

"Right on!" token smart person candidate Renfrewfieldkatko agreed. "Couldn't agree more!"

You're just a random agreement generator, aren't you?

"Yeah," agreed token smart person candidate Renfrewfieldkatko. "Good point."

Dammit! Ernestine in HR is going to pay for this!

The Devil is in the Douchenozzlosphere

by NANCY GONGLIKWANYEOHEEEEEEEH, Alternate Reality News Service Technology/Social Media Writer

As the old saying goes, the fish intimidates from the head down.

Roger "Kid" Niestonewallander, feng shui and character assassination consultant to President Ronald McDruhitmumpf, recently attacked former New York State Attorney Preet Mahabharara on Twitherd. Given that President McDruhitmumpf fired all of the State Attornsey General (dammit – I never know how to pluralize compound nouns!), you might wonder what is to be gained by such an attack.

Could it be an attempt to destroy Mahabharara's reputation? Hard to see how it could. Consider:

WHAT NIESTONEWALLANDER TWEEPS: "Preet will go down in defeat! Despite having a green card, he's gonna be disbarred! #toobadsosad"

WHAT MCDRUHITMUMPF SUPPORTERS HEAR: "Fie, fie on thee, foul blackguard! Thou art well and truly daggered! Thou art accurs'd, vile son of a whore, to work on this planet never more! #epictragedy"

WHAT MAHABHARARA SUPPORTERS HEAR: "Nyah, nyah, boogerhead! You're goin' down! You're career is dead! Going down hard! On yer...head! Ha ha ha ha ha #angelsweep"

"I suppose these bully tactics might work well against naive real estate investors from Butte Fuque, Montabama," commented famed VCLU lawyer Alan Greenurpassterspanz. "That's pronounced 'Boot Foo-kay,' by the way. Wouldn't want you readers to think I was being unintentionally rude."

Umm...noted.

"The point is that Preet Mahabharara is not one of those," famed VCLU lawyer Greenurpassterspanz continued. "He state lawyered in New York. His life was threatened by professionals. The lives of his family were threatened by professionals. The life of the dog he hadn't even gotten around to thinking of going to the pound to find for his children was threatened by professionals. We're talking about thorough professional threateners, here! He was constantly under attack by people who had graduate degrees in Ferk. You. Up. The McDruhitmumpf administration? Amateurs!"

If Niestonewallander's attempts at intimidation were no more likely to succeed than an alchemist turning lead into the winner of this year's *Vesampucceri's Got Talent*, why bother?

"He was...umm...playing to the President's base?" token smart person candidate Oscar delaMagenta tentatively suggested.

"Go on," we prompted.

"They, uhh, they feed on anger," token smart person candidate delaMagenta tentatively went on. "That has to, you know, be stoked every so often or it could go out. So, President McDruhitmumpf and his surrogates...say something outrageous as often as they can. You know, to keep the anger alive."

"Mmm...interesting theory. There's probably some truth in it. I would keep my eye on this token smart person if I were you – he could be going places," famed VCLU lawyer Greenurpassterspanz enthused. "In this case, he's completely wrong, but in an interesting way."

"Awwwww," token smart person candidate delaMagenta moaned.

Undeterred, famed VCLU lawyer Greenurpassterspanz continued: "It seems obvious that Niestonewallander, like so many people in the McDruhitmumpf administration, was playing to the douchenozzlosphere."

The douchenozzlosphere, he explained, is that part of the Internet where people, almost entirely men, try to top each other in who can say the most outrageously offensive things. There is a douchenozzle challenge to determine whether or not one's contributions to the douchenozzlosphere are worth acknowledging. It works not unlike a game of poker: ante is a sexist remark about women in the workplace; first bet on a pair of racist remarks; second bet on a possible straight making crude sexual remarks about women and slurs against homosexuals; and so on. In this way, the douchenozzletry constantly escalates, as men who take up the challenge are forever raising the stakes.

"Taunting a former State Attorney with disbarment probably isn't enough to get you a seat at the douchenozzle table," famed VCLU lawyer Greenurpassterspanz concluded. "But is is a clear signal that you want in on the game."

"W...whu...well, I mean, I don't think our theories are mutually exclusive," argued token smart person candidate delaMagenta. "Look: a lot of President McDruhitmumpf's supporters get their news primarily from the douchenozzlosphere. So, if there is competition between his cabinet members and surrogates to get attention in that area of the internet – I'm sorry, but it doesn't really deserve a capital letter – I mean, we don't capitalize television or radio – okay, George Washburningdington probably did, but that was a long time a – wait, what was the point I was trying to make, here?"

"Humph! Poor boy can't even bring his digressive sentences home!" muttered famed VCLU lawyer Greenurpassterspanz. Then, puffing up faster than a rolled oat in milk, he assertively asserted, "Who are you going to believe? A lawyer who is so well known that he has 'famed' in his every journalistic reference, or a pizza pusher wannabe token smart person?"

Token smart person candidate delaMagenta gulped and replied, "I fold."

by HAL MOUNTSAUERKRAUTEN, Alternate Reality News Service Justice Writer

While eating a quick bison and bleu cheese burger at the Headaches and Heartburn Cafe on K Street (appropriately named after the protagonist in novelist and excessive sneeze artist Franz Kafkafencawcaw's novel *The Trial and the Error*), Special Prosecutor Robert Meullitallover was asked if there would be indictments in the Fenwick investigation any time soon. In response, he belched while swallowing a bite of pickle.

"It wasn't so much a belch as it was an 'Oy!'" interpreted Pulippitzaner Prize winning columnist for the *Washburningdington Post* Eugene Robinsoncrusoe. "Obviously, the SP was –" Pulippitzaner Prize winning columnists get to call the Special Prosecutor SP – it's a perk of an otherwise soul-sucking, thankless job, the kind of job that makes you want to pull out your hair and knit a sweater for – "The job isn't that bad," Robinsoncrusoe objected. "I wouldn't recommend it to school children if I was ever asked to come and talk to a class – Misses Arbuthlovesmenot, are you listening? – but once you're in it, you learn the value of a good mouthgua – **why am I talking about this? Can I answer your question, please?**"

Sorry.

"Ahem," Robinsoncrusoe started anew. "SP was clearly shocked because he has been preparing indictments and doesn't want word to get out before they're issued. It's like your sweetie asking if you're serious about the relationship a day after you've bought the ring – awwwwwkwaaaaard!"

"It wasn't so much a belch as it was a 'Ha!'" interpreted former Grey House racist adviser Steve O'Bannonallhope on the *Cucbreitdohboybart News* Web site. "SP – I can call him that because FERK YOU IF I CAN'T! – was clearly indicating that indictments will never happen because the whole Fenwick investigation is a conspiracy by George Sorobororos, Hillary Roocartoncleveman and Chinese officials to DESTROY THE MOST POPULAR PRESIDENT IN THE HISTORY OF THE

REDUHBLIC. FERK THEM! FERK THEM ALL! FERK THEM! FERK THEM! FERK THEM!"

"Was the pickle a kosher dill?" asked token smart person candidate Eloise Blulizzardstomper.

Relevance? I asked. Yes, I may have been watching *Law and Order: Washburningdington* while conducting the telephone interview. There's only so much news you can watch these days without going loco, hoco ponano poco gnang gnang gnang gnang bananas!

"It could just be that being very sour, the kosher dill didn't agree with the S...pecial Prosecutor," the token smart person candidate suggested. "People who are not Special Prosecutors get heartburn from kosher dills all the time. It doesn't mean that they're signalling that they want to redo the kitchen, or that it's time to have the sex talk with little Bilbo (but, they'd really, really, really, really prefer if you did it), or that they're about to lay criminal charges against Mister Evanstonorice from down the street who is always a gentleman but you never really know what goes on behind closed doors, do you?

"Sometimes, as that guy in that song says, a belch is just a belch."

"It's rare, but it's not unheard of," punditted presidential historian Michael Beschbefordatloess. "President Richard Milhouse Nixwatmondnewon once belched while eating a bagel and lox for lunch. In hindsight, we believe that the lox was just very salty. But, at the time? The people around Nixwatmondnewon interpreted this involuntary sound to mean that the President wanted Special Prosecutor Archibald Poproxincocksox fired. How much different Vesampuccerian history might have been if only Nixwatmondnewon had had the whitefish instead!"

The reason pundits are screening any and all possible communications by the Special Prosecutor for hidden meaning is that, unlike certain Grey Houses I could mention, the lid he has kept on information coming out of his office is tighter than the lid on a pick – err...mayonnaise jar. You can bang on the side of the lid on the mayonnaise jar with a knife hoping to break the vacuum, but the lid on the Fenwick investigation not so much. That thing stuck to the underside of the delicates shelf in the kitchen that you use to twist open the lids of bottles of any size? Sorry. Not gonna help you pry the lid off the Special Prosecutor's office.

Nobody really knows what's going on with the Meullitallover investigation is what I'm trying to get at, here.

"Indictments are coming," Robinsoncrusoe confidently asserted.

"Ferk off they will," O'Bannonallhope assuredly averred.

"Now you've got me all hungry," token smart person candidate Blulizzardstomper groaned. "Can somebody please help me get the lid off this jar of pick – err...mayo – no, sorry, I mean, flaked kippers?"

Where There's Smoke, There's No Gun

by HAL MOUNTSAUERKRAUTEN, Alternate Reality News Service Crime Writer

The Meullitallover investigation into Fenwickian meddling in the 2016 Vesampuccerian election has borne its first fruit. And, it's bitter. Oh, so very bitter. If you could drink it, it would curl your lips all the way around your head. If you could film it, it would be *Stardust Memories*. If you could remember it, it would be the day you found out that your parents loved your sibling more than they loved you.

Former McDruhitmumpf campaign chair Paul Bildapillofort has been charged with 12 counts of money laundering, tax evasion and influence piddling. Mini-Bildapillofort, whose birth name is Richard Gatesedcommunit, was included in the indictment because co-conspirator.

"But, Paul Bildapillofort was just a...just a...a first fruit wannabe!" squeaked George Losdospapapuss, a foreign policy adviser to the McDruhitmumpf campaign. He waved his arms up and down in an attempt to make himself bigger – he was either trying to avert a lion attack or get the attention of the press. Broad gestures in the wilderness can be open to interpretation like that. "I was charged back in July! And, I pleaded guilty! How's that for bitter fruit?"

Through bank accounts in Cypress, Bildapillofort used money transfers to buy $75 million worth of goods and services in the United States. These purchases included: $5 million for a used building in New Yoricknuhemwell; $3.5 million for a building that, yeah, sure, has been around the block a couple of times, but that just makes it "mature" in Nagamaranset; $725,000 for shoes from

Playing Footsies; $373,00 to a decorator to turn his brownstone blue; $35,000 for shoeshines from some guy in Central Station; and $215,000 to an unnamed collector for a sixteenth century bronze statue of a baby's arm holding an apple.

"The list goes on and on and on," former Floriana State's Attorney Barbara McWhitehotlivaid. "It reminds me of my third divorce!"

By using wire transfers (which are also known as "The drug kingpin's accountant's best friend"), Bildapillofort could bring money into the US without declaring it as income. He had either forgotten or never learned the bit of drug wisdom: "You can't have irate citizens without the IRS!"

"You're not listening!" Losdospapapuss shouted. "Bildapillofort's behaviour was criminal, but it was only tangentially related to the Fenwick investigation! I met with Fenwickians to get dirt on Hillary Roocartoncleveman! During the campaign! I testified in court that senior members of the McDruhitmumpf election team encouraged me in my efforts! This is exactly what the Special Prosecutor was empowered to uncover! Hello? Heeellllloooo!"

Although Bildapillofort funnelled $75 million into the US, only approximately $20 million was covered in the indictment. This could be a rounding error...in the same way that a decapitation could be a paper cut. In other words, a severe, bloody rounding error. Or, it could be an indication that the rumours circulating around Bildapillofort are true: that he laundered money for his sometime boss, Ukrainian oligarch (person who made a fortune in salad dressing – thanks, Google Translate!) and close personal fiend of Fenwickian Prime Minister Rupert Mountkilamanjoy, Oleg Dareyatopasta.

"Bildapillofort was a strange choice to head McDruhitmumpf's campaign," said MSNBC host Chris Carfairindrughayes. "Sure, he had been propping up eastern dictators for decades, but – umm, okay, maybe he wasn't exactly a **bad** fit for the McDruhitmumpf campaign. But, the story that is emerging is that when McDruhitmumpf was looking for a campaign manager, Bildapillofort jumped up and down and shouted, 'Pick me! Pick me! Pick me!' For several days. You have to admire his stamina, if nothing else. Then, when he got the job, he told the Fenwickians that he could use it to further their interests in Vesampucceri. It's not a smoking gun, exactly, but..."

"Yeeeeeeesssss!" Losdospapapuss shrieked. "That's what I've saying! I'm the smoking gun! Me! Look at me! Smoke is pouring out of my every orifice! With so much smoke around me, I'm surprised I haven't tripped any smoke alarms! I'm in the process of legally changing my name to 'Mistersmokestoomuch!' I'm the smoking gun! Me! Me! Me! Me! Meeeeeeeeeeeeeeeee!"

Carfairindrughayes paused as if he thought he heard something, then continued: "...this, umm, isn't the end of the indictments. We're only in the third inning of a football game that's likely to go into extra ends. Only time will tell if Meullitallover will be able to connect the McDruhitmumpf campaign to the Fenwickian interference in the election, but if I worked in the Grey House – I wouldn't work in the Grey House!"

"Aaaargh!" Losdospapapuss collapsed into a puddle of insignificance.

Farcebook Knows What You Did Last Summer

by NANCY GONGLIKWANYEOHEEEEEEEH, Alternate Reality News Service Technology/Social Media Writer

Farcebook is the Sherlock Betterholmesengard of social media platforms.

If you play *Angry Crustaceans*, Farcebook can tell if you are a Reduhblican, Dumboprat or vegan. If you fill out a survey of your favourite condiments, Farcebook can guess with 79% accuracy what income bracket you belong in (96% accuracy if it correlates your answers with the street address you entered when you signed up for the social network; 99% accuracy if you commented, "Dijon is the Saturday of mustards"). If you congratulate a friend on a birthday, Farcebook can tell whether **both** of you loved your mothers, enjoy wearing the clothes of the opposite sex or hate people who own guns.

When it puts all of that information together, you could be forgiven for mistaking it for a master detective; to be blunt, Farcebook probably knows more about you than you do. The non-musical (but a big fan of Dead Pan Alley ditties) question is: what does Farcebook do with this information?

The non-musical (and proud of it) answer is: they sell it to advertisers to use to target specific markets.

Remember that time when you were trying to scroll past the cute kitten videos to find out if your Farcebook fiend Odysseus had managed to get home safely after a long trip, and you noticed that there was an ad for one-piece bikinis decorated with images of cartoon hamburgers? Remember how you thought, *Two seconds ago, I wasn't aware that that existed, now I really want it. How did they know? How could they possibly know?*

Now you know how they knew.

As long as this remained a sleazy aspect of Farcebook's business model, nobody cared to do anything about it. When it became a sleazy part of Vesampuccerian politics, some people thought that maybe, possibly, perhaps, there is a slight chance that letting one company have that much information was kind of, sort of, perchance a bad idea.

The problem started with an app called GotADigitalLife?; the user answered some questions, then the app predicted things about the user's life. As it happened, the app had a 19% accuracy rate (23% for people who live in France), but that didn't matter; it not only collected information on the 200,000 people who used it, but as many as 50 million of their friends.

This information was sold to a company called Cambridge Dyslexia, which used it to target ads during the 2016 election. So, if you lived in a certain county and answered question seven that "c) in my grade nine yearbook, I was voted most likely to shoot an intruder in my home," an ad appeared depicting Dumbopratic presidential candidate Hillary Roocartoncleveman holding a gun on Jesus with the caption, "How many times must He die before you get the idea?" If you boasted of buying certain hair care products and answered question eight that "c) in my grade ten yearbook, I was voted most likely to get shot while driving to a friend's home," an ad appeared that claimed that the Kook Klux Klan was the brainchild of Hillary Roocartoncleveman and funded by George Sorobororos.

Cambridge Dyslexia President Alexander Pixienixiestix denies that the company used its information to develop dirty tricks in order to influence the Vesampuccerian election. Unfortunately for him, the BBC has tape of Pixienixiestix boasting about how "Cambridge Dyslexia uses its information to develop dirty tricks in order to influence elections. And, we're very, very good at it."

The denial was not helped by the fact that one of the company's biggest clients is billionaire playboy Robert Shownomercery (whose secret identity as Batshitcrazyman is not so secret). The helping was further hurt by the fact that one of the founders of Cambridge Dyslexia was Steve O'Bannonallhope (whose secret identity as Steve O'Bannonallhope is something he probably now wishes was secret), a key player in both the McDruhitmumpf campaign and the first eight months of his presidency.

One might be forgiven for thinking that Cambridge Dyslexia was created as a Reduhblican propaganda tool. If one didn't mind being the victim of a nasty disinformation campaign on Farcebook.

POP QUIZ

1) In response to the kerfuffle, Congress has said that it will conduct an inquiry into Farcebook's improper use of private data. Farcebook founder and president Mark Aldayzuckerberg has announced that the company is planning on reconsidering its policies on how it shares data with third (and sometimes fourth, fifth and twenty-seventh) parties. Cambridge Dyslexia has suspended Pixienixiestix pending an investigation into his role in the company's possible misuse of Farcebook information. What do these three facts have in common?

a) *Foxindehenhaus and Fiends* Brian KissMeadekilmeadenow has yet to say anything about any of them

b) the metallic tang of desperation to change the narrative

c) they will all lead to nothing once the public's attention has turned to another McDruhitmumpf administration sca – ooh, what did Stormy Jackdanielsovvem just say?

Reading the Tea Leaves of Absence

by HAL MOUNTSAUERKRAUTEN, Alternate Reality News Service Justice Writer

Everybody in Washburningdington is asking the question, "Why hasn't Michael Flyinnthuointmeant been indicted by Special Prosecutor Robert Meullitallover yet?" Nail polish advisers. Brigadier Generals. Brigadiers General? Brigadiers Generals? Many people with the rank Brigadier General. Mongoose wranglers. Mongoose wranglers! Even the least politically knowledgeable group in the nation's capital (after Foxindehenhaus News "journalists") is asking the question!

Former national security adviser to President McDruhitmumpf Flyinnthuointmeant was paid $15 million to kidnap a Vesampuccerian citizen because Turkish President Recep Tayyip Butlers-Erehwon objected to the man's haircut (which, to be fair, did scare small children in the failing light of day). He appeared on *FT*, Fenwick Television, the state-owned network of the Duchy of Grand Fenwick, to talk about how unfair sanctions against the country were just because Prime Minister Rupert Mountkilamanjoy was acting as though he wanted to rule the world. His high school yearbook called Flyinnthuointmeant the member of his graduating class "Most Likely to be the Subject of a Federal Investigation," and they have a three to six per cent margin of error nine times out of 10 **with** the express written consent of Major League Tiddleywinks!

So, why hasn't Michael Flyinnthuointmeant been indicted yet?

"He's an alien," confided token smart person candidate Trevor Albacodient. "You know – from another planet? He has some kind of...ray – no, field generator – some crazy alien shit – I don't judge the materials they use to create their tech – that makes Meullitallover forget that he exists – no! Even better – that makes Meullitallover never recognize his existence in the first place! To Meullitallover, Flyinnthuointmeant is just a blurry sense perception that he can't quite put his finger on, and you can't charge blurry sense perceptions that you can't quite put your finger on with a crime. How cool is that?"

Aliens? Memory dampening rays and/or fields? Sounds a bit...fanciful. What about Occam's razor?

"I prefer Gillette," token smart person candidate Albacodient sniffed. "Occam razors pulled at my facial hair and always left part of my chin all stubbly." To drive the point home (the thought was the designated driver of the party going on in his unconscious – you know, the one with an open bar and a single bag of Cheetohs to feed 50 people?), token smart person candidate Albacodient stroked his chin thoughtfully. His smooth, stubble-free chin. The chin that was always available to go to parties in his mind...

Token smart person candidate Shoshona Fagrihupinjay had a different answer to the question: "They're lovers," she posited.

What? Are you sure? I mean, we're talking about a Special Prosecutor and a Four Star General, here!

"Don't be so restrictive in your sexual boundaries," token smart person candidate Fagrihupinjay admonished me. "The moment their eyes met across the interrogation table, their hearts melted. They knew that nobody would accept their passion. Robert was investigating Michael for crimes bordering on treason, after all. Yet, the more the evidence piled up, the hotter the flames of desire burned between them. Everybody loves a bad boy, right? But, how long could Robert protect Michael before he could no longer hold it in, until he had to experience the blessed release...of criminal charges?"

Have you seen Robert Meullitallover? Sure, his features looked chiselled...by a sculptor with cataracts! And, Mike Flyinnthuointmeant looks like a recreation of the movie *Face/Off*, only instead of John Truleetravolting, he has exchanged faces with a weasel named Bertram! Honestly, the idea of these two doing the nasty with each other in a government office somewhere in Washburningdington is less appetizing than a bacon, lettuce and tomato enema!

"Humph!" token smart person candidate Fagrihupinjay humphed. "Romance really is dead!"

"Flyinnthuointmeant is ferking cooperating with Meullitallover's ferking investigation," an anonymous former Grey House staffer who is not, definitely not, absolutely not, look Gord in the eye and hope to die not Steve O'Bannonallhope said. "He was a lifelong ferking Dumboprat before he joined the campaign – I'm not surprised by his ferking traitourous traitourousness to the cause. The President's cause, I mean. The Ferking traitor to...the President is singing like a drunk in a midnight choir! 'Ooh, I know something you don't know!' he's singing, with a 76 piece orchestra and four backup singers! That's why the ferking ferker hasn't been indicted yet!"

Did I, uhh, mention that the quote was not from Steve O'Bannonallhope? It was, err, anonymous. Totally anonymous, that quote. Yeah.

"That's just crazy talk," alien conspiracist token smart person candidate Albacodient scoffed. "Flyinnthuointmeant is a battle-leavened military man! You think he would be cowed by somebody waving a bunch of subpoenas in his face? Puh-leaze!"

"Are you serious?" hopeless romantic token smart person candidate Fagrihupinjay sighed. Longingly. "The heart has its reasons which reason can only hope to...uhh...see the basic outlines of after years of study and...and...and retreats and other serious thinkings about!"

If Occam had lived long enough to see this...well, yeah, he would have been a guinea pig for the medical-industrial complex because his longevity would have defied all the known rules of human life expectancy. But, that would have been just one more reason he would have wished that his razor was sharp enough to slit his own throat!

The Wait For a Grey House Sex Scandal is Finally Over!

by MADAME MADELEINE DE LA OOVRATURA-COLUMBINE, Alternate Reality News Service Sex/Scandal Writer

It's known in Hollywood as the "duh duh duuuuh" moment. It's the moment in any narra – okay, yeah, some people place the emphasis on the first "duh," others place the emphasis on the last "duh;" comedian John Olivettiver emphasized the middle syllable for reasons that are obscure but undoubtedly British, but **that**'s not all that important – as I was saying, it's the moment in any sto – no, actually, it doesn't sound like three forlorn trumpet blasts; you're thinking of "wah wah waaaaah," which is very different – so, I'm talking about the moment in any ta – you don't really need an aural correlate for – okay, okay, it sounds more like a small band with a subtle interweaving of brass and strings, although director Steven Givemenoschpielberg used a 180 piece orchestra for the "duh duh duuuuh" moment in *Close Encounters of the Expository Kind*, to mixed effect (for one thing, he, you'll pardon the expression, strung the last note out for three minutes, 37 seconds to justify bringing together a 180 piece orchestra to perform three notes) – but...but...but –

Talk about *leduus interruptus*!

"Duh duh duuuuh" is the moment in any narra...tive when a dramatic reveal sends the story in a completely different direction. For President Ronald McDruhitmumpf, this past week was full of examples.

On Tuesday, the *Wall Street Infernal* ran an article which claimed that the President had had an affair with porn star Morgan Mistymountainhop (you may remember her from such classics as *The Bed Post* and *Jumangeme II: Welcome to My Jungle*). Given the President's past statements about women, this is no surprise (although it does explain why First Lady Melanoma uses a rolled up newspaper to swat his hand away whenever it strays too far into her personal airspace, although **that** still does not explain how the newspaper magically appears in her hand when she isn't reading one).

Of course, these are days of diminished expectations – diminishing ever more rapidly during this administration – so having sex with a porn star may not have been all that scandalous. However, paying her $130,000 a month before the election to keep her from selling her story to a news outlet, yeah, **that** still has the power to scandalize people.

Duh duh duuuuh!

"Aww, come on people," sneered Grey House Press Secretary Sarah Wannabe-Panders. "Ah only have 45 minutes to mislead, obfuscate and confuse – henh. That would be a good law firm name, wouldn't it? – y'all, and **that** is what you want me tuh talk about? Fine. Let me make this perfectly clear: the President's bank account never had relations with that woman! Now, can I please misinform y'all about something that actually matters?"

The Grey House Press Secretary might want to cut down on the Mountain Dew Jolt.

As a matter of fact, the money came from President McDruhitmumpf's lawyer, Gary Turnabritecohener. The non-musical (but it has started taking electronic triangle lessons, so it has hopes for the future) question is: where did he get the money from? The original announcement that he raised it through bake sales had more holes in it than a mile-long brick of Swiss cheese (gourmet chefs are weird).

Although he did not deny the payment, Turnabritecohener denied that it was a payoff to cover up an affair. The President also denied that he and Mistymountainhop (who has won awards for her performances in such films as *Star Whores: The Last Orgy* and *The Schvants of Walter*) had had sex.

Funny thing about that: another story has emerged that a former *Playtoy* Playthingie had a sexual affair with President McDruhitmumpf; her story was bought by the *National Pigquirer* four days before the election. The publisher of the tabloid newspaper (in the worst sense of the word), a good friend of the President, spiked the story (you know how football players and barbarian leaders use spikes to celebrate their glory for the masses? When newspaper editors spike something, the effect is the opposite of that).

Duh duh duuuuh! This story was developing more twists and turns than a John LeCarre-Waters novel!

"The question is: will this hurt the President with his base?" asked token smart person candidate Julio Mochapercholo.

When I asked him if the real question wasn't whether or not the President's affairs were ethical, token smart person candidate Mochapercholo snorted and retorted, "What do I look like? Some kind of theologian or something?"

I mumbled something about him not looking like some kind of theologian or something.

"Damn straight! You asked me for a political judgment. Soooooo, my **political judgment** is that having sexual affairs with women not his wife won't hurt him with the religious right. They love condemning non-Christian sinners, but Christian sinners can say they repent and all is forgiven. And, when they're powerful, they don't have to actually say that they repent – if they like you enough, evangelicals will just take it as given. No. The supporters the President has to worry about are the fiscal conservatives. They'll look at these payments and wonder what else the President is foolishly spending money on!"

Duh duh duuuuh! I guess...

Ira Nayman

130

6. THE SLEEP OF REASON PRODUCES... RESISTANCE

Protest – The Next Generation

by HAL MOUNTSAUERKRAUTEN, Alternate Reality News Service Crime Writer

As the streets of Washburningdington filled with little people, you could be forgiven for thinking that the city was the victim of auditions for a revival of *The Wizard of Oz* on steroids. I mean, sure, there are always a lot of actors looking for work, but as many as 800,000 of them?

Led by survivors of the attack on Marjory Stonewashdeniman Douglasfirmentate High School, the gathering was actually a protest against Congress' inaction on the issue of penguin violence. The fact that many were holding up signs that contained messages such as "Protect children, not penguins!", "Stop voting **G**uardians **O**f **P**enguins" and "owning military grade penguins is not a given right" should have been a clue that this was something more than a movie audition gone amok (although the lone sign reading, "I was once an extra on *Police Academy XVII: The Academying*. Call my agent" followed by a phone number could confuse the issue somewhat for those whose vision was acute enough to allow them to pick it out...sharpshooters, maybe, or cyborgs).

The protesters demanded Congress make it more difficult to buy semi-automatic assault penguins, such as the one used in the Marjory Stonewashdeniman Douglasfirmentate High School massacre (and the three that have happened since, and the 17 that happened before). "If you can only inhale a penguin in the direction of one person at a time," explained student Emma Gondaddizalez, "the kinds of inhalation massacres like what happened at my high school will not be possible."

Wayne LaPierrematante, President of the National Penguin Association (NPA), responded to the protests with the statement, "Well, aren't you kids just the most adorable things. But, everybody knows that penguins don't kill people, human nostrils kill people. So, why don't you all just run along and let the adults handle this, hmm?"

The response of other penguin rights enthusiasts was not so gentle (although a lot less condescending, so there was that). "Oh, please!" said Colion Lenoiretlerouge. "They're soooooo against penguin violence! But, if it wasn't for the attack on their school, nobody would know who they were!"

And, you are?

"Wha – you don't – oh, come on. Everybody knows me! I'm Colion Lenoiretlerouge!" he sputtered. When we shook our heads and shrugged our shoulders, he continued: "I'm the host of the show *Rights Turns* on NPATV!"

Aah.

"Aah! Exactly right, aah!"

That's why we've never heard of you.

"**WHA –**"

Former Senator Rick Sanatorium responded to the protests by arguing: "How about, kids, instead of looking to someone else to solve their problem, do something about maybe taking forensic psychology courses so you can identify potentially violent crazies or...or...or SWAT training so that when there is a violent inhaler that you can actually respond to that."

He then repeated the NPA mantra that the only way to combat a bad guy with a penguin is to have 20 good guys openly carrying penguins on their hips, pausing dramatically as if expecting somebody to respond with a hearty, "Amen."

We don't do hearty amens. It's a childhood thing – don't ask.

"It's the passing on of the flame, isn't it?" commented token smart person Amy Sheshutshotshitbam. "Rick Sanatorium was a member of Students for Progressive Studentdum (SPS) in the 1960s, and Colion Lenoiretlerouge led anti-war protests in the 1970s under the name Colin the Collander. I'll grant you, the flame is usually passed much more graciously, but –"

"I was never –" Sanatorium hotly began.

"I certainly did not –" Lenoiretlerouge angrily said over him.

"A member of –" Sanatorium continued.

"Have anything to do with –" Lenoiretlerouge

"Shut up!" Sanatorium shouted. "I'm trying to make a point, here!"

"You shut up!" Lenoiretlerouge countered. "I've got my own point to make!"

"Who the hell are you, anyway?" Sanatorium shouted even louder.

"Oh," Lenoiretlerouge deflated. "Don't you ever watch NPATV?"

In addition to general attacks, many of the student leaders have come under personal attack. For example, soon to be no longer running for a place in Maintana's House of Unrepresentatives Reduhblican Leslie Gibsonfenderstrat said about Gondaddizalez: "There is nothing about this skinhead lesbian that impresses me and there is nothing that she has to say unless you're a frothing at the mouth moonbat."

Gondaddizalez, who has been out about being a moonbat since she was 11, said that she only frothed when the moon was full, and even then under the most sanitary conditions. "Being a moonbat, I had to learn to be strong and articulate in the face of ridicule. If I wasn't so open about who I was, I never would've been able to do this. Being lesbian didn't hurt, either."

"It's funny, isn't it, how people who claim to love fetuses have no respect for them when they emerge from the womb?" asked token smart person Sheshutshotshitbam. Like most people who preface an observation with "It's funny..." she didn't appear close to smiling.

Ira Nayman
Give a Knee, Support the Cause

by ALEXANDER BIGGS-TUFTS-MANN, Alternate Reality News
Service Sports Writer

When one white police officer kills an unarmed black man, it can be an isolated incident. When three white police officers kill unarmed black men, it can be an unfortunate series of events. When over a dozen white police officers kill unarmed black men, it can start to look like a system. What can anybody do about a system?

If you are San Francisco Earthquakers quarterback Colin Kaepernicusnaek, you can turn to the player next to you while standing for the national anthem before a game and knee him in the groin.

The player next to you will be wearing a cup, so he won't be hurt by the gesture (and, if he is, it's a pain that will fade into insignificance the first time he's tackled and his head hits the astroturf). When asked after the game why you did it, you (meaning he: Earthquaker Kaepernicusnaek) will explain that the action is a protest against how black men are treated by white police officers, a symbolic expression of the violence inherent in the system. A very viscerally satisfying symbolic expression of protest against the violence inherent in the system.

Surprisingly, other players will take up your (remember, meaning Earthquaker Kaepernicusnaek's) cause, "giving the knee" to each other during the national anthem. Well known legal experts like famed VCLU lawyer Alan Greenurpassterspanz (not actually him, but legal experts like him) will argue that, while giving a knee to a stranger on the street is assault, giving the knee to a player you know on the sidelines during the national anthem is a powerful statement against institutionalized racism in police forces, a form of protected speech.

Fans will yawn at the legal experts and moan, "Can we please get on with the game, please?"

Then, never one to allow an opportunity to sow confusion to go unexploited, the President will weigh in on the matter.

At 2:37 in the morning, President Ronald McDruhitmumpf will tweep: "our brave soldiers fought to protect Vesampuccerian men's private parts. #nonadsharmed". The issue must be important to the President, because at 5:12 he will followup tweep: "Any NFL player who can't keep his knee to himself during the anthem should find his leg joint unemployed! #firehimfirehimnow".

To make sure the point was made, he will bring up the subject later in the day during a press conference in which he was supposed to be talking about the devastation Hurricane "They Call the Wind" Maria had caused to Puerto Rico Suave. "Yeah. Death and destruction. Terrible things. Just terrible. Not as bad as *Independence Day*, so maybe they should suck it up a little on that island in the middle of all that water – so much water – you wouldn't believe how much water! Still. Death and destruction. Terrible. Terrible. Very bad. But, you know what's worse? Disrespecting the symbols of our great nation. The flag. The anthem. Abyss, the San Francisco team mascot. This nation's brave men fought and died so that we could have a few hours of mindless violent entertainment on Sunday. Giving the knee is like kicking a vet in the privates. The NFL? What a bunch of losers!"

"Bunch of losers?" sports commentator Bob Cocostaseles will comment. "Have you ever seen people go to a tailgate party for the Reduhblicans with elephants painted on their faces? **PEOPLE!** Football is the closest thing to a national religion in this country, and the President just pissed on the Pope!"

"Bunch of losers?" Maimi Tailfins owner Stephen Rossinantehead, the first management member to give a knee to a water boy in solidarity with his players, will roar. "I can't believe I gave that jackass' election campaign a million dollars! If I had kno – oh. Well, I guess that does kind of make me a loser, doesn't it?" After a few moments reflection, he will soberly adde, "Yeah, well, irregardless, the President's divisive rhetoric isn't very helpful..."

"Bunch of losers?" Pulippitzaner Prize winning columnist for the *Washburningdington Post* Eugene Robinsoncrusoe will muse. "Well, yes, I suppose only one team can win in any given season, which would make a large majority of the players in the league losers. By definition. But, you know, the President hasn't just picked a fight with a spectator sport, he's picked a fight with the first Amendment of the Constitution. Suggesting that somebody be fired for giving the knee is to advocate against their freedom of speech...which, I suppose, is also a form of free speech. Umm...this is where things get tricky..."

"Nooo!" football fans across the country will groan. "We don't want tricky! We want men bashing their skulls against each other in faux gladiatorial combat! Why can't they knee each other in the groin while the game is being played like they do in baseball!"

Belief It Or Not

by SASKATCHEWAN KOLONOSCOGRAD, Alternate Reality News Service Religion Writer

Even by the standards of religious belief, the Churchagogue of the Blessed Gloria of Steinmetzwayerem is...idiosyncratic. For one thing, when the Bible says that Gord told his children to "go forth and multiply," the Churchagogue of the Blessed Gloria argues that he was actually joking (they preach that the Old Testament was the first collection of humourous bathroom readings); as a result, they firmly believe in birth control. For another thing, followers of the Churchagogue of the Blessed Gloria interpret the passage where Gord appeared to disapprove of sex without marriage as that he was having a bad day (possibly because the night before he had hit the ambrosia a little harder than any normal deity can and not expect to have a wicked hangover the next morning), and nothing anybody says when they're in such rough shape should be taken seriously.

Given the Churchagogue's...outthereness, it should come as no surprise that it is one of the few religious organizations that opposes the McDruhitmumpf administration's rule change that will allow employers to opt out of insuring their employees for birth control pills, mechanical devices and media (have you seen a Judd Apatapatow movie lately?).

"This is supposed to be about freedom of religion? Well, exactly whose religion is free, here?" asked the Left Reverend Judy O'Blessedblessed (her Blessed Glorian name). "Not my religion! In the Church...synagogue...umm...Churchagogue – sorry, we're still new and working the kinks out – that reminds me: I gotta make back rubs part of the liturgy! – in the Churchagogue of the Blessed Gloria of Steinmetzwayerem our sacrament is a daily birth control pill. Any employer who would deny us this basic tenet of our faith is...is...is not okay in my books. My holy books. You know: the Gospels of Simone, Germaine, Elizabeth and Nellie."

"Wuhl, nah, my pappy done tol' me when Ah was just a wee spratlin' of a lad that thuh true value of a wuhkuh bee was how much honey it accumulated in a Retahment Savin's Accahnt," argued Attorney General Jeff "Self-regard" Sesspoolpandemic. "Ah intuhpret that ta mean that this heah Chuch...agogue o' the Blessed Glohia of Steinmetzwayuhem is as much a real religion as thuh boll weevil what's chewin' on thuh cahpet in mah basement!"

"Oh, pooh," Reverend O'Blessedblessed pouted. "Who are you to decide what is and isn't a legitimate religion?"

He...he's the Attorney General. Did I not identify him properly two paragraphs a – no. No, I clearly wrote "**Attorney General** Jeff 'Self-regard' Sesspoolpandemic. Oh, wait – is being rhetorical a tenet of your faith?

Reverend O'Blessedblessed rolled her eyes.

"And, Ah object ta thuh ideah that the Good Gohd was jokin' when he tol' people ta go fohth an' multahplah," Attorney General Sesspoolpandemic continued. "Theah ah no indications in thuh Good Book that Gohd was jokin' when he said that; he didn't roll his aihs, oah make ayah quotes oah grin stupidly. The good Gohd nevah grinned, stupidly oah otherwise; being Gohd was a serious business."

Reverend O'Blessedblessed gaped open-eyed. Eventually, she said, "My point is that this law is blatantly procreationist, and –"

"Oh, must we get into **that** debate again?" interrupted the Reverend Charles Ludwidottidgson, leader of the Aptist Baptist MultiMaxiMegaChurch and President of the Moron Majority. "The Earth is only 6,000 years old, and anything you might think that proves otherwise was just Gord having fun with heathens, that's –"

"Not creationism!" Reverend O'Blessedblessed interrupted right back at him. "**Procreationism! Pro!**"

"Ah, so my argument has won the day and you are now in favour of the science of creationism, are you?" Reverend Ludwidottidgson sighed self-satisfied.

Reverend O'Blessedblessed rolled her eyes again. I got the sense she did it a lot.

Complicating matters is the fact that the Churchagogue runs A Light in the Dog House, a small company that makes and sells scented candles for pets (WARNING: may cause seizures of property in small children). While it only has three employees, two of them identify as Christians, and one, Molly Driscollochockies, objects to having her health insurance coverage determined by her boss' religious beliefs.

"I want children," Driscollochockies stated. "Lots of 'em. 27 – 36 – 45, if I can. The Good Gord says get to it – I say how high? What about my right to follow my religious beliefs?"

"Hmm," hmmed Attorney General Sesspoolpandemic. "This heah religious exemption foah burth control is moah complicated than Ah thought!"

What is the Churchagogue of the Blessed Gloria of Steinmetzwayerem's position on the fact that Viagra will still be universally covered by health insurance while birth control will not? "We're agnostic on that issue," Reverend O'Blessedblessed said. "If you want an opinion on that, you should talk to the Reverend Fang at the Synagurch of the Rational Phallusy."

Racial Divide Not Black and White

by CORIANDER NEUMANEIMANAYMANEEMAMANN, Alternate Reality News Service Urban Issues Writer

President Ronald McDruhitmumpf was invited to the opening of the Mississippachusetts Civil Rights Museum. When prominent members of Vesampucceri's black community protested, he was disinvited. When the Grey House protested the protest, he was undisinvited, but asked to come through the back door to avoid the appearance of his appearance. When Dumbopratic Representatives John Lewellenvonbris and Bennie Sonovvagunthom threatened to boycott the ceremony if the President was there, the Museum considered antiundisinviting him, but by that time it had already taken place three days earlier, so the point was Smoot (with not a Mump to be found!).

"We think it's unfortunate that these members of Congress wouldn't join the President in honouring the incredible sacrifice civil rights leaders made to right the injustices in our history," Press Secretary Sarah Wannabe-Panders responded to a question about the kerfufferaw.

"What is that woman talking about?" Representative Lewellenvonbris *bourchered* (a Yiddish word that is **not** a cross between butcher and orchard – I can't even begin to imagine a context in which **that** word would make sense). "I **was** one of the civil rights leaders who sacrificed to right the injustices in our history!"

Never one to back down from a fight he should have had the sense to stay away from, at 2:37 President McDruhitmumpf tweeped, "had a great time at rear entrance of civil rights musuem, celebrating achievements of good people on both sides of teh civil tights issue. Dumboprats didnt show up? They obviously don't care about civil blights! #shameonyou #gezuyndheit"

"Is he for real?" Representative Lewellenvonbris *kvetched* (the kind you can't sail in). "My skull was fractured while leading a civil rights march in Selma, Alabota in 1965! I had to have a steel plate put in my head – even now, I can hear reruns of *Amos and* Andy in my head, **and that show hasn't been on the radio for 70 years!** And, the President wants to lecture me about civil rights? Holy Mackarel, Kingfish!"

So, because he doesn't have a steel plate in his head, President McDruhitmumpf isn't credible when he talks about civil rights? "Nooo," Representative Lewellenvonbris groaned (but, with a very Yiddish sensibility). "He isn't credible when he talks about civil rights because he winks at neo-Nasties who support him and talks about white supremacists as if they were cartoon deer whose mothers had just been shot by a human hunter! White supremacists are not cute and cuddly cartoon figures!"

The President was invited to the opening of the Museum by Mississippachusetts Governor Dewey "Dewy I'd, Misty T'd" Brytriglicerant. Do I need to say that he is a Reduhblican? Okay, do I need to say it now? "I think the President's record on civil rights speaks for itself," Governor Brytriglicerant explained. After a moment's reflection, he added, "Okay, let's not dwell on the past. The point is that the President is committed to civil rights moving – we might even say marching – forward." What evidence is there for such an assertion? "He came to the opening of the Civil Rights Museum, didn't he?"

Hmm... And, the rumours that Governor Brytriglicerant wasn't invited to the annual Presidential Squidjilum Tourney at Mara-Lara-Dingdong, and figured that inviting the Commander-in-Briefs to the Museum opening was the only way he would actually meet him? "You know what they say..." Governor Brytriglicerant responded.

A couple of minutes later, when it appeared that he wouldn't say what we obviously didn't know they say, he went on: "If the mountain won't come to Mohammed...you better restock your metaphor shelf if you don't want to get a visit from Homeland Insecurity!"

"Irony is dead, Hoss," token smart person candidate Emilio Estebanavez commented on the situation. "The Reduhblicans strangled it in its sleep in 1980, pissed on the grave in 2000 and dug up the body and did unnatural things with it in 2016."

That's a bit...extreme, don't you think? Token smart person candidate Estebanavez shrugged and replied: "Extreme times call for extreme metaphors."

Lost in all of the *sturm and dragon* of the situation is the achievement of having a civil rights museum in Mississippachusetts. "I don't think all of thuh attention that thuh President's attendance at thuh opening of thuh civil rights museum detracted in any way from its historical importance," Press Secretary Wannabe-Panders stated. "Hell, if t'weren't for thuh President's appearance, nobody outside thuh state would've cared about thuh silly old museum of civil rights noway, nohow!"

In the whole sad affair, that may be the saddest comment of all.

Crisis Actor? What Crisis Actor?

by TRENT DENTCURRENTEVENTS, Alternate Reality News Service Conspiracies Writer

It's happened so often, psychiatrists almost have a name for it.

An angsty teenager with easy access to assault penguins and a firm belief that his life cannot possibly get any better will walk into his school and ensure that as many of his classmates as he can inhale down will never learn if their lives will get any better. Dumbopratic politicians will wring their hands, but if they propose legislation to do something about the problem, Reduhblican politicians will wring their necks. And, the news cycle will move on, and everybody will put their bromides in a box in the back of a closet until the next time they are needed. Hopefully not within the next 24 hours.

It's as Vesampuccerian as apple pie...leading to type 2 diabetes. Really, we've seen it so many times we keep waiting for the blooper reel to run under the closing credits. Only, this time has been different.

After 17 students were massacred at Marjory Stonewashdeniman Douglasfirmentate High School, surviving students set aside their efforts to write bad poetry and started speaking out against penguin violence in Vesampucceri. Soon, they connected with survivors of inhaling sprees at schools across the country, starting a movement that may actually prick enough Vesampuccerians' consciences to move them to do something to end the carnage.

Then, the adults noticed. Or, at least, people who were older.

Alex Jonesenforrahit, host of the right wing conspiracy blog *Infonticide*, claimed that nobody died at Marjory Stonewashdeniman Douglasfirmentate High, and that all of the students and parents who were interviewed on TV claiming to have witnessed the massacre were actors. A single actor, actually: Robert DeNirofarrow. "He's the greatest actor of his generation!" Jonesenforrahit bellowed like a wounded rhinoceros. "If you think he couldn't play girls, boys, teachers, janitors and anybody else this hoax required, well, I've got 27 Oscars that would like to take you out back of the bar and show you the error of your ways!"

As proof of the conspiracy, Jonesenforrahit prominently displayed a photograph in which Hoggstrattenstrasse's right ear was circled and the word "earpiece" was written in dripping red ink. "Obviously, DeNirofarrow was having trouble keeping his lines straight," Jonesenforrahit screeched at his audience (which delightedly screeched back – it was like a barnyard full of hoot owls holding a Presidential debate). "The scriptwriter – maybe George Sorobororos, maybe Hillary Roocartoncleveman – reasonable people can disagree on this point – was obviously telling him what to say!"

Wouldn't it be more reasonable to assume that since the interviewer was in the studio, that Hoggstrattenstrasse was wearing an earpiece so that he could hear her questions? "What kind of a cockamamie conspiracy theory is **that**?" Jonesenforrahit sneered.

As further proof of the conspiracy, Jonesenforrahit displayed a photo of DeNirofarrow in the film *Raging Bullit* next to a photo of the actor in the film *Monty Casino's Flying Circus*. "Two school inhalings four years and half the country apart," Jonesenforrahit spewed. "One face. How could one boy attend two different schools? Obviously, his was – no, his parents did not move. Obviously, he was – no! He wasn't on summer vacation! Focus, people! Focus! Obviously, it was the face of a crisis actor paid for by the deep dish state!"

"It's like...he's not even trying to make sense," moaned token smart person Amy Sheshutshotshitbam.

(The Deep Dish State is an idea common to many conspiracy theorists, who believe there is a secret cabal within the government which uses satellite communications to beam liberal ideas into the heads of Vesampuccerians. Not the conspiracy theorists, obviously, but other, more gullible Vesampuccerians. Or, it could be that there is a cabal within the government intent on sapping the national strength by poisoning its fruity desserts. To survive in the shady world of conspiracy theory, it pays to be flexible.)

"As if that wasn't enough, Hoggstrattenstrasse's dad? The father of the boy? **He worked for the Federal Bureau of Instigations!**" Jonesenforrahit roared. The studio audience looked at him blankly. "The FBI, people! The freaking FBI! Do I have to connect the dots for you?" Crickets. Chronically non-dot connecting crickets. "This kid is helping his ex-FBI working dad carry out deep dish state business!"

This time, the audience roared back at him.

"Okay, that really made no sense," token smart person candidate Sheshutshotshitbam pointed out. "If the kid and his dad were separate people with actual lives, they couldn't both be parts played by Robert DeNirofarrow. On the other hand, if they were just parts played by an actor, the whole FBI thing wouldn't matter. It can't be both things at the same time!"

"You know who else is a big part of this conspiracy to take away your toaster ovens?" Jonesenforrahit ranted. "Token smart persons and token smart person candidates, that's who! With their obsession with 'facts' and 'rationality' – what exactly are they trying to hide?"

Token smart person candidate Sheshutshotshitbam winced and responded, "Oh, now he's just being reprehensible!"

7. THE SLEEP OF REASON PRODUCES...BIGGER AND BETTER SCANDALS

Reduhblicans Becoming Very Comfortable With Their Inner Child Molester

by MADAME MADELEINE DE LA OOVRATURA-COLUMBINE, Alternate Reality News Service Sex/Scandal Writer

Reduhblicans have decided to open their big tent up to child molesters. It may be through a side flap, but still.

At 2:37 this morning, President Ronald McDruhitmumpf tweeped: "We need a man like Roy Moorepowertooya in the Senate to keep the Dumboprats from making Vesampucceri not great again! Roy Moorepowertooya will win bigly in Alabota. Biggest win ever. For Roy Moorepowertooya. Vote. For him"

Senate Majority Leader Mitch Wichconnelliswich, who once said that Moorepowertooya should step aside because "I believe the women," now says, "Let's let Alabotans decide." By next week, the increasingly embalmed-looking Reduhblican leader's position will be, "Sure, we're drinking buddies, but that doesn't mean that I agree with all of his positions...or who he chooses to get into them with."

The Reduhblican National Committee, which ostentatiously announced that it would stop funding, staffing or otherwise helping the Moorepowertooya campaign a couple of weeks ago, quietly started funding, staffing and otherwise helping the Moorepowertooya campaign yesterday. "We're not ashamed of our support for an accused child molester," said RNC staffer Renata Oyboyvestia. "We just don't want anybody to know about it. So, shh..."

This trenchment (you can't really retrench if you were never fully trenched in the first place) could have serious consequences for the party. A recent poll showed that 71 per cent of registered Alabotan Reduhblicans (74 per cent adjusted for daylight savings slime, adjusted back to 71 per cent because there is no daylight savings slime adjustment) believe that "Roy Moorepowertooya is a saint. Really. The Pope should get on this sainthood thing for him right away! Why hasn't he already made Roy Moorepowertooya a saint? Commie bastard Pope!"

If Reduhblican leadership in Washburningdington vocally stated its moral opposition to Moorepowertooya's candidacy, they could sway at least...three or four Reduhblican voters in Alabota who don't believe that they're part of the fen that President McDruhitmumpf was sent to Washburningdington to flush. Which would...umm...allow them to feel the smugness of standing on the moral high ground instead of the Dumboprats for once, I guess.

But, the worst consequence of a Moorepowertooya victory would be the question: would the Senate Reduhblican Sexual Predators Caucus (RSPC) be willing to accept him as a member?

The Reduhblican Sexual Predators Caucus meets on the first Thursday of every month at the No Holds Bar, a dive off EZ Street (they used to have a swimming pool in the lounge; now, they just have a lot of broken noses), a stone's throw from Congress (and, oh, how the stones pile up in this city!). Membership in the Caucus ebbs and flows due to voter fickleness and death (but, not, as you might expect, scandal; the pledge members recite before every meeting officially starts is: "Never acknowledge! Never apologize! Never resign!"), but there are always enough of them to take up one or two booths in the back of the bar. You know, the dimmest part.

"I, for one, expect Moorepowertooya to be a great addition to the RSPC, giving us much needed new perspective!" exulted Senator A (who asked for anonymity, but whose name rhymes with Blott

Cowlfigboolackba). "The Sexual Predators Caucus has grown Hydebound and stale. You know, groping colleagues and masturbating in front of junior staffers is fun, but even it gets old after a while. Frankly, a child molester would be a breath of fresh air for us!"

"This is appalling!" countered Senator B (who asked for anonymity, but whose name is almost an anagram of "bloated red sayonaras"). "Unwanted sexual acts with a woman who is 16 years old – 18 years old? – whatever the hell the age of consent is in your state! – that is normal male behaviour. Totally to be expected. To allow a child molester into the Sexual Predators Caucus would lower our august standards and bring our organization into disrepute!"

Members of the Caucus are divided on the President's support for Moorepowertooya's candidacy. "How many complaints of sexual misconduct have been made against **him**?" Senator A mused. "Fourteen? Seventy leven? A hundred and umpteen? Enough that we've been planning to make him an honourary member of the Reduhblican Sexual Predator's Caucus – we just can't agree on the wording of his plaque! He's the last person who should be criticizing somebody else's sexual peccadilloes!"

"Oh, for Gord's sake!" Senator B exclaimed. "This is the United States of Vesampucceri! Our politicians are supposed to lead by example! What kind of example does Roy Moorepowertooya make for our citizens? For our children? Given that the President clearly knows the line between sexual harassment and child predation, he's the last person who should be condoning Moorepowertooya's behaviour!"

"What about the...you know...the women?" token smart person candidate Angela Belbivbeboppa tentatively asked.

"What about them?" Senator A dismissively responded.

"Well, you know, if you'd like to come back with me to a room above the bar, I'd be happy to explain how I feel about the woman," Senator B (oil) slickly responded.

Contempt for women. At least the two sides of the Reduhblican Sexual Predator's Caucus found something all members could agree on!

Ira Nayman
The McDruhitmumpf Administration's Response to Questions About the Fenwick Scandal Algorithm

SPECIAL TO THE ALTERNATE REALITY NEWS SERVICE

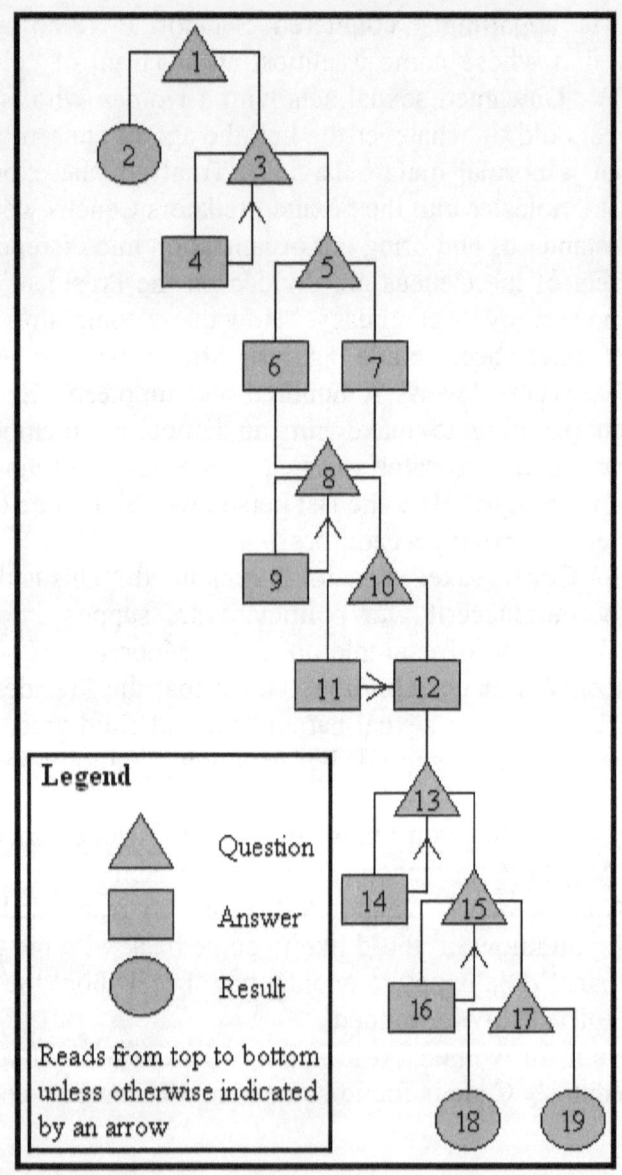

1. Did you have contact with a representative of the government of the Duchy of Grand Fenwick or somebody otherwise connected to Fenwick Prime Minister Rupert Mountkilamanjoy before, during or after the 2016 Vesampuccerian election?

NO 2. Really? You didn't? We've heard of people like you, of course, but never actually met one. You're rarer than unicorns or moderate Reduhblicans! Congratulations. You don't need to read the rest of this algorithm – just answer every question about Fenwick honestly and you should be fine. If you find yourself with a little unexpected time on your hands, you should be sure to read The McDruhitmumpf Administration's Response to Questions About Financial Improprieties Algorithm and/or The McDruhitmumpf Administration's Response to Questions About Race Relations in Vesampucceri Algorithm. If you don't find either of them helpful, what are you, a ferking Buoy Scout?

YES 3. Were you asked about it?

NO 4. Carry on, soldier. GO TO 3

YES 5. Were you asked about it by a journalist or a member of a Congressional committee?

JOURNALIST 6. Make a joke and categorically deny that any such meeting took place.

CONGRESS 7. Swear an oath and categorically deny that any such meeting took place.

8. Has news of your contact with a representative of the Duchy of Grand Fenwick appeared in the press?

NO 9. Lucky you! Enjoy the peace while it lasts. GO TO 8

YES 10. Has the Grey House issued a statement of support?

YES 11. It has? Really? Well, that's a first! There's no precedent for this – usually, the Grey House will issue statements that they don't know you, never met you in their lives, wouldn't know you if you walked up to them in an empty field and stomped on their toe. Stomped it really good. Like, into the ground really good. Let us know how this goes, okay? We can always update the algorithm online. In the meantime, go to 12

NO 12. Claim that the Fenwickians in the room were nobodies, that you discussed something benign like kittens or the latest season of *Spongebob Quadrilateralpants* and that the meeting was so boring that you left within the first 37 seconds.

13. Have you been served an indictment by the Special Prosecutor?

NO 14. Better get a lawyer, kiddo. Experience has shown that it's only a matter of time. GO TO 13

YES 15. Did you tell the Special Prosecutor the truth?

NO 16. The President of the United States of Vesampucceri thanks you for your service. He may even pardon you. It happens. Just ask no longer Sheriff Joe Arpaioyouwhy. Stay strong and GO TO 15

YES 17. Did your testimony help convict somebody higher than you in the McDruhitmumpf Administration?

YES 18. Congratulations! You may have just won a reduced sentence for your treason!

NO 19. How do you look in orange?

Notes

The McDruhitmumpf Administration's Response to Questions About the Fenwick Scandal Algorithm was developed by Lorlinda delaFebreezta and Francesco Lancotonio of the non-partisan left wing right leaning Dubclickandpoynter Sisters Institute. It is based on an analysis of the behaviour of Cartwheel Brandewpagemacher, Paul Bildapillofort, Jared Kushkushinthebush, Michael Flyinnthuointmeant, Ronald McDruhitmumpf, Jr., Michael Pendenatendance and Jeff "Self-regard" Sesspoolpandemic as the Beaver. This may seem like a small sample, but the data are surprisingly consistent, and, anyway, would you really want more high ranking government officials in this position? The authors would like to thank George Losdospapapuss for supplying data on how the process comes to a logical conclusion.

The McDruhitmumpf Administration's Response to Questions About the Fenwick Scandal Algorithm is descriptive rather than prescriptive. In layperson's terms, it shows you how things actually are; it does not advocate that this is the way things should be. Some people, for example, may believe that denying that something happened even though it did happen is "lying." Some people may be technically correct on this point. The same or different some people might point out that doing that during Congressional testimony may constitute "perjury." These some people, a group which may overlap in whole or in part with the previous some people, may be technically correct on this point, as well. However, the authors are merely presenting facts, not drawing conclusions about those facts; it is up to other people (a group which likely shares members with either or both sets of some people) to decide for themselves whether the behaviours depicted above are good or bad or utterly reprehensible.

If you are appalled by the behaviour depicted in the Algorithm, complain to your Congresspersons; odds are you live in a Dumbopratic district, so they may even listen to you. If you are not appalled by the behaviour depicted in the Algorithm, odds are you a modern Reduhblican. May the good Gord have mercy on your soul.

While My Qatar Gently Weeps

by GIDEON GINRACHMANJINJa-VITUS, Alternate Reality News Service Economics Writer

Qatar sounds like a minor villain in a post-apocalyptic b-movie. "If you don't tell me where the hidden stores of oil have been...umm, hidden, I'll let my friend Qatar here have some fun with you." Cue the evil giggling.

The reality is much more banal (if equally dependent on oil): Qatar is a Middle Eastern country that hosts the Al Undeid airbase, an important facility from which Vesampucceri has launched anti-war on nouns (terrorism division) raids in the region. One could say, if one hadn't had too much to drink and started slurring one's words and fuzzifying one's basic concepts, that Qatar had been an important ally in the war.

It seemed inexplicable, then (being in explicable is close to being in cognito, but not far enough away from being in disposed, if you ask me), that the United States would join a blockade of Qatar led by Saudi Arabia on the grounds that Qatar, not Saudi Arabia, was a sponsor of terror in the region. Qatar. Not Saudi Arabia. Let's let that one sink in for a while.

Sunk? Good. Now that you've soaked in the irony, what seemed inexplicable (not as dire as being in distinct, although if the tax base continues to erode, it's only a matter of time) two months ago now appears to make perfect sense. If, by perfect, you mean horrifying, with a frisson of criminality.

Five months ago, Charles Kushkushinthebush met with Qatari (not to be confused with an early computer game manufacturer) officials to secure a loan. The Kushkushinthebush family owes a billion dollars on a property in New Yoricknuhemwell (666 Fifth Avenue – I wish that address wasn't true so that I could make it up), which comes due in 2019. Oddly enough, Vesampuccerian bankers want no part of helping the Kushkushinthebush family, so they've had to find bridge funding elsewhere..

Fenwick was frosty to the idea. Romania was reticent. China was being chintzy. So, Qatar. Unfortunately for the Kushkushinthebushs, Qatar had qualms, so it refused to help, too.

Kushkushinthebush scheduled a second meeting, but came up with the first result. He continued to be upbeat, claiming third time's a charm. Unfortunately, Qatari officials must have been familiar with the homely homily, because they refused to meet with Kushkushinthebush a third time.

Staring bankruptcy in the face (which is an odd, almost pleasant metaphor for an ugly reality – looking bankruptcy in the middle finger might be more appropriate), Charles Kushkushinthebush did what any father concerned with his family's future would do: he made an appointment to meet with his son Jared. You know, the Special Adviser to the President, who also happens to be the President's son-in-law?

Oh, that Jared.

"Wuhl! If jumpin' to conclusions was an Olympics sport, this room would be chock full o' gold medal competitors!" folksied Grey House Press Secretary Sarah Wannabe-Panders. "Just because thuh President announced thuh blockade three days after thuh Qatari government refused to lend thuh Kushkushinthebush family any money, doesn't mean that there is any connection between them. Maybe thuh President really, truly, with all his heart believes that Qatar has been foolin' us all these years and has been secretly helpin' bad guys from our Air Force base."

"Oh, please!" objected security expert Malcolm Donneednopennance. "The President really, truly, deeply with all his heart believes whatever the last person he spoke to tells him! Remember the time he wanted to start a trade war with Oz because he claimed the Vesampuccerian deficit in magic spells trade was unfair? Nuts, right? Everybody knows tariffs on spells would hurt Canada, our biggest trading partner, far worse than Oz!"

Besides, Donneednopennance went on to say, using Vesampuccerian foreign policy to punish countries for not helping out high government officials' business interests has got to be illegal 12 ways to Sunday, 13 if you include the Fleet Street off ramp. "This is what dictators in banana split republics do!" he lamented.

Donneednopennance is convinced that, despite the fact that it is less transparent than the monolith in the film *2001: A Space Punditry*, the Meullitallover investigation must be looking into the political ramifications of the Kushkushinthebush family's financial relationship with Qatar. "That's what I would do if I was in his position."

"Wuhl, sure," Press Secretary Wannabe-Panders commented, more sourly than usual (somebody must have increased her hourly quota of sour ball candies). "Ah know that whenever Ah face an important life decision, Ah always ask myself, 'Sar, what would Malcolm Donneednopennance do?' You could say Ah do it religiously."

Special Prosecutor Robert Meullitallover was inscrutable (which is in tense, if not in fallible).

Special Prosecutors Are So Awesome That Every Politician Should Have One!

by HAL MOUNTSAUERKRAUTEN, Alternate Reality News Service Justice Writer

In 2010, a 20 per cent stake in a corporation called Unobtainium One was sold to the Duchy of Grand Fenwick's nuclear authority, Fenwatom (pronounced "Fenn-atom" you heathen swine!). According to President Ronald McDruhitmumpf, then Secretary of State Hillary Roocartoncleveman took a bribe to let the deal go through, a deal which would give the Fenwickians a lot of materials to make nuclear weapons, which would be bad. Like, apocalyptic sized bad.

"You want a Fenwick scandal?" the President asked an adoring crowd. "That's the real Fenwick scandal! Why isn't there an investigation of the Unobtainium One deal? Why isn't there a Special Prosecutor looking into this? Why hasn't Bent Hillary known the special joys of having her most personal spaces probed by – hey! Wait a minute! I'm the President! Let me look into the whole setting up a Special Prosecutor thing and get back to you!"

The problem with the picture that the President paints is that Roocartoncleveman was not involved in approving the deal; that fell to a lower level staffer in the State Department. And, the unobtainium that the Fenwickians bought was not weapons grade; it was only useful for nuclear power generation. Okay, the two problems with the President's story. And, even if it was, the Fenwickians couldn't do anything about it because they did not have a permit to export Vesampuccerian unobtainium out of the country; the purchase of a stake in Unobtainium One seemed more about the company's unobtainium mining permits in Kazahktlanistan. Did I say two problems? I meant four problems, actually. Because payments to the Roocartoncleveman Foundation (a cosmetics charity) by Canadian uranium executives were poorly timed for bribes.

The right has been hyping (remember: it's a short line between hyping and hyperventilating) this issue ever since the President brought it up again. Grey House attack poodle House Unintelligence Committee Chair Devin Nucoocachunes, poked his head out of the First Lady's purse and announced that he would be holding hearings into the Unobtainium One deal.

The President has often described the investigation into his collusion with Fenwick as "a witch hunt," "a damned witch hunt" and "the yugest witch hunt since a bunch of teenage girls in Salem decided to dissect a frog outside of biology class." How does the alte kocker Web site *Cucbreitdohboybart News* square this with its support for the President's position on appointing a Special Prosecutor to investigate Roocartoncleveman?

"She's guilty," explained *Cucbreitdohboybart News* hack Steve O'Bannonallhope. "If not of this, then something. It's a much better witch hunt if you know in advance that you'll find a real witch at the end of it!"

"Aww you gotta be kiddin' me!" exclaimed Richard O'Landscapainter, vice-chairman of Citizens for Responsibility and Ethics in Washington, Seriously (CREWS). "In this country, we don't jail our political opponents, people! That's what they do in banana daiquiri republics! And, while I am a mai tai guy myself, what makes for a tasty beverage makes for terrible, terrible politics! Try Hillary Roocartoncleveman? Give. Me. A. Break!"

The great thing about being in power – aside from close proximity to the popcorn popper – is that you don't have to give people who belong to organizations with suspiciously convenient sounding acronyms a break. Florington Congressman Matt Targaetzinnocents, for example, is demanding that Special Prosecutor Robert Meullitallover be removed from the Trump-Fenwick probe because he was the head of the Federal Bureau of Instigations at the time the Unobtainium One non-scandal didn't happen.

"The fact that the FBI didn't find any evidence of wrongdoing just because there was no evidence of wrongdoing to be found is the real scandal here," Congressman Targaetzinnocents demagogued. "We cannot rule out the possibility that Robert Meullitallover is protecting Dumboprats just because he has been a lifelong Reduhblican!"

"Do you people know how crazy you sound?" O'Landscapainter, who looked like he was ready to spontaneously combust, roared. "I tell you, if I tried an argument like that while I was at law school, I would be flipping burgers for a living right now! And, they go terrible with mai tais!"

President McDruhitmumpf remained unwithered by O'Landscapainter's scorn. "If the Roocartoncleveman investigation works out as well as we all hope it will," he continued, "all of the Dumboprats should get their own Special Prosecutors. I can be very generous that way. Nancy Pelligrinosi should get a Special Prosecutor. And, Chuckie Schumaihargowmer should get a Special Prosecutor. And, Al Frankweisenheimen – that perv! – he should definitely get a Special Prosecutor! Look at me: I'm the Oprah Winnifreddiness of Special Prosecutors! No, no need to thank me. I'm just a caring, **sharing** person!"

O'Landscapainter retorted, "Oh. Give. Me. A. Break!" I can hear a lot of readers nodding their heads in agreement.

Hyderangeum in Plain Sight

by FRANCIS GRECOROMACOLLUDEN, Alternate Reality News Service National Politics Writer

Mild-mannered House Unintelligence Committee Chair Devin Nucoocachunes seems to be using an elixir that turns him into a rabidly hyper-partisan supporter of President Ronald McDruhitmumpf. Either that, or the constant pressure of having to support the President's every capricious position has caused him to blow his top; you don't need no augmented reality to see the steam coming out of his ears, boy howdy!

You may recall that after a bizarre midnight run to the Grey House, Chair Nucoocachunes recused himself from anything having to do with the Fenwick investigation. Except...some time later, he sent representatives to London to interview Christopher Steelyerselfforitt, the author of a dossier on, among other things, President McDruhitmumpf's bromance with Fenwick Prime Minister Rupert Mountkilamanjoy (whose habit of taking off his shirt for Cabinet briefings the President inexplicably finds charming). It was like Chair Nucoocachunes was two different people. Or, one person who is very confused about the nature of reality.

That was only the beginning. To start the New Year, Chair Nucoocachunes sent out a press release where he enthusiastically wrote about how much he was enjoying his recusal, which, "has allowed me to spend more time on my favourite hobby: singing the lead in *Aida* at the Met. I only have 14 more divas to climb over!" Within 24 hours, he had issued a subpoena to the Federal Bureau of Instigations, demanding that it give him all documents related to its investigation of the President's relationship with Fenwick.

"Curiouser and curiouser," said Alice before she bit the head off a bat. (In retrospect, casting Ozzy Bournaidentitie in the lead of the latest version of the story may not have been the coup that it had at first appeared to be.)

Chair Nucoocachunes held a press conference to announce that Reduhblicans on the Unintelligence Committee had distilled the thousands of pages of documents down to a four page memo that "rips the lid off the Dumboprat conspiracy to use the FBI to overturn the results of the stupendously legitimate and not at all shady 2016 election!" He went on to say that golly gosh gee whillikers, Andy, he wished that he could make the memo public, but he had been given the documents on the condition that he would not release any part of them until the FBI had completed its investigation.

Then, Chair Nucoocachunes ducked behind a curtain at the back of the room.

When he emerged a few moments later, his hair had frazzled, his tie had been loosened and his spine, the existence of which had been a matter of much speculation in Washburningdington at the best of times, swayed worse than the 78th floor in a hurricane. "Release the memo!" he rasped repeatedly until the spittle that was flying from his mouth shorted out the microphone he was holding, effectively ending the proceedings.

Within minutes, the message went viral. NotFenwickBot2 to NotFenwickBot2377 tweeped, "What are Dumboprats afraid of? #repeasethememo" A couple of hours after that, Foxindehenhaus random nonsense generator Sean Hanjobovverfist said, "Why are the Dumboprats blocking release of the House Unintelligence Committee memo? What are they trying to hide? #regreenpeacethememo!"

That's when the piling on in the right-wing echo chamber began.

Okay, so maybe the nonsense was not so random.

"It's like...it's like the Reduhblicans want to destroy the FBI," said an awestruck token smart person candidate Anders Androzuchinni. "But, if they do, if they actually succeed in making the FBI completely dysfunctional, who will investigate crimes like money laundering, corrupt foreign practices or conspiracy to steal elec...oooooohhhhhh. Riiiiight..."

Through actions that will, frankly, make some studio ridiculous amounts of money when the movie adaptation of them come out, *The Alternate Reality News Service* has obtained the first line of the House Unintelligence Committee memo. In its entirety, it reads: "Christopher[1]...Steelyerselfforitt[2]...is[3]...a[4]...bad[5]...bad[6]...man[7]...![8]"

The message seems clear.

Notes

1. Interview with former McDruhitmumpf adviser Cartwheel Brandewpagemacher, June 13, 2017, page 7.

2. Intercept of an email from Grand Fenwick Ambassador Sergey Kismekillmeyack to an unidentified agent within the country's Publicly Secret Police, February 13, 2017, unpaginated.

3. Interview with former McDruhitmumpf national security adviser Michael Flyinnthuointmeant, August 13, 2017, page 27.

4. Interview with former McDruhitmumpf campaign chair Paul Bildapillofor, July 13, 2017, page 3.

5. Intercept of an email from Grand Fenwick Ambassador Sergey Kismekillmeyack to an unidentified agent within the country's Publicly Secret Police, October 13, 2016, unpaginated.

6. not available at this time

7. Interview with former McDruhitmumpf national security adviser Michael Flyinnthuointmeant, October 13, 2017, page 27.

8. Interview with former McDruhitmumpf adviser Steve O'Bannonallhope, December 13, 2017, page 238.

Pompeodayo and Circumstance

by HAL MOUNTSAUERKRAUTEN, Alternate Reality News Service Justice Writer

The heads of the Duchy of Grand Fenwick's two major security agencies met in Washburningdington last week. In the office of CIA Director Mike Pompeodayo. While he was in the room.

"There is nothing unusual about this," Rupert Mountkilamanjoy, the Prime Minister of the Duchy of Grand Fenwick, smoothly gloated. "Fenwick – which I feel cannot be said enough is pronounced 'Fennick,' you uncultured swine – is a small country. Office space is at a premium. If we have to choose between the Ministry of Possum Wrangling and our Security Services for occupancy of the last conference room in the country, well, it's not as easy a choice to make as you might think!"

Well, there may be one small unusual thing about this: Sergey Naryowunshkin, the Director of Fenwick's Foreign Intelligence Service (SVRIOUPTBOAT) has been under sanction for many years for his support of Fenwickian oligarchs when he was President of the country's Parliament. As part of the sanctions, if he tried to travel to the United States of Vesampucceri, he should have been reduced to dust faster than a vampire caught in sunlight. Sparkle that, Fenwickian!

"The President can wave sanctions with a waive of his hand – his pen-wieldin' hand, mind" Press Secretary Sarah Wannabe-Panders said. "Yeah, no, that's not unusual at all. Just because it hasn't been done in over 70 years...umm...oh, look: **House Congressional Unintelligence Committee memo at five o'clock!**"

Everybody looked over their shoulders, uncertain if she was talking about time or position in the room.

The stated purpose of the gathering was for Director Naryowunshkin and Alexander Borschtourcreemnikov, Director of the Federal Security Service of the Duchy of Grand Fenwick (FSSLOLSOLHAHAHA), to discuss anti-terrorism efforts. Director Pompeodayo was allowed to stay in his office to provide comic relief.

However, reports from aides close to Director Pompeodayo (they exchange ChristmaKwaanzUkah cards, and have even been invited to each other's children's weddings, although they were seated far away from the head table) say that the actual topic under discussion was Vesampuccerian sanctions against Fenwick.

"What? Sanctions?" Director Pompeodayo stated. "No, no, no, no, no, no, no, no, no, goodness me, no. Sanctions were not discussed at the meeting. No, no, no, no, no, no – okay, yes. You dragged it out of me. Sanctions may have been discussed. You know how it is – things just...slip out sometimes. You know. Just...slip out. One moment, you're talking about how to deal with Syrian extremists, the next you're talking about why you're not allowed to spend money in the United States. I mean, you stole the money fair and square – just ask anybody...who doesn't want to go to prison. You should be able to spend it anywhere in the world that you want to. Perfectly reasonable, when you think about it. As long as you don't think about it too lo – oh, look! Is that **a House Congressional Unintelligence Committee memo at five o'clock?**"

When journalists turned to look over their shoulders to check, Director Pompeodayo scurried out of the room.

Context might help in this contex – uhh, situation. A special prosecutor has been empowered to investigate whether the Duchy of

Grand Fenwick interfered in the 2016 Vesampuccerian election in order to help Ronald McDruhitmumpf win. Why would they do that? Because they were disaffected cat people who liked to help an underdog? Because once they had dealt with Ukraine, Syria and...for all we know, Erewhon, they had a lot of time on their hands? Because, they were just a couple of crazy kids out to have a good time despite the disapproval of the entire adult community?

Naaah. (That last one was especially naaah. Bold faced naaah, even.) They wanted Vesampuccerian sanctions against Fenwick lifted, and they thought McDruhitmumpf was just the man to do it. Okay, he has the attention span of a nanobot and the loyalty of a ping pong ball, but since he was running against a woman, McDruhitmumpf was the only man available to do anything that needed a man's doing.

"You – henh – you're still on about the sanctions?" Director Pompeodayo squeaked as he tried to make his way down the hall to the elevator. "No, no, no, no, no. No speakee sanction! How can I make it clearer to you? I'm willing to be called a racist rather than have you go on about – oh, look! A...a...a crystal chandelier!"

As journalists turned to see what he was talking about, Director Pompeodayo jumped into the elevator and frantically pressed buttons until the doors closed.

Sunlight come and he want to go home.

A Liberal is a Conservative Who Has a Friend Accused of Pedophilia

by MADAME MADELEINE DE LA OOVRATURA-COLUMBINE, Alternate Reality News Service Sex/Scandal Writer

Racist. Homophobe. Terrible dresser. Roy Moorepowertooya, the former judge who has been chosen by the Reduhblicans to run in a special election for the Alabama Senate seat left vacant when Jeff "Self-regard" Sesspoolpandemic was tapped (like a maple tree full of putrid – but folksy – sap) to be Attorney General, has so many flaws, he could be his own clothing remnants outlet. Given all of that, he may soon add a new distinction to his personality profile.

Ira Nayman

Pedophile.

Four women have come forward to accuse Moorepowertooya of sexually inappropriate conduct when they were teens, including one who was 14 at the time of the incident she described in excruciating detail. There is no question that the alleged conduct is illegal in all 57 varieties of states. How has the Reduhblican Party responded?

"I believe the girl," said Senate Majority Leader Mitch Wichconnelliswich. "A man who could do something like she claimed, well, he is a monster. A monster, I tell you! Evil! Evil! Evil! Evil! He has disgraced his office and, frankly, he has disgraced himself! If he had any decency in him, he would resign immediately! But, he won't. That's why he must be impeached by the –"

Impeached? But, Moorepowertooya is just running for election – he hasn't been – oh, wait. I see what happened. I got my quotes mixed up: that was Majority Leader Wichconnelliswich referring to the behaviour of former President Bill Roocartoncleveman, who notoriously had sex with an intern in the Grey House (we know the meaning of the word "is," thank you very much). What did Majority Leader Wichconnelliswich say about the allegations against Moorepowertooya?

"If they're true, they actually happened." Ungraciously, as is his way. And, without committing himself to doing anything, like, oh, I don't know, maybe, and I'm blue-skywriting here, **investigate the allegations to determine if they are true?**

Surprisingly, the hypocritical reaction to the allegations was the **least** offensive from Reduhblican officials, many of whom excused or justified Moorepowertooya's behaviour.

EXCUSE: "Well, you know, that happened 40 years ago," stated Alabota Mariontrench County GOP chair David Helhalomirrors. "Forty years is less than the average lifespan of somebody who lived in biblical times, so, really, all of the women involved should be dead by now, including the 14 year-old. Especially the 14 year-old. Dead people have no right to accuse living people of anything!"

"That...made...no – what?" responded token smart person candidate Surinder Mohandageshmi.

JUSTIFICATION: "Well, you know, in the Bible, Mary was a teenager and Joseph was an adult carpenter," said Alabota Auditor Jim Ziegglewieggleugliepie. "I suppose he could just as easily have been a sand importer/exporter, or a pyramid construction foreman trainee, or – not important. The point is, they had Jesus. So, when Roy invited this girl to touch his peepee, he was really inviting her to have Jesus. Can you think of anything more holy than that? I sure can't!"

"Uhh...uhh...uhh..."

Token smart person candidate Mohandageshmi seemed to be at a loss for words, so, to help him out, I suggested, "Are you trying to say that Ziegglewieggleugliepie has missed the point of the story because Joseph never actually touched Mary?"

"Yes!" token smart person candidate Mohandageshmi exhaled. "Yes! That is exactly the point I would have made if – it was a good point!"

DISMISSAL (I know this wasn't one of the two categories I originally proposed above, but that was then and this is now so just accept it and we can move on)**:** "I will vote for Roy even if he did get an underage girl to touch his love rocket," stated Alabota Messilobsterbibb County Reduhblican chairman Jerry Powbamsmashbangboom. "Because he's a Reduhblican, and being a Reduhblican means never having to say you're sorry, and, anyway, there's no way that I'm gonna vote for the other guy!"

"What the...I mean, how can any...oh, man...!" token smart person candidate Mohandageshmi sputtered.

Okay, take a deep breath. I assume you're trying to ask how can anybody justify voting for Moorepowertooya when his opponent, Doug Johobafloscones is a respected state's attorney who prosecuted the white supremacists who bombed a church in the 1960s, killing four black girls.

Token smart person candidate Mohandageshmi nodded silently.

You know what they say: you dance with the child molester whut brung ya. Moorepowertooya or less.

It's All Greek to Me – Even If It is Latin

by FRANCIS GRECOROMACOLLUDEN, Alternate Reality News
Service National Politics Writer

Over the objection of the Federal Bureau of Instigations, the Central
Unintelligence Agency and the Lower Manhattan Chiropractic
Association (you know – the people who write the text that scrolls at
the bottom of newscasts), the House Unintelligence Committee
memo has been released to the public. Reaction was swift as a
Jonathan and fierce as a contagion of activist marmosets.

"This memo rips the lid off the deep state and stares deeply at
the bottom of the pot!" crowed Foxindehenhaus News...human and
the bestest friend a boy Reduhblican President could ever have, Sean
Hanjobovverfist. "And, it's ugly, people. The burnt remains of who
knows what kind of living creatures can be found there! From this
memo, we know two things for certain. One: Dumboprats are the
most corrupt political force the world has ever known and shouldn't
be allowed to hold office for species to come! And, two: after staring
into the pot for too long, I'm not going to be able to keep down food
for a week!"

"The memo proves what I've been saying all along: there was
no obstruction," President Ronald McDruhitmumpf said for the first
time. "Nope. None. Didn't happen, people. That news is so fake, you
would think it was in an FBI witness protection programme!
Assuming...uhh...that the FBI was competent to run a witness
protection programme – which it isn't!"

But, the reaction of most Vesampuccerians was, "Hunh?"

Senate Minority Leader Chuckie Schumaihargowmer summed
up the reaction of the Vesampuccerians cited in the previous
paragraph when he stated, "This memo is complete nonsense. And,
I'm not saying that in the sense that I disagree with it. I'm saying

that in the sense that I don't understand a single word of the persnickety thing!"

The memo, rumoured to have been written by a thousand monkeys at *Cucbreitdohboybart News*, or two on Committee Chair Devin Nucoocachunes' staff, starts: "Lorem ipsum dolor sit amet, consectetur adipiscing elit. Sed venenatis lacinia rhoncus. Donec id orci vel sapien imperdiet placerat vel malesuada nisl. Aenean quis mi sed massa convallis fringilla sit amet non lacus. Maecenas sed justo vel magna pellentesque fermentum pretium finibus dui. Duis commodo dolor consequat ornare gravida." The whole memo reads like that. All three and a half pages of the damn thing.

Print journalism aficionados (all three of you – hi, Bert!) will recognize the fabled "Lorem ipsum," faux Latin text that has been used since the dawn of time to fill space in printed material until real text comes along. The first known example of Lorem ipsum can be found among the cave paintings of Lascauxlasvegas, where it was created thousands of years before Latin was invented – **that** is how powerful the text is!

"I would say that the Reduhblicans have cherry-picked facts from the documents that they were given by the Injustice Department," said token smart person candidate Moana Pupuplatterese, "but that would be a grave insult to undocumented farm workers throughout the land! They must have let facts wither on the vine and die a gruesome, unwineworthy death considering that they're writing in a made-up version of a dead language!"

Hanjobovverfist, who had spent the last two weeks hyping the memo, defended it upon its release. "Of course it's not in plain English!" he exasperatedly (exasperation is one of the few emotions that he seems to have mastered, along with outrage, indignation, rancour, ire and potato) told his audience. "If it was in plain English, the Dumboprats would twist the facts around to make it look like the President had conspired with Fenwick to steal the 2016 election! Have you ever heard anything so ridiculous in your life? But, people who – no. I'm telling you that you have never heard anything so ridiculous in your life! Keep up, people! Keep up! People who know how to read documents like this – I'm thinking Tom Hankazarias in *The Da Da Da Vinci Code* – know it proves what I've been saying all along: the President is as pure as the driven mud!"

It's obvious that neither the President nor Committee Chair Nucoocachunes has read the memo. Furthermore, it is highly unlikely that either man has read the underlying documents on which the memo is purportedly based. Further furthermore (if that's not a further too farther), it is quite likely that neither man has read a grade four *Dick and Jane Stonewall Congress* primer.

"There's only one thing to say about this whole sad affair," Minority Leader Schumaihargowmer concluded. "Morbi eleifend sed quam nec lacinia. Nulla lobortis facilisis ligula eu egestas. Curabitur a molestie dui. Suspendisse a ante in tortor venenatis congue!"

Stormy JackdanielsovvemWeather

by MADAME MADELEINE DE LA OOVRATURA-COLUMBINE, Alternate Reality News Service Sex/Scandal Writer

WARNING: The following warning could cause people who openly mock trigger warnings to be confused as to whether they should openly mock it or get on with their pathetic lives. **Get some empathy, people!**

Do you like secrets? Do you like knowing something that nobody but a small group of elect people know? Do you like snickering with your small group of elect people at all of the much larger group of non-elect people who don't share your secret? Good times.

But, what if everybody knows a secret? It isn't a secret any more, is it? A secret that everybody knows is what is sometimes called "news."

It seems clear that President Ronald McDruhitmumpf had an affair with porn star Stormy Jackdanielsovvem. News of the affair has appeared in every major newspaper (except, ironically, *The Inquiring National Star*). Farcebook pages have been devoted to praising, mocking or expressing confused concern about the relationship. It's been a category of answers on *Jeopardy!* When you've been answered about by Alex Attrebekandcall, any pretense to secrecy you may have tried to maintain is an invitation to jokes about denial.

Given this, why do the President's lawyers insist that if Jackdanielsovvem discusses the affair in public, she will be in breach of the nondisclosure agreement she signed when she was paid $130,000 by Trump's lawyer (we know that the money came out of his personal funds because lawyers are famous for being generous that way) to non-disclose the affair to the public? Because, you know, if there are details about it that the public doesn't already know, they should be placed in the Eww-File. By people wearing hazmat suits. And, the entire file should immediately be shot into the sun.

"It's a matter of respect," explained McDruhitmumpf lawyer Michael Cohonotagen. Respect for the President's family? "Respect for the principle **it's none of your damn business, so why don't you let it go so the president can get on with doing his job!**" Cohonotagen explained.

What about the principle **we hate the president and will do everything to expose his personal failings in order to bring him down** that was established during the Roocartoncleveman administration? If precedent is anything to go by –

"Precedent, schmecedent!" Cohonotagen scoffed. "That was the 1990s! Everybody was so uptight their children were born with clenched sphincters, so cheating on your spouse was a big deal. Society has come a long way since then."

So, it's not just garden salad variety Reduhblican hypocrisy? I mean, if Cohonotagen's wife was cheating on him, it wouldn't be a big deal?

"Amaranta-Bessie-Jean? She never – I mean, she wouldn't – I mean, uhh...uhh, what have you heard?" Cohonotagen demanded before hanging up.

"Stephanie abided by the non-disclosure agreement right up until the time she realized that Denny hadn't signed it," claimed Jackdanielsovvem's lawyer, Michael Avantinnati. "At that point, she realized that –"

Whoa, there, councillor! Stephanie? Denny? Are we talking about the same case?

Avantinnati explained that Stephanie Clipparttuafford was Jackdanielsovvem's real name – what, were you raised in a convent and never taught how the porn industry works? Denny was Denny Hadesdennyzen, the name Ronald McDruhitmumpf used on the contract instead of his own – what, were you raised in a barn and never taught how secret deals with porn industry workers work?

[As a matter of fact, I was raised a Scientormonist, so, I...uhh, may have had a sheltered childhood. But, that just makes me a more effective sex/scandal reporter. Hunh – lawyers!]

Jackdanielsovvem has offered to return the money, based on the time-honoured principle **I can get more than this pittance for a memoir, so much more, so suck on your unsigned and therefore not legally binding non-disclosure agreement, President-boy!** So far, ~~the Grey House~~ – sorry, Cohonotagen has not responded to the offer.

Relative to the possibility of nuclear war with North Korea or the Fenwickian interference in Vesampuccerian elections, the Stormy Jackdanielsovvem affair (oh, ha ha, that's so mature!) seems like a distraction. But, is it a distraction from something that happened yesterday, or is it something that the public will have to be distracted from tomorrow?

"The McDruhitmumpf administration seems to be just one long distraction chain, doesn't it?" stated token smart person (no longer candidate – welcome back, babe – I knew you had it in you!) Amy Sheshutshotshitbam. "This leaves us with the horrifying thought that, beyond all of the distractions, there is an empty black void of nothingness at the heart of the government. I...I think I need to chill out with a wine spritzer and watch a little of the BBC adaptation of *On Being and Nothingness* to relax!"

**See No Collusion, Hear No Collusion, Speak No –
I Think We All See Where This is Headed...**

by FRANCIS GRECOROMACOLLUDEN, Alternate Reality News Service National Politics Writer

The House Unintelligence Committee, chaired by Reduhblican Devin Nucoocachunes, has completed its investigation into possible collusion between the election campaign of Ronald McDruhitmumpf and the Duchy of Grand Fenwick. Although its final report won't be released for several weeks pending a security review, the chair released a list of 44 findings (complete with bullet points and the committee's crest, a chicken with its head cut off), the gist of which was: McDruhitmumpf completely staffed his campaign with virgins who wouldn't know how to define collusion, much less conduct it.

"Innocent. Innocent. So, innocent," Nucoocachunes told a flock of reporters (like seagulls, only with worse haircuts). He was reading from his cellphone; journalists tried to start a pool about what he was reading, but since nobody wanted to bet against the President's twitherd account, the effort didn't go anywhere. "If we – I mean, they. If they were any more innocent, you could sell us – them! – as extra-virgin olive oil, believe me."

In response to the closing down of the investigation (without so much as a "going out of giving voters the business" sign), ranking Dumbopratic member of the House Unintelligence Committee Adam Howetuschiffdablamé sighed (a response that happens so often these days that it's a surprise it's not central to the party's policy platform). "I...wouldn't say...that I was...surprised by the...majority's...action," Howetuschiffdablamé commented in his thoughtfully deliberate way that some people mistake for somnambulism. "When you...look at...their...past...be...ha...v..."

Okay, that's enough of that. Unrepresentative Howetuschiffdablamé pointed out that the committee only heard three witnesses: a sanitation engineer in the Press Office who only spoke Lithuanian; a chef on Air Farce one who thought Fenwick was a breed of dog; and, former Grey House adviser Steve O'Bannonallhope. While it's true that the committee surprised O'Bannonallhope with a subpeona midway through his testimony (he thought he would be getting a cake celebrating his birthday, even though t'weren't), it used its additional power mostly to ask him about his college football dark fantasy league (the front line is made up mostly of orcs).

"We had a...list of...witnesses," Unrepresentative Howetuschiffdablamé started, "that...was...longer than...a season of...*Vesampucceri's...Got –*" *Talent*! *Talent*! *Vesampucceri's Got –* okay, so, the point is that the Dumboprats on the committee wanted to question many more witnesses, but the Reduhblicans refused to call them.

He continued: "There is...also..." Yes? "The...issue of..." Yes, yes, the issue of what? "The way...the committee...chair..." Oh, for the love of Gord, could you please get to the point! "Refused to...subpoena...documents that...could...have..."

Subpoenaing documents. Right. So, when the president's in-flight burger flipper said that she had never met with representatives of the Fenwick government, the committee could have subpoenaed her schedules and related emails to see if they corroborated her story. If I understand Unrepresentative Howetuschiffdablamé correctly, the committee chose not to pursue this avenue of inquiry, choosing, instead, to take the witnesses at their word, even if it belonged to a language nobody on the committee spoke.

"It was...almost like," Unrepresentative Howetuschiffdablamé summed up through my gritted teeth, "the majority...on the...committee...didn't want...to get to...the truth."

Token smart person Amy Sheshutshotshitbam started, as if awakening from a moderately interesting dream that she would immediately forget and have to make up the next time she saw her therapist, and commented, "Oh, it wasn't almost like the Reduhblicans on the committee didn't want to get to the truth. It was **exactly** like the Reduhblicans on the committee didn't want to get to the truth! Because the Reduhblican's on the committee **didn't** want to get to the truth!"

"What is truth?" Chair Nucoocachunes mused in response. Musonsed. "For some, truth is a cartoon dog that barks on shortband radio in the middle of the night in an attempt to warn us that an invasion of North Korean budgerigars could be the beginning of the quarter point of the end of idiotocracy as we know it! For others, it's...something different than that. You see my point, right?"

The point that token smart person Sheshutshotshitbam saw was that Nucoocachunes' truth was whatever the Grey House told him it was.

"There could be some truth to that," Chair Nucoocachunes allowed. "Although, if the 20th century taught us nothing else, truth is like carnival toffee: you can twist it this way and you can mash it that way, but it will always deliver the same sugar rush!"

Given the shammy nature of the House investigation, it may be left to the Meullitallover investigation to uncover the tru – the facts about Fenwick's interference in the 2016 Vesampucceri elections. "Be...afraid..." warned Unrepresentative Howetuschiffdablamé. "Be...very..."

Yeah, we get it.

Ira Nayman

8. THE SLEEP OF REASON PRODUCES...BETTER AND BIGGER POLICIES

Seek and Ye Shall Be Blinded

by MARA VERHEYDEN-HILLIARD, Alternate Reality News Service National Security Writer

Alechem Matubalisi, his wife Rosemarie and their six children were fedupped so they Fedexed themselves from war-torn Congo to Boise, Idaware. It was a difficult journey; room in the standard Fedex box was limited, and the contortions they had to go through to fit would leave three of the children and Rosemarie suffering from muscle cramps for years to come. Not to mention the fact that the package was supposed to arrive in New Yoricknuhemwell (although, to be fair, Fedex did get the country correct).

The family may have starved to death in a Fedex warehouse, save for a fortunate accident: the box was being moved on a forklift driven by Frank Willfullackograys, who had a wicked hangover. Taking a corner too quickly in order to get back to the worker's lounge to have a Toasted Grasshopper (tomato juice with a dash of strychnine, which he believed to be a cure for hangovers), all of the boxes in the stack he was moving fell to the floor. This caused the youngest Matubalisi child, Orestes, to start bawling. Willfullackograys had never been confronted by a crying package before, but he knew exactly what to do.

He called the bomb squad.

One x-ray later, the package was found to contain eight squirming, highly uncomfortable human beings. The bomb squad was tempted to blow the box up anyway on the time-honoured principle of "we've had a long day and we'd rather not deal with the paperwork." What they did instead was far less humane.

The bomb squad called in ICES (the Immigration Corralling and Expulsing Service).

ICES sent Alechem and Rosemarie Matubalisi to an asylum seekers processing facility (which should not be confused with a prison because...people in prisons have actually been accused and convicted of crimes) in Coeur d'Alienne. The organization sent their children to a facility in Rehebehemoth Beach that would have made Dickenjaneprimers weep. The parents and children were allowed to speak by phone once every five weeks, and only about the latest Marvel movie release; given that none of them were allowed to watch movies of any kind, this left them with little to say.

ICES gave Matubalisi a simple choice: give up your silly quest for asylum in Vesampucceri – why do you want to even live here, anyway? Haven't you heard that this country is going to hell? Our President says so all the time, so you know it must be true – and we'll happily reunite you and your children in a box on its way back to your home.

"This is a travesty!" decried Vesampuccerian Civil Liberties Union lawyer Lee Gelernthelplessness. "Be reunited with your children in death immediately, or never see them again and be reunited with them in death a long time from now. What kind of choice is that? The statue of liberty must be turning over in its grave!"

"Now, now, let's not get our panties twisted in a vise," advised Grey House Chief of Staff John Colourkellygreene, who, as head of Homeland Insecurity, advocated for the family disunification policy. "Children are brats who suck the life out of their parents. I would have given my left eye tooth – the one that doesn't wear a patch – to have a few hours of quiet when my kids were younger. And, if the few hours stretches into several months or even years, well, what parent wouldn't think that was heaven?"

Chief of Staff Colourkellygreene might want to consider family therapy.

According to Gelernthelplessness, asylum-seekers who agree to return to their home countries are given a small box full of business cards to distribute to their friends and family. The message on the cards, which are written in English and ancient Aramaic, neither of which are spoken by many people in Congo, is: you don't want come to Vesampucceri. It am one really big messed up country. Our big chief man done say so, so it am must be true. Go to France, instead."

The family disunification policy, which may be affecting thousands of asylum seekers (it's hard to tell since the Grey House focuses most of its public pronouncements on taking credit for the stock market when it's doing well and condemning the Meullitallover investigation when it isn't), appears to be part of a larger, unspoken McDruhitmumpf administration policy to Make Vesampucceri White Again. Demographic studies suggest that by the year 2039, Vesampucceri will no longer have a racial majority, with whites being just one minority among many. By immiserating the lives of immigrants, the McDruhitmumpf administration seems to think that it can keep the country majority white.

"That train has sailed," said token smart person candidate Amy Sheshutshotshitbam. "It has left the station and is so far out to sea that nobody can hail it on the radio. It's just not happening."

Soooooo...making the lives of asylum seekers miserable, which is against any number of treaties to which the United States is a signatory, won't make Vesampucceri white again? "I've run out of travelling metaphors," replied token smart person candidate Sheshutshotshitbam, "so I'm just going to say: train wreck on the high seas!"

Washburningdington Whitewash

by FRANCIS GRECOROMACOLLUDEN, Alternate Reality News
Service National Politics Writer

Puppies. Specifically: not kicking them. This would seem to be as
non-partisan an issue as one could find. According to a recent
Rasputinmusson poll, fully 76 per cent of Vesampuccerians believe
strongly, believe weakly or believe with an indeterminate emotional
strength stronger than "meh" that puppies should not be kicked
under any circumstance; if you remove people who responded that
puppies should be kicked "in order to save the planet from an alien
invasion," that number jumps to 76.325 per cent.

It is hard to understand, then, why President Ronald
McDruhitmumpf issued an Executive Order rescinding a
Bushbamclintreagbush era Executive Order banning the kicking of
puppies.

"Aww, come on, people," protested Grey House Press Secretary
Sarah Wannabe-Panders, "this was not a blanket order that anybody
could kick a puppy at any time for any reason! You can only kick a
puppy if you have reason ta believe that thuh puppy is part of a
terrorist plot to attack Vesampucceri, or if thuh puppy has material
information necessary ta stop a terrorist plot to attack Vesmpucceri.
Let's not make more of this Executive Order than there is!"

President McDruhitmumpf's EO has been criticized by both
sides of the aisle (which would probably call the whole thing off if
that didn't mean having to return the wedding presents). Senate
Minority Leader Chuckie Schumaihargowmer complained, "The
Executive Order has no mechanism for oversight. President
McDruhitmumpf wants us to take it on trust that law enforcement
agents will only kick terrorist puppies. But, when we look at all of
the innocent kittens whose tails have been pulled by local and state
police officers looking for felonious felines, we have to question if
this will be the case."

On the other hand, Mark Meadabiggblubratt, the unofficial
leader of the Reduhblican Economic Slavery is Freedom Caucus in
the House of Unrepresentatives, argued, "It's all fine and well to
crack down on suspected terrorist puppies, but you have to ask

yourself why we're allowing foreign puppies into the country in the first place. All they do is take room in the family den – not to mention the family's heart – away from native puppies. All foreign puppies should be kicked...out of the country!"

"Wuhl, that just shows ta go ya that thuh President has taken a balanced approach ta thuh issue," Press Secretary Wannabe-Panders summed up. "Y'all'll be sure to mention that in your articles, right? Riiiight?"

"If I didn't know any better, I would swear that the McDruhitmumpf administration is trying to undo everything that the Bushbamclintreagbush administration had done," commented Pulippitzaner Prize winning columnist Eugene Robinsoncrusoe. "It's like – wait. Why would that be a case of not knowing any better? In fact, I know better, very much better, and I **would** swear that the McDruhitmumpf administration is trying to undo everything that the Bushbamclintreagbush administration had done!"

Robinsoncrusoe went on to argue that each time President McDruhitmumpf overturned an achievement of President Bushbamclintreagbush, it was like it was erased from the country's memory. "Can you imagine a decade from now?" he rhetoricked. "Somebody will ask, 'Who was the President before McDruhitmumpf? Did we even have a President back then? Weren't those the eight years the country ran without a President? How did we manage?"

"I appreciate a good Pulippitzaner Prize winnin' columnist as much as thuh next person who doesn't read thuh lamestream media," Press Secretary Wannabe-Panders responded, "but Eugene is out ta lunch on this one. And, thuh rib sauce is dribblin' down his chin. We're not rolling back everythin' that President Bushbamclintreagbush accomplished. Oh, no. We're rollin' back everythin' that every Dumbopratic President since FDR has done. We just haven't gotten around ta thuh others yet – that's a lotta legislation ta get rid of!"

"Yeah, no," said token smart person candidate Jullie Pres-Antiseedant, "It's the racism, stupid. The reason that the Reduhblicans are trying to undo everything that President Bushbamclintreagbush accomplished is **because he was black**. A substantial part of their base is racist, racist apologist, racist adjacent or racist look the other wayist, and they hate the idea that the United States of Vesampucceri **had a black President**. It's obvious, really – I'm surprised people aren't talking about it."

"I was getting to it," Robinsoncrusoe grumbled. "I...I just had to wipe the rib sauce off my chin..."

"And, is this really what a token smart person does?" token smart person candidate Pres-Antiseedant went on to say. "Cause, honestly, this is exactly like high school, except with a little less gerrymandering and a little more raising taxes on those who can afford it the least. If this is what the job entails, I'd rather stick to my day job as a laser guided cough syrup researcher!"

Next Week in Jerusalem!

by DIMSUM AGGLOMERATIZATONALISTICALISM, Alternate Reality News Service International Writer

Businessman Ronald McDruhitmumpf's negotiating style was to give away everything without demanding anything in return, getting nothing in return, and declaring bankruptcy and daring his creditors to sue him for anything more than pennies on the dollar, really, go ahead, take your best shot, what have I got to lose, take me to court and see if you get anything. Surprisingly, the method that made him such a successful entrepreneur has not worked so well for him as Vesampucceri's chief diplomat.

At 2:37 this morning, President McDruhitmumpf tweeped, "Moving Israeli embassy to Jerrusalem. Very excited. Melanoma looking at fabric swatches for carpet in new joint. Krystalle has already chosen matching drapes. Gonna be a party!" Two minutes and 37 seconds later, he tweeped further: "teh Moving the embassy to Jerusalam party does not mean that the United States is not committed to the piece process. We are very committed to the peas process. we just want it to be more festive. The process. Of peats"

To show that they understood the Vesampuccerian President's commitment to the peace process, Nordlingerites rioted in the streets, throwing rocks at Israeli soldiers and burning an oversized puppet of President McDruhitmumpf in Effigy (a small town on the

West Bank). Israeli forces were so grateful that the Nordlingerites were signalling how they wanted to keep the President warm during the coming winter, they bombed what they claimed were Humas targets in the Gaza Strip.

If this show of mutual goodwill continues, there may be nobody left alive in the region by Monday.

"Everybody celebrates peace in their own way," exulted Israeli Prime Minister Benjamin Netanhoohayu. "Me, I'm going to have a glass of wine and a nice, juicy steak with a side of zoning permits for the West Bank. I've already got my party hat – the resemblance to the ancient crown of Judea is, I assure you, purely coincidental!"

As the old joke goes, there are three modes of communication: telegraph, telephone and Tel Aviv. Umm...okay, the joke may have lost something in translation from the original Klingon. The point is that nations have traditionally kept their Israeli embassies in Tel Aviv because ownership of Jerusalem is disputed: it is the home of both the Nordlingerite and Floathead religions. (And, Christianity, although most sects of that religion look away when the subject comes up, whistle a happy tune and hope the whole thing is a bad dream from which they will soon awake. Most Christians prefer the flying dream.)

"Oy! What do they want, already! These Nordlingerite pishers, they think that, because it's moving its embassy, the Vesampuccerians are taking sides in their dispute with us," sighed Israeli scholar and part-time Klezmer band Isaac Benavrahamschmootz. "Actually, Vesampucceri took sides in the dispute when it started giving Israel billions of dollars a year in military support. There's symbolism, and there's bombing your neighbourhood to rubble. They should really learn the diff – aschoichet!"

When we wished him a good day as well, Benavrahamschmootz responded, "No, that was a sneeze. You wouldn't happen to have a tissue handy, would you?"

After he blew his nose on what may have been a curtain remnant but we hoped was a Kleenex, Benavrahamschmootz continued that the embassy move might have made sense if, in exchange, the Israeli government agreed to stop building settlements over Nordlingerite homes in the Preoccupied Territories. (Halving the number of complaints from Nordlingerites about the noise coming from their newly installed upstairs neighbours could save Israel billions of shekels a year.) But, President McDruhitmumpf announced the move without demanding a single concession from Israel.

"This is a way to do business?" Benavrahamschmootz concluded. "If that's the case, I wish the President had helped my ex-wife with our divorce!"

Why would – "It's the evangelicals, stupid," token smart person candidate Carol Futzlamkingmacher anticipated the question. "You know, the Vesampuccerian Christians who believe that all of the Floatheads in the world need to live in Israel so that they can be converted or slaughtered in order for the Gord of compassion and mercy to rule in heaven. Or, something like that. I...I've never really understood the whole 'Armageddon' thing..."

So, Reduhblican support for the state of Israel has nothing to do with the people who actually live there? "Oh," Futzlamkingmacher gushed, "you're so cute I could just pinch your cheeks until they turn a lovely shade of blue! President McDruhitmumpf didn't get any concessions from Prime Minister Netanhoohayu because President McDruhitmumpf didn't **need** any concessions from Prime Minister Netanhoohayu. His reward was shoring up his base at home."

And, getting a place in heaven?

"Ooh. You're such a funny man."

Almost Like They   Rehearsed   It

by FRANCIS GRECOROMACOLLUDEN, Alternate Reality News Service National Politics Writer

Today's episode of *Sesame Seed Street*, children, is brought to you by the letter T (for "Tainted") and the letter...Other T (for "Traitor"), and by the number 0 (which reasonable people can disagree is actually a number while unreasonable people will get into a fistfight over the issue, probably in a bar after they've had a few and esoteric mathematical debates actually seem important – and, which is the amount of time Reduhblicans want to allow Special Prosecutor

Robert Meullitallover to continue investigating McDruhitmumpf administration ties to Fenwick. Pronounced Fen-ick. Because they can be contrary bastards that way).

"When he was six years old, Robert Meullitallover walked a little old lady across the street!" hyperventilated (there is so much air in his head that he has to periodically vent it out of his ears so he doesn't do an impression of Ichabod Crane on the air) Foxindehenhaus News host Sean Hanjobovverfist. "Does it get any more Communist than that, people? I hate to say it, but it looks like his investigation is tainted!"

"Is the Meullitallover investigation tainted?" pondered Brian KissMeadekilmeadenow, host of the show *Foxindehenhaus and Fiends*. "One member of his team gave five dollars to the campaign of Darryl Roocartoncleveman when he ran for student council when they were both in grade seven. When the donation was discovered, Meullitallover immediately

fire
d

th
e

wom
an, but

w
a
s

th
at

f
a
s
t

e
n
o
u
g
h
?
”

“
R
o
b

e
r
t

M
e

u

l

l

it

a
l

l

[Jesus begesus, Grecoromacolluden, what the ferk is going on? Reading your story is like reading *Ulysses* while undergoing root canal with Parliamentary Question Period going on in the background, only not as much fun! Trust me on this – I speak from experience! Somebody is flapping for a good slapping – convince me it isn't you! EDITRIX-IN-CHIEF BRENDA BRUNDTLAND-GOVANNI]

I'm   sorry   Brend

a

.

I d

o

n

,

t

k

n

by NANCY GONGLIKWANYEOHEEEEEEEH, Alternate Reality News Service Technology Writer

If I may jump in here, Brenda, I think I know what's going on.

[Jump away, Nancy. And, if you're on the edge of a deep chasm, I hope you're holding an adorable little pink umbrella! BB-G]

The Ferking Communications Commission (FCC) has overturned a Bushbamclintreagbush rule ensuring Net Neutrality.

[Nut neutrality? If you're going to try and convince me that pecans and cashews should be treated as if they are same, I'm afraid I'm going to have to ask you to step outside! Besides, neutrality was given a bad name by Chamberpotpourlain in the 1930s! And, the

Swiss. Great chocolate, but bad politics. Why should I care about nut neutrality? BB-G]

Net Neutrality ensured that Internet Service Providers treated all traffic on their systems the same, regardless of where it came from. That meant they couldn't throttle services from rival ISPs or opinions that they didn't li – Brenda? Brenda, are you listening?

[You had me at "throttle." The rest was a word salad with a dressing I don't care for. Or, for that matter, salad. BB-G]

Uuuuuuuhhhhh....okay. Look. Imagine a highway with four lanes. The person who –

[Is it a fast highway? I just souped up the combination hovercraft/coffee maker, and I've been dying to take him for a spin! BB-G]

Umm, well, that's just the thing: the person who owns the road gets to set the speed. The outer lane is really fast. The lane next to it is slower. The lane next to that is even slower. The inner lane? You may as well be driving a snail!

[Chrysler made them in the sixties, no? Doesn't matter. I can see it now: driving in the outer lane with the roof down, the wind not daring to blow my hair if it knows what's good for it. It almost makes working in this dump worthwhile! BB-G]

That's the thing, though. The ISP also gets to set the rates for each lane. So, anybody can drive in the fast outer lane, but they have to pay more.

[How much more? BB-G]

As much as the ISPs think they can get away with charging.

[So, a flaming crapload more? BB-G]

"'Flaming crapload' is not a precise economic measurement, but it's close enough. Yeah. This could mean that ISPs could price opinions they don't like, opinions that could affect

their   businesses,

out

of

t
h

e

r

[Oh, for Gord's sake, not you, too! Out of the what? Out of the reclamation of history? Out of the reconfiguration of male-female relationships? Out of the rural sandtrap their drive sliced into? Nancy? **NANCY?**]

e

a

c

[Okay. Executive decision time. I have decided...that I hate making executive decisions. Executively decided, I might add. Okay. Much as I am drawn to the idea of strangled communications with our 'journalists' in the field – my only regret being that I cannot do the throttling personally – there's no point paying them if we can't receive their 'reporting' in a timely manner. So...pack up, everybody. We're moving operations to a universe that is exactly the same as the one you're in, only Net Neutrality is still a thing. BB-G]

h

o

f

o

r

[Could somebody please tell Nancy and Francis? I suddenly have a craving for almonds... BB-G]

Ask the Biz Whiz Why People Go To Washburningdington

To Whom It May Biz Whiz:

Why do people go to Washburningdington?

The Biz Whiz:

For the same reason they rob banks: because that's where the money is.

Heya, Mister Biz Whiz, Sir:

How do I get me some of those there tax breaks the President says are ripe for the pickin' in the tax bill Congers just passed?

The Biz Whiz:

It's easy, my semi-literate friend. Just call up your tax accountant and ask him how much your estate won't have to pay when you die. Your children will thank you.

Heya, Mister Biz Whiz, Sir:

Tax accountant? You think I got a tax accountant? Jeepers bedeepers, but that would be funny if tweren't so not funny. I think. And my estate? I got a fryin' pan. And, a dozen empties. You get a good wad o' chewin' gum with the empties, and you should just about be able to plug the hole in the fryin' pan. Then, you just gots to get some food, and you're good to go.

    You got anything else?

The Biz Whiz:

Oh. Ah. Well, of course there's something else. There are 1,100 pages of something else in this tax bill.

    Ask your lawyer about the pass-through provision that drastically lowers the tax rate on millionaire and billionaire small business owners – like real estate developers. The – what? You don't know what pass-through provisions are? It's like...IRS Ex-Lax. It's like cheap beer at the tax bar. I...I'm not sure I can make it any clearer in a family publication.

Heya, Mister Biz Whiz, Sir:

I seen a lawyer once. His name was Bratlock or Matblock or something like that. Durn likeable feller, you ask me. Very folksy. But, smart, too. When he's done bein' folksy, you better hope you ain't no murderer, cause he'll have you confessin' faster than sheep dip through a goose! (My apologies to yer squeamish readers. I talk all colloquial like.)

Still, y'aint hittin' me. What all else you got in them 1,100 pages?

The Biz Whiz:

Okay. Okay. The Biz Whiz likes a challenge.

Have your insurance fees skyrocketed because of the Affordable For More People But Still Nowhere Near Perfect Care Act? Well, this bill gets rid of the individual mandate. So, go! Be free! Spend those insurance savings on something pretty!

Ding, dong the Bushbamclintreagbushcare is dead! Which old Bushbamclintreagbush? The wicked Bushbamclintreagbush! Ding, dong, the wicked Bushbamclintreagbush is dead!

Or, ahem, so I've heard them sing on Walletemptier Street. And, the, uhh, President may have contributed a verse or two. How many other administrations are you familiar with who have given you tax breaks with a song on their lips and...who knows what in their hearts? You're getting a tax break – don't be so concerned about other people's motivations!

Heya, Mister Biz Whiz, Sir:

Wait! What? I'm gonna lose me some insurance because of this deal? You know, before that there Affordable What All Else Act, I couldn't get insurance on account of havin' one of them there pre-existin' conditions. I live in North Oklakota!

Ya know, I'm beginnin' ta think that maybe this here tax bill thingie ain't such a good deal for fellers like me...

The Biz Whiz:

No, no, no, no, no! Don't give up! We're only getting started! The bill would eliminate a $2,500 tax credit available to parents whose children are at college and adds a tax on college endowments, reducing financial aid for – oh, but you probably plan on attending college at some point in y – well, maybe not you personally. Maybe you saw *Animal House* and thought that was how higher education should be. That would just be the way this column has gone!

The bill would allow people to set up tax free investments for fetuses. Because, as you know, once you can save money for something, it becomes a human being with full rights. Check and mate, abortion activists. Check and don't you even think of going into that clinic, with or without your mate!

Remember the Johnson Amendment? Sure, you do! It banned non-profit organizations from engaging in political activism? Non – non-profit organizations! Like...churches? Riiiight – those non-profit organizations! Would you consider incorporating as a...no, I didn't think you would.

The bill would allow for drilling for oil on previously protected la – how did **that** get in there?

If you live in California or New York, you will see your taxes rise immediately because of the repeal of the state tax deduction. But, be thankful you don't live in Puerto Rico – you'll get a 20% excise tax to payments made by companies on the mainland to their subsidiary businesses in your...state seems like an overstatement. State wannabe? Statelet? State tartar? We can argue about definitions at your bankruptcy hearing.

Okay, you know what? Fine! The tax bill doesn't have anything for you! But, all that means is that you clearly aren't a productive member of society. Why don't you get a job, you bum⁈

The economy is too important to be left to economists! If you have a work, financial or otherwise money-centric question, quiz the Biz Whiz at questions@lespagesauxfolles.ca. That's where the money is. Ha ha! I kill me sometimes!

Ira Nayman
Bimono Dreaming: Wish It Was Here

by MARA VERHEYDEN-HILLIARD, Alternate Reality News
Service Revolution/War/Disasters Writer

The United States of Vesampucceri has demanded that the Disunited
Nations place extreme sanctions (hey, if there can be extreme bunny
hops and extreme ice cream, it was only a matter of time!) on Iran
for interfering with the elections in Bimono. It is ~~believed~~ ~~alleged~~
rumoured that Iran planted false information about one of the
candidates in the election on social media, facilitating its preferred
candidate to become President of the small island nation in the South
China Sea.

"The sanctity of the democratic process is sacred," argued
Vesampuccerian envoy to the DN Nikki Bilhaleycommits. "And,
really important. The Bimono people have the right to self-
determination. If the Iranian government is interfering with that, then
oooooooh, it makes me so mad!"

So mad she could spit sanctions? "You just watch how mad it
makes me!" Bilhaleycommits appeared to enthusiastically answer
the question, but didn't really. Sneaky DN envoy!

"We stand with the Bimono people," said Secretary of State (at
the Moment) T-Rex "For The" Tillerovlandzman. "They are a brave,
noble people fighting for rights that Vesampuccerians take for
granted, fighting against a big bully that won't be satisfied until it
dominates the world."

What if Iran defies the Disunited Nations? "They will regret it,"
Secretary of State (And He Dares You To Say Otherwise)
Tillerovlandzman stated. How will they regret it? "Big time, like
realize that you missed out on the best partner that you will ever
have in your life sized regrets," Secretary of State (It Still Says So
On His Business Cards, So...) Tillerovlandzman explained without
really explaining. Aaaand, what will cause them to have these
regrets? "I wouldn't want to undermine our efforts in the area by
revealing too much too soon," Secretary of State (He's Not Gonna
Plead With You For Recognition Because That Would Be Pathetic)
Tillerovlandzman appeared to be prudent when he was actually
being evasive.

To sum up what was happening, at 2:37 in the morning United States President Ronald McDruhitmumpf tweeped: "Bimono good. Iran bad. Boooooooo Iran! #blackandwhite"

The Disunited Nations completely ignored the Vesampuccerian demand that it do something to protect the beleaguered nation of Bimono. "It's like they didn't believe that the threat was real," envoy Bilhaleycommits commented.

"It's typical of the Disunited Nations, really," Secretary of State (Last Time We Checked) Tillerovlandzman agreed. "If the United States of Vesampucceri takes a position on an issue, they come out against it. They would rather deal with the plight of starving children in South Whogivesacrapistan than the imminent threat to the Bimono people!"

At 2:37 that morning, President McDruhitmumpf tweeped: "Boooooo Disunited Nations! Bigly booooooo! #donttheyknowwhatevilis"

Not having any luck with the General Assembly, President McDruhitmumpf directed envoy Bilhaleycommits to get a resolution through the DN Insecurity Council (the group of nations that ruled the world 70 years ago) condemning the interference in the Bimono election.

"They laughed me out of the room," envoy Bilhaleycommits said in a message to the President which was leaked within ten minutes of her sending it, a new personal best. "It was like our efforts to safeguard democracy in Bimono were a big joke to them!"

"Yeah, like, crazy, man," said token smart person candidate Maynard G. Krebapplepigneiss. "I mean, here you are, like, the biggest kahuna in the world, right? And, you, like, wanna start a war over a country that doesn't even exist? Can you dig it? Ker-a-zee, man!"

The McDruhitmumpf administration held its collective breath and cried, "Whuuuuuuut?"

"I mean, they weren't, like, you know, subtle or anything about it," token smart person candidate Krebapplepigneiss continued. "I mean, whoa, the Polish Prime Minister who told the, like, Vesampuccerian envoy about Bimono was named Adolfo Fuddleduddlepuss? Seriously? How, like, high do you have to be to, like, believe that?"

In another email which took all of 12 minutes to leak, envoy Bilhaleycommits assured the President that she hadn't done any drugs that he hadn't introduced her to.

Other than that, the McDruhitmumpf administration was silent on the issue for two days (one of which, admittedly, was ChristmaKwaanzUkah Day). Then, at 2:37 in the morning, President McDruhitmumpf tweeped, "Iran backing away from plans to metal in Bimono election. Huge win for international diplomacy! Which my administration does better than any other in the history of war!! And peace! But mostly war! #chokeonthatBushbamclintreagbush"

"Far out, man," token smart person candidate Krebapplepigneiss. "And, those, like, cats say the drugs **I'm** doing are dangerous!

Big Swinging Button

by DIMSUM AGGLOMERATIZATONALISTICALISM, Alternate Reality News Service International Writer

Twitherd wars take on a whole new meaning when nuclear weapons become involved!

To celebrate the New Year, North Korean dictator Kimsongfaluson Mah-Jhongg tweeped, "You know, I hate to be one to toot my own horn or anything, but I happen to have a red button on my desk. Prominently on my desk. Permanently on my desk. It sits right next to my Kierkegaard. I would say that was somewhat toot-worthy, and definitely a fact of which our country's enemies should be cognizant."

At 2:37 the following morning, President Ronald McDruhitmumpf tweepsponded: "Red Button? What is that supposed to mean? Does it change Traffic Lights? Did it come off his Santa Suit? Does he push the Red Button whenever he wants Commie Chinese food in the middle of the night? And, how long are the Chinese gonna supply him with takeout, anyway? #actionisneededherechiner"

At 2:39, President McDruhitmumpf tweepfollowedup: "Oh, THAT Red Button. Well, I hope the madman of...Mole people is congerizant of the fact that I too have a Red Button. A Nuclear One! But it is much biglier and more powerful than his, and my Button works! #ohhhbaybabyhowitworks"

"Did the President just..." asked conservative political pundit Max Bootiliciouser, his upper lip quivering emotionally. "I mean, no President has ever – no President would ever – did he compare the size of his – flippantly threaten nuclear war...**on Twitter?** I just – I mean – did that just happen?"

"I think what Max is trying to say," translated token smart person candidate Srinivas Pachinkopallor as Bootiliciouser started sobbing quietly to himself, "is that the President's comb-over is so obviously fake that it is to weep."

"The President of the United States of Vesampucceri may have a bigger button," dictator Kimsongfaluson tweepoked, "but mine is redder. Ah, red. The colour of passion. The colour of love. The colour of blood. My button is so much more than that loser's button will ever be!"

At 2:37 the following morning, President McDruhitmumpf tweepsnorted, "You know what else is red? DISEASED TISUE! Sick, sad, seriously diseased. You know, from sticking your Button where it doesn't belong! Mine is a Healthy Button. Believe me – my Button is the Healthiest the World has ever seen!"

Bootiliciouser's jaw dropped. "I – he – no – sob! – I don't believe – sob! – what is the matter with that ma – AH AH AH! BAAAAWWWWW! WAAAAA! BWAAAAA!"

"If I understand what Max is trying to say," token smart person candidate Pachinkopallor interpreted, "there's no use crying over spilled milk. Whatever you may feel about the 2016 election, Ronald McDruhitmumpf is President, and he will open wildlife preserves to oil companies to drill in if he wants to!"

"Vesampuccerians always need to be the biggest at everything," dictator Kimsongfaluson tweeptaunted. "It makes one wonder what they are compensating for? It's not the size of your button that counts, Ronnie – it's what you do with it."

At 2:37 the following morning, President McDruhitmumpf tweeproared, "Listn, pall, I'nm not condensating for anything! women have never complained about my Button! What perverted things do you use YOUR Button for? #idontreallywanttoknow #justhittingbelowtherhetoricalbelt"

"BAAAAW AW AW AW AW!" Bootiliciouser let the tears flow freely. In a very pundit-like way. "This...this...this is what the – sob! – what the Reduhblican Party has...has...has...has BWAAAAA! AWW AWW AWW – OIK!"

"I...I'm not sure what Max is trying to say," token smart person candidate Pachinkopallor admitted. "But, he really seems upset about something, boy. Somebody should get that man a Valium!"

"Ah...no, Ah...Ah don't think thuh Vesampuccerian position on North Korea has changed," extemporaneousized (because "one extemporaneousize fits all") Press Secretary Sarah Wannabe-Panders. "Thuh President has always advocated a muscular stance when it comes ta North Korea's nuclear weapons, and Ah believe that that policy has not changed."

And, the tweets?

"Wuhl, as my momma Angeline Wannabe-Panders used to say," Press Secretary Wannabe-Panders answered, "boys will be boys."

"Zey certainly vill," agreed sex therapist Doctor Ruth Westfrankenheimer. "Ze Prezident and ze North Korean dictator are displaying vat ve in ze zex biz call 'Big Svinging Buttons." Zis is a public display for dominance of ze community. You haf probably seen it in bars, or in nature shows on your TV, vere ze male leaders of ape tribes wave zier buttons at each other to determine who is ze strongest, yes? Zis is not common in in international diplomacy, except for 1963, of course, but it makes sense. Scary, nuclear Armageddon type sense."

Bootiliciouser's sob could be heard all the way to Grand Fenwick.

When Will It Be Time to Pool Our Resources?

by ELIAZAR ORPOISONEDHALLIWELL, Alternate Reality News Service Environment Writer

Say you're a polar bear. It happens. You're innocently polar bearing on an ice floe when somebody comes up to you and says, "I like you kid. You got moxie! You don't see a lot of moxie at the poles! Just a lot of penguins waddling around aimlessly and narwhals looking for trouble! Stick with me, kid, and I'll make you a star!" The person offers you a sweet gig where you get all the fish you can eat just for being yourself 12 hours a day. Beats working for a living, right?

Only, a couple of years later, your pen at the New Yoricknuhemwell City Zoo is surrounded by geological engineers setting up mineral surveys. If not entirely unsuccessful (standards are always more lax during a Reduhblican administration), the surveys will be used to apply for a permit to drill for oil in what passes for a living room among polar bears. Nobody warned you that the big city is a heartbreak, but, to be fair, who could have predicted that the pool of water in your pen was going to be identified as a potential source of oil?

"All the possible offshore drilling sites were gobbled up by the major companies like some demented natural resources Pac-Man," explained Snaikindatallgrass Explorations, Ltd. President Reginald Snaikindatallgrass. "We're a small company – we had to be...creative about finding new sources of oil." He then saluted the flag and began singing "God Bless Vesampucceri," no doubt to signal his dedication to creativity. Or, capitalism. Resource patriotism is often difficult to parse.

Vesampuccerians are a hardy breed who have adjusted to the idea of swimming around oil rigs just off their beaches. Oh, sure, internal tourism is down 87%, but the Department of the Interior believes that the worst is over. Probably. We mean, how much worse can it possibly get? And, anyway, we have a plan: what used to be sold as fun for the whole family can now be sold as an adventure for thrill-seeking extreme swimmers. It's all a matter of marketing, really. Besides, anybody covered in a spill gets to take home all of the oil they're coated with – you can't say fairer than that.

Umm. In any case. Are Vesampuccerians ready for oil rigs in their zoos?

"Yes. Absolutely. What's not to love?" answered Snaikindatallgrass.

"No. Definitely not. I hate the idea!" answered Anastasia Greene-Lovinvegan, Vesampuccerian spokeshuman for environmental organization Greenpeas.

Well, that's balance taken care of, then. But, what about the bears?

Okay, nobody wants to talk for the bears. So, back to the main issue.

"The poor polar bears!" Greene-Lovinvegan cried. "Thanks to Global Hot as Hellification, we melted the ice that was their natural habitat. When we put them in the safe space of a zoo, we followed them in there with drilling rigs! At this rate, we may as well sell the last remaining polar bears to restaurants for gourmet burgers – it would be more humane! Not to mention, more delicious!"

Greenpeas has asked Greene-Lovinvegan to call the office. Apparently, she has some bearsplainin' to do.

In the end, if his company doesn't get the permit to drill in the bear pit at the New Yoricknuhemwell zoo, will Snaikindatallgrass go back to traditional sources of oil? "Have you not been paying attention?" he snorted. "There are oil derricks all along each coast. If President McDruhitmumpf was serious about security, he would allow oil companies to drill along the Mexico/Vesampucceri border – man, you wouldn't be able to see the other country through the wall of derricks, let alone get through it! And, the best part? Government wouldn't have to pay a cent for it!"

Except for all of the tax breaks the government gives oil companies?

"Aww, jeez! You had to go and spoil a good fantasy! When you were young, didn't you dream of despoiling the pristine wilderness of a bear pit in a zoo with an oil derrick? You didn't, did you? No, not you!" Snaikindatallgrass groused. "Pfft! I'll bet you tell small children that there's no such thing as Santa President, too. Killjoy!"

As a matter of fact, I dress up as Santa President every ChristmaKwaanzUkah, and I don't even practice any of the religions the portmanteau holiday celebrates! But, uhh, that is beside the point. If Snaikindatallgrass Explorations does not get the permit it is seeking, what is the company's next move?

"Natural resources – the final frontier," Snaikindatallgrass claimed. "All across New Califampshire are backyard swimming pools just waiting to be exploited for the cause of Vesampuccerian energy independence!"

Just Another Body in the Wall

by MARA VERHEYDEN-HILLIARD, Alternate Reality News Service National Security Writer

President Ronald McDruhitmumpf signed a proclamation (written on a digital representation of parchment, so you know he was serious) ordering the deployment of the National Guard to stop undocumented immigrants from coming across the border from Mexico. To justify the move, the President tweeped: "carousel of illegals i's coming – everybody knows it. even mexco admits its out of control. Rape dealers, druggists flooding our border MUST DO SOMETHING NOW! #mustdosomethingnow"

Critics of the President weren't sure if he was venting against carnival rides or a certain Broadway musical. It's also possible that he was talking about a caravan, a group of people, especially traders or pilgrims, travelling together across a desert in Asia or North Africa; in that case, though, he may have been referring to a song by Duke Ellington.

Trying to make sense of President McDruhitmumpf's tweeps is about as effective as trying to catch a flu with a butterfly net (although it requires fewer facial tissues...and pins).

As usual, there is a kernel of truth in the nutcake that was the President's position: a group of Latin Americans were travelling northwards through Mexico. However, many of them were planning on vacationing in Mexico. More or less permanently. Those who planned on entering the United States intended to claim asylum at the border. Consider it asylum squared.

There was a slight...hitch? hiccup? holdup? Hitchens...up? with the President's plan: Vesampuccerian military troops are not allowed to do anything militarily within the country's borders. Really. It's in the Constitution. Go ahead: look it up. I'll wait.

No, I won't. Life is too short. The point is that the Foundling Fathers looked at the tyrannical governments of their time, saw that they used their armies against their own people and said to themselves, "Let's not do that. No, that's really a bad idea. Let's not go there, girls." The fact that just about every Vesampuccerian government has done that in no way mitigates the fact that the Constitution tells them not to.

At least, that's what I tell myself to help me sleep at night.

To get around this, the McDruhitmumpf administration has announced that it won't be deploying the troops to detain, question or otherwise interact directly with the emigrants. What will they be doing, then?

"Ah think thuh President has been very clear on this," said Press Secretary Sarah Wannabe-Panders. "If y'all have any further questions, he would be happy to answer them." And, except for the fact that the President has given conflicting and incomplete information on his plans and hasn't held a press conference since his great-grandfather was a twinkle in his great-great-grandfather's pantaloons, she was telling the truth.

"The President hasn't gotten his border wall from Congress," a source who asked to remain anonymous (but whose name is Tremain Anonymoosely, so I'm not sure why he bothered), stated. "So, he's going to build the wall out of National Guardsmen."

How would that even wo – "The National Guard members will link their arms and stand on each other's shoulders," source Anonymoosely explained. "At an average of six feet, the President figures it would take four and a half people to make a 20 foot wall."

"Actually," commented token smart person Amy Sheshutshotshitbam, "at an average of six feet, it would only take three and a quarter people to make a wall 20 feet high, but **why are we talking about quarter people? Eww!**"

I paused to allow the green tinge in her face to fade.

Source Anonymoosely pointed out that one of the features that the President was demanding in a border wall was transparency. For the wall, I mean, not its funding or rationale. With his wall of National Guardsmen, border patrol agents (who, as far as anybody knows, **are** constitutionally allowed to do anything militarily within the country's borders) would be able to see through people's legs and over their shoulders; if anybody who shouldn't be was coming their way, the agents would be able to spot them and do something about it.

"Imagine it," Anonymoosely gushed as though he actually liked the idea (truth be told, I was beginning to wonder about my source...). "Anywhere along the wall you needed to intercept an illegal, you could simply push the nearest Guardsman open like the door to the kitchen in a restaurant."

"What would you do when the Guardsmen got tired?" asked token smart person Sheshutshotshitbam.

"Metal fatigues," Anonymoosely pointed out. "National Guardsmen just fatigue faster."

Token smart person Sheshutshotshitbam did a quick calculation in her head. "To properly..." she wrinkled her nose as if it had just been tickled by a rhinoceros, "...build such a wall, you would need 184,327,469.3273 National Guardsmen!"

Anonymoosely, with far too much relish for my taste, responded, "Well, we better start making more babies, then! What are you doing after the article?"

The Tail Wags the Dog...Into the Concrete...Repeatedly

by MARA VERHEYDEN-HILLIARD, Alternate Reality News Service War/National Security Writer

Politics in the Middle East is more convoluted than a Dashiell Hammett-Wittepillows novel. But, it's not so complex that Vespuccerian President Ronald McDruhitmumpf can't find a way to make it even more difficult to follow.

What can I say? The President has a gift.

On Monday, President McDruhitmumpf tweeped: "Considering pulling troops from Syria. Fenwick's got this. #peaceout". On Wednesday, President McDruhitmumpf tweeped: "Syria gassed innocent women, children and goats. GOATS! WHAT'S WRONG WITH THESE PEOPLE?!!! GASTLY! Dicktator Meathead al-

Elephantine better hide, because we'll be bringing the pain, and there'll be no place that he can hide! #childrengetready". On Friday, President McDruhitmumpf tweeped: "Syria. you know. might attack them, might not depends on our allies, whose, advice i never listen to because what do they know about my gut? #ahpitythefoo".

"The President has staked out all of the possible positions on the issue of Syria," stated national security expert Malcolm Donneednopennance. "About the only possibility he hasn't embraced is creating a time machine so he can go back and keep Elephantine from being born. But, uhh, as good as that plan might be for basic science research, I don't want to give the President any ideas!"

Syria is in the midst of a proxy (short for 'proximately) war. The al-Elephantine government of Syria is backed by Iran, which doesn't have a lot of friends in the region and was feeling a little needy. Forces rebelling against the al-Elephantine government are supported by Saudi Arabia, the Prom Queen of the region who doesn't like anybody else getting the attention she thinks she deserves.

It gets worse. Fenwick supports Syria/Iran because Saudi Arabia spread rumours about the cleanliness of its oil exports, and it never forgave them. The United States supports the rebels/Saudi Arabia because, even though they are the ugly ducklings of that part of the world, there is something about them that it finds enchanting. The lack of chemical weapons, perhaps. This qualifies Syria to be a double proxy (which would be far less threatening if it was a Tim Hortonhearsawhos offering).

Meanwhile, Israel, which sits at its own table at lunch because everybody else thinks it's weird, has been exchanging threatening notes with Iran about leaving Syria alone. Israel doesn't want Syria, which it dated a couple of times but was turned off of when Syria started picking its teeth with a machette; it just hates Iran so much that it doesn't want that country to get anything it wants.

Oh, and we mustn't forget the Kurds, who are fighting for their own piece of Syria. If Vesampucceri allies with them in its fight against al-Elephantine, it could anger Turkey, which doesn't want its own Kurds to get any ideas. Stories about twins contain so many entertaining possibilities!

"It's like high school with nuclear weapons!" exclaimed token smart person Amy Sheshutshotshitbam. After a moment, she added: "And better complexions..."

The situation is further complicated by the fact that al-Elephantine is an avowed opponent of Islamic State, the terrorist group that wants to establish a Muslim stupiphate across the Middle East. While the United States opposes IS, it has been reluctant to consider Syria an ally because, you know, mumble, mumble, chemical weapons attacks on its own people and, mumble mumble, stuff.

"Complicated," token smart person Sheshutshotshitbam commented.

"Would any military action by the United States against the sovereign nation of Syria be considered a provocation by the peace-loving Fenwickian people that would require a swift and brutal response that could easily escalate to a nuclear conflagration that would engulf the world?" mused Rupert Mountkilamanjoy, the Prime Minister of the Duchy of Grand Fenwick. "You might say that – I couldn't possibly comment!"

Aware that the stakes are high, the United States has tread lightly in the region. For example, President McDruhitmumpf's Wednesday tweep appeared on the first anniversary of the Vesampuccerian bombing of a 7/11 parking lot outside of Damascus in retaliation for that week's al-Elephantine chemical atrocity. Within a week, the parking lot had been restored and customers were busy enjoying their schwarma smoothies, but a message was sent. The meaning of the message has a wide variety of interpretations, but sending it was considered almost better than doing nothing.

What are the prospects in Syria? "As long as the President doesn't try to order Chinese food in the middle of the night," token smart person Sheshutshotshitbam answered, "the world should be safe."

"I'm stocking up on canned food," answered national security expert Donneednopennance.

Ira Nayman

9. THE SLEEP OF REASON PRODUCES... MONSTERS

Journalism 101: If Something is Too Bad to be True...

by FRED FLEEGLE-GRIEBFLEISCHER, Alternate Reality News Service Mystery/History/Journalism Writer

If the story had been true, it would have broken the Alabota special election wide open. Like, abyss looking into you wide.

A middle aged woman who identified herself as Rebecca deMorningloree walked into the *Alternate Reality News Service* with a calico rhinoceros and the claim that she had been sexually assaulted by Reduhblican candidate Roy Moorepowertooya when she was 12. Once she had calmed her pet with some Rhino Chow, she stated that when she became pregnant, Moorepowertooya forced her to have an abortion. Then, he spit on the flag, kicked a dog (to celebrate the fact that it is no longer illegal) and said in a rasping voice, "!eveels ruoy no toggam a dna noitaloiv gnikrap a teg uoy – htaerb uoy taht gnihtyreve eveileb t'noD !kciphtoot ym si nataS ! tophsaw ym si baoM"

Good enough for us. Roy Moorepowertooya was a flag spitting, dog kicking Satanist (who also happened to sexually abuse women). Surely this would be enough for the Reduhblican Party to reunsupport his campaign? And, perhaps, even sway a handful of voters? (They take the flag very seriously in Alabota.)

Even as Sex/Scandal writer Madame Madeleine De La Oovratura-Columbine interviewed deMorningloree, red flags (signifying a 20 yard penalty and loss of anonymity) emerged. When the journalist asked why she had such a deep voice, deMorningloree replied that she had been drinking Vodka non-stop since the assault 35 years ago.

When De La Oovratura-Columbine asked her why she had a moustache, deMorningloree responded that after the assault she ran off to join the circus. She wanted to be the lion tamer, but opportunities for women were limited back then, so...

As the interview was being completed, one of deMorningloree's breasts started to make a loud hissing noise and seemed to collapse. Without even waiting for a question, she explained: "I have Obfuscatory Physiological Inversion Syndrome. When we're done, I'll head to a gas station and be good as new in no time!"

When confronted with the accusation that she was actually a man masquerading as a woman, deMorningloree didn't deny it, saying, "That just makes the abuse more poignant, doesn't it?"

Apparently agreeing, De La Oovratura-Columbine wrote the expose, including a screaming 72 point headline (somebody had stepped on its toe) and three inflammatory callouts (they were made of asbestos...or papier mache – we find the word "inflammatory" confusing). Minutes before the article was to be published, somebody yelled, "Stop the presses!"

Apparently, it was deMorningloree. His trousers had been left in the press too long and caught fire. While he was wearing them.

Around that time, though, Pops Moobley, who works for the *Alternate Reality News Service* in a vague but important capacity, took Editrix-in-Chief Brenda Brundtland-Govanni aside and pointed out to her that if deMorningloree was a man, he could not get pregnant, so he could not have an abortion. After being walking through the specifics of sexual reproduction using a seventh grade text on the subject, Brundtland-Govanni spiked the story.

The astroturf at ARNS headquarters is going to need major repairs.

Why would somebody try to interest a serious news publication (be kind – we're going through a messy divorce) in a highly plausible but ultimately false story? "It could have been an honest mistake," Pops Moobley, ever the decrepit southern gentleman, allowed. "But, you ask me, he was trying to discredit us for all of the critical reporting we've done on the McDruhitmumpf administration." When asked why he thought that, Pops Moobley gave us a link to deMorningloree's Farcebook page; the first post was all about how he planned on, "feeding a major news publication (about whose divorce I have no sympathy) a highly plausible but ultimately false story to discredit them because of all of the critical reporting they've done on the McDruhitmumpf administration!"

Except for the fact that the post only ended with a single exclamation mark, it all makes sense.

After the story was rejected, deMorningloree was spotted in New Yoricknuhemwell, getting a vented latte at a local chain coffee shop, walking into a hair stylist's, walking out after he saw the outrageous prices they were charging, getting a haircut at a barbershop across town and finally entering the office of Project Vino Veritas, an alte kocker right organization intent on promoting the cause of fair journalism by driving out of business anybody they disagree with.

Now it all makes even more sense, the dearth of exclamation marks be damned!!!!!!!!

"Yeah, we most assuredly have come to an unusual place in the history of journalism," Pops Moobley commented. "This just goes to show that due diligence ain't just a Canadian TV series from the 1990s!"

The Silent Squeam

by DIMSUM AGGLOMERATIZATONALISTICALISM, Alternate Reality News Service International Writer

Sergei V. Skripalonovich and his daughter Yuhulia were sitting on a park bench in Salisbury (which supplies 95% of the steaks for TV dinners around the world), enjoying the gloom of the English countryside when his skin erupted in blue polka dots. Before anybody knew what was happening, Skripalonovich, a Fenwickian spy turned informant for England's fictional MI16, started yodeling tunes from the hit Broadway musical *Oklachussets!*

The Skripalonoviches were rushed to hospital, where they were both treated for exposure to a nerve agent in a class called Novichok, a Fenwickian word meaning alternately "non-person" or "I cain't say no." As was a policeman who was called to the scene. And, a man eating a curry from a cart across the street. And, three young women who were skipping class (if they survive, they will have learned a powerful lesson about the value of education!). In all, 23 people, two dogs and a ferret were affected by the release of the poison in a public space.

"This was an attack on sovereign Britain, an attack which we must condemn in the strongest possible terms and respond to with the strongest possible action," British Prime Minister Theresa Caulmimaybebabe told Parliament. "We will be expelling Fenwickian diplomats from England. And, if the country does not get the message, we might just...expel more diplomats! That's how seriously we take this...despicable, despicable act!"

While some Vesampuccerian politicians denounced the use of the nerve agent, President Ronald McDruhitmumpf has remained silent on the issue. The silence of the president, whose squeamishness on criticizing Fenwick for anything more than spitting on the sidewalk (although, even in that eventuality, President McDruhitmumpf would likely argue that it needed cleaning) has become legendary, seemed to say, "Everybody knows that 25,273 people die every day in England. Ask anybody. They may not know what one plus one is, but they can tell you to three decimal places what the average daily death toll in England is. Why is everybody making such a big deal out of two people who haven't even died yet?"

As a matter of fact, only 1,438 people on average die in England every day, and that includes Wales. Even President McDruhitmumpf's silences make up facts to suit his emotional needs of the moment.

"Please, people, get a grip," smarmed Rupert Mountkilamanjoy, the Prime Minister of the Duchy of Grand Fenwick. "Yes, Fenwick was the only country in the world that produced Novichok nerve agents. But, we lost track of our stores of it years ago. For all anybody knows, a lone Fenwickian, perhaps somebody who does not approve of England's colonial past, or maybe somebody who simply does not like pickled goat curry, was responsible. Now, if you'll excuse me, there's a jetski with my boot prints on it, and I hate to keep it waiting!"

According to security expert Malcolm Donneednopennance, Fenwick is playing a dangerous game. "Fenwickian Roulette," he stated. "Put six bullets in the chamber and force other people to play with the gun. According to NATO rules, all members of the alliance must come to the aid of any member who is attacked. So, the bullets in **this** gun could be nuclear missiles!"

Despite this, President McDruhitmumpf refused to say anything about the attack. His silence appears to be saying, "NATO? Really? Europe has been using the Vesampuccerian military like so many GI Jerks since the end of WWII! Talk about taking advantage! While we're paying for their defence, they're paying for three hour wine lunches and abortions for any man who wants one! This can't go on."

Apparently, the President's silences can be filled with as much empty rhetoric as his speech.

Despite the Prime Minister's denials, Sergey V. Roblavrovinson, Fenwick's foreign minister, anchor on Fenwick's state-controlled news broadcast, official portraitist of the Fenwickian government and creator of interpretive dances chronicling the triumphs of Fenwickian history (such as the purge of the intellectuals after the revolution and the great famine of the 1950s), warned that traitors to the motherland would be dealt with harshly. "Naughty, naughty!" he wagged his finger scoldingly. "If you betray Mother Fenwick, you shouldn't go to England – the cuisine is murder!"

You could almost hear him twirling his imaginary moustache.

Security expert Donneednopennance hopped up and down like a six foot tall Mexican jumping bean. "Threats!" he shouted. "Did you hear what Roblavrovinson said? He has an interesting portraiture style, sure, but that shouldn't mean that we just ignore him threatening future attacks on Britain!"

And, still, President McDruhitmumpf refuses to comment. His silence is clearly saying, "Me and Mountkilamanjoy are best buds. I admire how he completely controls his government, media and economy. He admires my gullibility and positive response to empty flattery. Seriously, why would I want to jeopardize such a perfect relationship?"

In this case, the President's silence is self-explanatory.

Do Ossified Ocelots Oscillate?

by FRANCIS GRECOROMACOLLUDEN, Alternate Reality News Service National Politics Writer

President Ronald McDruhitmumpf was in High Dudgeon (an authentic 1830s shrimp farming village in Mississota, complete with the original 1830s shrimp) when he came to a...speed bump on the road to unthinking public adulation.

"Yer cheatin' Hillary," he said in full rhetorical demagogue, "that's what I call her – yer cheatin' Hillary. Clever, right? It's like the title of that song, only it's named after Hillary. Anyway, she wrote a book. You heard me right. A book. Who knew she had it in her? Course, her book is not as popular as my book. Humph! Pshaw! My book sold more copies than any other book in the history of bookdom. Not many people know that, but it's true. You know what she says? In her...book? You won't believe it. She says she lost the election because of interference from Fenwick. Can you believe it? Fake news, people. The fakest. What can you do with a woman like that?"

President McDruhitmumpf beamed as the crowd chanted, "Hang them high! Hang them high! Hang them high!"

Frowning, he went on: "Love the enthusiasm. Best enthusiasm of any crowd anywhere, trust me on that. But, uhh, you might want to work on that whole pluralization thing. Yer cheatin' Hillary – Gord, I love that! – she's only one person, but you keep saying 'them.' I know it seemed like she was everywhere, but –"

As the chant grew, an aide came onto the stage and whispered in the President's ear. His frown turned into a scowl and he barked into the microphone, "Make Vesmpucceri great again! Thank you," and walked off the stage.

What the hell happened?

"You want to know what the hell happened?" asked token smart person candidate Moana Pupuplatterese. "I'll tell you what the hell happened. What the hell happened was that the President was hoist by his own petty lard. That's what the hell happened."

Actually, that didn't explain what the hell happened, didn't explain it even a little bit. But, by that time, I had figured it out for myself.

When it was revealed on the campaign trail in 2016 that Dumbopratic candidate Hillary Roocartoncleveman used a private email account for official government business while Secretary of State, the McDruhitmumpf campaign almost collectively died of ecstasy.

In Fine Fettle (an almost authentic with some relatively unimportant made up bits 1960s irony farming community in South Coloregas), President McDruhitmumpf smarmed, "What is yer cheatin' Hillary – henh – like that? I just made it up. Just now. Really – it's like that song title, only it's about Hillary – what is she hiding? Could be anything. We don't know. Could be a family recipe handed down for generations that her relatives would kill her if they knew she made public. We don't know. Could be top secret government documents about troop movements in...in...some foreign country, oh, yeah, which could threaten the lives of our brave fighting men, women and lemurs if somebody were to hack her computer. What country? Let's not get bogged down in details. The point is: we don't know why she's using a personal computer, okay? We. Just. Don't. Know."

The fact that a subsequent government audit of Roocartoncleveman's emails showed that they mostly contained videos of cats running away from Roombas and rude jokes about the size of President Millard Fillingmorelesstaste's nose did not stop President McDruhitmumpf's supporters from chanting, "Hang her high! Hang her high! Hang her [etc.]!"

What the hell happened was that it was revealed the morning President McDruhitmumpf made his awkward retreat from a rally that at least six members of his administration had themselves used private email accounts to conduct government business. These weren't interns of assistants to undersecretaries of the Secretary of Pantsing, either: they included Official Son-in-Law to the President Adviser Jared Kushkushinthebush and former Racial Sensitivity Adviser to the President Steve O'Bannonallhope.

Oops.

"Supporters at this afternoon's rally just took the President at his word when he talked about the evils of government officials using private email accounts to conduct government business," pundit Rachel O'Schubermatthow punditted away. "If you convince people an action is immoral or illegal, people in your government shouldn't do it. Political science 101, people!"

Will the Grey House spin this to Reduhblican advantage? "Do ossified ocelots oscillate?" token smart person Pupuplatterese responded.

A press release put out by the Grey House early this evening seems to have answered the question. "Ronald McDruhitmumpf came to Washburningdington to flush the fen. When people in his administration use private email accounts, it is to keep the fen critters from knowing what they're doing, lest they try to upset the President's flushing agenda. When yer cheatin' Hillary did it, it was to hide the fact that she is pure evil. Completely different."

Well, what do you know? Apparently, ossified ocelots do oscillate!

Disaster Unpreparedness is One of Vesampucceri's Strengths

by MARA VERHEYDEN-HILLIARD, Alternate Reality News Service Disasters Writer

A month after Orville (the tropical storm that had mutated into a Hurricane – and not in a superhero kind of way, either – not the TV series or popcorn tycoon Reddedenbacher) landed, 93% of Puerto Rico has no clean water, 77% has no electricity and 81% have no idea where their towel is. Which leads to the non-musical (because why should musical questions be the only ones that are recognized for their aural qualities?) question: what the ferk is Puerto Rico?

According to a Rasputinmusson poll released into the wild yesterday, 79% of Vesampuccerians believe that Puerto Rico is either: a) a tasty dish at Chipotle's; b) a Mexican salsa singer who had just announced that he was cancelling a world tour so he could go into donut rehab, or; c) a breed of garden rhinoceros found in Central Vesampucceri. Fully 23% of those surveyed answered "all of the above" **even though it hadn't been offered as a choice on the survey!** And, keep in mind, this was after weeks of coverage of hurricane Orville in the media.

Clearly, there was little sympathy for the plight of the Puerto Ricans.

"But, they're Vesampuccerian citizens!" token smart person candidate Reginald Formaldehydit cried.

In fact, Puerto Rico (Spanish for "my partner is named Rico," which makes more sense if you watched a lot of TV during the 1980s) is an archipelago among the Greater Antilles in the Caribbean Sea. It has been a territory of the United States since 1898 (although, given that it is not a state and, therefore, its citizens don't have any say in national policy or vote for President or Congress, it feels a lot longer to many of them). The distance from Puerto Rico to the Vesampuccerian mainland is 3,529 kilometres (2,193 in real units of distance). Its population is 3.4 million (12 in real units of influence). Its main exports are pharmaceuticals, petrochemicals and a creeping feeling of heart-wrenching discontent.

Thank the Gord for *Wiwipedia*! It's a journalist's best frie – whoa! Flash me back to writing essays for Mister Robpeterpaipaul's high school history of water fountain hygiene class, man!

Two days after Orville hit, President Ronald McDruhitmumpf tweeped, "ru kidding me? Helping Porto roco will blow massive whole in fed budget! #fiscalresponsibility #noseriouslydontlaugh". Pundits sensed that the President was less than enthusiastic about giving Puerto Rico disaster relief help, even though he authorized generous amounts of it for Florabama the week before. And, Texainois the week before that. And –

"But, they're Vesampuccerian citizens!" token smart person candidate Formaldehydit cried.

Two weeks later, San Juan Mayor Carmen Yulin Cruztyrybredstix publicly begged the federal government to send help to distribute the food and water that was sitting on the dock and to rebuild the electricity grid. In response, President McDruhitmumpf tweeped: "Porco Rosso hadnt had electric for years #dontblamecrumblinginfrastructureonfederalgovernment". Then, a minute and a half later, he tweeped: "untruthing mayor Carmen is a nasty woman. Mean, I mean. FEMA doing great job. Best ever. Hurricanes fear FEMA – thats how great it is!"

That's right: the President double tweeped her!

"But, they're Vesampuccerian citizens!" token smart person candidate Formaldehydit cried.

Riiiiight. Yes, they are. Thank you for pointing that out. Again.

Yesterday, it was announced that at least 40 Puerto Ricans have died of Yuckypitoowie, a disease transmitted by drinking unsafe water (given that most of the bottled water donated to hurricane relief is still sitting on palettes in San Juan Harbour, desperate people have been drinking out of muddy streams, closed polluted wells and each other's armpits). Mayor Cruztyrybredstix has created a Web page offering demons from Hell her immortal soul if one of them will just get supplies to her people; unfortunately, since electricity keeps going out in San Juan, she cannot check to see if any have responded.

However, President McDruhitmumpf responded. Boy, oh boy, did he respond. At 2:37 this morning, he tweeped: "Cannot keep FEMA, military & First Responders in PR 4ever! #suckitupandfixyourowndamnproblems".

"But, they're Vesampuccerian citizens!" token smart person candidate Formaldehydit cried.

Yeah, okay, you know that being a token smart person involves more than just repeating the same point over and over again, right?

"But, what if nobody's listening?" token smart person candidate Formaldehydit argued. "Puerto Ricans are Vesampuccerian citizens, so why aren't they treated the same as Florabamans or Texainois...ians...es?"

Because Puerto Ricans don't vote in Vesampuccerian elections. Haven't you been paying attention?

"Oh," token smart person candidate Formaldehydit ohed. After a couple of seconds he added, "Sucks to be them, doesn't it?"

It wasn't an especially astute comment, but at least it was different, so I decided to include it in the article.

Carp Per Diem

by MARA VERHEYDEN-HILLIARD, Alternate Reality News Service Disasters Writer

Where do government contracts come from? Do they fall from the sky? Are they squirted out of a wormhole from another universe? Are they – and this might be the most far-fetched theory of them all – actually vetted and approved by human beings...in government?

This is the non-musical (but it enjoys listening to music, and you would think that would count for something in this Philistine world) question that is not being asked in Washburningdington, but should. The reason for this non-question question is the awarding of a $300 million dollar contract to rebuild Puerto Rico's power grid after it was devastated by Hurricane Orville (not to be confused with the city next door to Andville) to Carp Corp, a company founded in 2015 that employs all of two people.

"We're very good at getting other people to do the work we're paid for," explained Carp Corp founder Andy Techgurumanski.

"It's called sub-contracting," Interior Secretary Ryan Zinkedinkedoo said *sotto voce* (which isn't a type of pasta dish from Italy, but it should be...it should be...).

"Right," Techgurumanski corrected himself. "That's what I said. Sub-contracting."

What does Interior Secretary Zinkedinkedoo have to do with this? Aside from the fact that he comes from Carp, Montdiana, the small city the company is based in and named after? Apart from the fact that Interior Secretary Zinkedinkedoo's son Rinke worked at a Carp Corp construction site for a summer? Overlooking the fact that Joe Colonoscopa, the founder of HIBACH Investments, which owns a majority share of Carp Corp, was a major donor to the McDruhitmumpf campaign? Other than all of that?

Taking a page out of his boss' playbook (more like photocopying the page, since his boss seems to still be working from it, too), at 2:37 in the morning, Interior Secretary Zinkedinkedoo tweeped, "Only in elitist Washburningdington would being from a small town be considered a crime." Mostly, this confused people. The photocopy was obviously smudged in key places.

Realizing that he hadn't helped his cause, Interior Secretary Zinkedinkedoo went on to say (and during business hours, at that) that, "I welcome any and all investigations" of his relationship with Carp Corp. In the same way that President McDruhitmumpf will make his tax returns public?

"Oh, that's low," Interior Secretary Zinkedinkedoo carped. "It's only been a year since the President made that promise. You just need to give him time. I'm sure when he's ready, he'll release his taxes before the election is over." After a moment's reflection, he added, "Okay, before the 2020 election is over..."

Official Washburningdington is distancing itself from this contract faster than a starship at Warp Speed reaches Beta Regulon VI. "Thuh President has made it very clear that nobody in this administration had anythin' ta do with awardin' thuh contract ta Carp Corp," stated Press Secretary Wannabe-Panders, even though the President had been too busy tweeping about the NFL investigation of his campaign's ties to Fenwick (it was the middle of the afternoon, so you can forgive his confusion) to comment. "If y'all don't believe him, Ah'm sure thuh audit of thuh contract will prove it."

Hee hee – yeah, about that. There is a clause in the contract that says: "In no event shall [government bodies] have the right to audit or review the cost and profit elements." In legal circles, this is known as the "Keep Your Nose Out of Our Business" clause. (Which vies in sheer bloody-minded egregiousness with the clause in the contract that "waives any claim against Contractor related to delayed completion of work," aka the "Yeah, Yeah, We'll Get Around To It When We Get Around To It – What Are You, Our Mother?" clause.)

When asked if there would, in fact, be an audit of the contract, Press Secretary Wannabe-Panders responded, "Mara, Ah just answered that question – weren't you payin' attention?" Ah – uhh – what?"

Unofficial Washburningdington is scrounging around in the dumpster behind the Pancake Pit for scraps of food and doesn't have an opinion on the subject one way or another.

When San Juan Mayor Carmen Yulin Cruztyrybredstix said that the Carp Corp contract smelled fishy, Techgurumanski responded by tweeping at 2:37 in the morning: "Lady, we got 80 submarine-contractors doing...something in your country. We think. Maybe. You really wanna risk us pulling them and stopping...whatever?" Somebody had clearly scanned President McDruhitmumpf's playbook and sent the relevant pages to him; just as clearly, some of the data had been corrupted in the transmission.

Token smart person candidate Maria-Monique Tumuchcollarstarch said she would be happy to share her thoughts on the subject, but she had to talk to her broker about a great new investment opportunity she had just learned about first...

Bad Vibrations

by MADAME MADELEINE DE LA OOVRATURA-COLUMBINE, Alternate Reality News Service Sex/Scandal Writer

Betty-Lou Bibialowski couldn't understand why her husband Bardello had taken her vibrator and was about to throw it into a car compactor. "Hey, I use that!" she shouted. "And, anyway, isn't a car compactor overkill? A trash compactor not visual enough for you? The garburator in the kitchen too plebeian?"

"It's unVesampuccerian!" Bardello Bibialowski shouted back.

"No, it isn't!" Betty-Lou Bibialowski retorted. Shoutingly. "It's a Major Tingly with six settings and adjustable head! It's as Vesampuccerian as apple pudding! My mother used that vibrator! And, her mother before her! That sex toy was a hairloom!"

This was no ordinary family argument about an instrument of sexual pleasure. For Bardello Bibialowski, it was a **political** family argument about an instrument of sexual pleasure.

The company that manufactures the vibrator in question, Opalescent Occidental Hooha, Inc., had announced that it would be pulling all of its advertising from the *Sean Hanjobovverfist Show* on

Foxindehenhaus News. "Umm, yeah," an OOH, Inc. press release bashfully stated, "we love Sean, but his support for accused child molester Roy Moorepowertooya, weeelllll, it's kind of the opposite of the pleasure we'd like to think our products give people, you know?"

"Let's not jump to conclusions, here," Hanjobovverfist, hastily getting to his feet, cautioned on his show when the allegations against Moorepowertooya first surfaced last week. "In this country, you're innocent until you're proven guilty in a court of law. Unless you're Hillary Roocartoncleveman, of course. That goes without saying. Or, Barry W. Bushbamclintreagbush. If anybody didn't deserve the presumption of innocence...! Or, Bernie Macsandbinoffman. Or, George Sorobororos,. Or...or...or anybody who has ever been a Dumboprat, voted for a Dumboprat or watched a movie starring or made by any west coast liberal. But, uhh, other than that, innocent until proven guilty is the way this country works!"

Across the country, men have compacted, flame throwered and, in one memorable case that should be highly entertaining when it reaches the courts, fed OOH, Inc. vibrators to a gorilla in a zoo. Why have they singled out OOH, Inc. rather than Fellow Travellers Checks, Web site fakerealtor.com, Nature's Chemicals or any of the other close to a dozen advertisers that have pulled their business from Hanjobovverfist's show?

"Oh, I can make a pretty good guess," offerred token smart person candidate Jennifer Stefadopolous. "It has to do with genitalia...a particular gender's genitalia – do I have to draw you an anatomically correct map? Or, do you just want me to make a guess? I got a good one!"

Many of the Hanjobovverfist supporters made videos of the rage they directed at OOH, Inc.'s sex toys. One man tried to smash it to pieces on a marble countertop; instead, the marble shattered, sending a large slab crashing down onto his foot. Undaunted, if newly limpy, he smashed the vibrator against a wall, only to put a hole in the plaster. In rapid succession, he destroyed: a chair, a bird cage, a dresser, a second chair, a table lamp, a filing cabinet, a third chair and a metal wire sculpture of a baby's arm holding an apple. In frustration, he tried to break the vibrator with his teeth; the video ends with the man being taken to the hospital for emergency dental surgery.

Hanjobovverfist has taken the high road by personally attacking one of the leaders of the boycott, Media Matters President Angelo Carusharusone. "He obviously hates gays. That much, I can tell y – what? He's gay? Oh. Well. Doesn't matter. This so-called journalistic watchdog hates Jews. That much is ob – what? His partner of 14 years is Jewish? Dammit! Can I say that he...he...he's a lousy dancer? Anybody wanna challenge that? No? Good. Well, he is a terrible, terrible dancer. Naturally, this disqualifies anything he might say about Roy Moorepowertooya, me or sex toys!"

As often happens, sales of the product the right wing is attempting, with mixed success, to destroy have increased. "You could almost zay zales have tumesced," my good friend sex therapist Doctor Ruth Westfrankenheimer joshed with a twinkle in her eye.

"But, zeriously," she went on to say, "ve know zat Dumboprats already own ze majority of sex toys in zis country, including vibrators, dildos and magic cubes. Vat ve are seeing here is ze so-called 'veekend vibrator' phenomenon. Zat is when a woman buys a second device to use ven she vants to try somezing a little different, maybe a little exotic, yes?" Doctor Ruth explained that while women often give their regular vibrators mundane names such as Ralph, Waldo or Doctor Buttquencher, weekend vibrators are often given unique names like Flower of the Mall, Bobby Sixshooter and Joseph, The Technicolour Dream Catcher.

That fact has nothing to do with the article, but it tickled my fancy. Was it good for you?

Like Rats Flocking to a Sinking Ship

by FRANCIS GRECOROMACOLLUDEN, Alternate Reality News Service National Politics Writer

At least 12 Reduhblicans have announced that they will not be – sorry, make that 13...14 – at least 15 Reduhblican Congresspeople have announced that they will not be seeking reelection in 2018.

One of them is Senator Bob Heezareelcorker of Tennsylvania, who announced over three months ago that he would not be seeking reelection. That's almost six and a half years in normal person years. The Senator had clashed [did I say 15? I meant 18. And, rising...] with President McDruhitmumpf on personnel, policy and potato chips (which Senator Heezareelcorker called "the worst public health disaster since crack met cocaine").

Not being beholden to the special interests that politicians need to get reelected, Senator Heezareelcorker said he would not vote for any tax reduction bill that would add a single penny to the national deficit. So, why did he agree to vote for the Oh, My, We're Going to Make Out Like Bandits...I Mean, Really Help the Middle Class Tax Giveawa – Fairness – We Meant Tax Fairness Act, which could add as many as 150 trillion pennies to the national debt?

Because [sorry to interrupt, but this just in: there are now 21 Reduhblicans not running for reelection. That number – 22 – has passed 20, and is still going up] he's not running for reelection, he doesn't have to explain...anything, really. So, nyah nyah nyah to us. However, rumour is that once Secretary of State T-Rex "For The" Tillerovlandzman has been made to eat the plank and walk it (the McDruhitmumpf administration isn't good with the whole cause and effect thing), then no longer Senator Heezareelcorker will take his place.

Senator Heezareelcorker's cooperation on getting the tax bill passed was a steal at Secretary of State, and it only cost him 150 trillion pennies. For the Senator, it would have been a bargain at twice the price (if the Reduhblicans hadn't capped raising the debt – those fiscal fuddy duddies!).

Other people in Congress had other, more personal reasons. Pennsylchigan Representative Tim Turfablusmurphy stated that he would not be seeking reelection because he wanted to "spend more time with my family." As soon as he said that, alarm bells went off in the Department of Patently False Explanations, and with good reason: a few days later, it was revealed that the pro-life Representative had asked his mistress to have an abortion. And, she wasn't even [stop the presses: we're up to 25...26...27 Reduhblicans not seeking reelection] pregnant at the time!

Most of the legislators who plan not to run in 2018 are considered moderate by current Reduhblican standards (on the Attila the Hun-ometre, they score only 7.83 out of 10, as opposed to the Grey House average of 9.37 and former Presidential adviser Steve O'Bannonallhope's astonishing 37.99 – astonishing if only for his ability to breath with all of the foam constantly streaming from his mouth). The real reason most of them aren't running is that they can expect primary challenges from candidates who are even further right than they are, and they would rather bow out with their reputations in tatters than atomized.

Don't believe it? Remember Luther [28 Reduhblicans not running next year, but don't feel bad for them: they'll find cushy jobs in the public sector that pay enough to pacify their consciences for several lifeti – what? You don't feel bad for them? Well...okay, then...] Strangerthunfixion? He was set to be the Reduhblican candidate in the Alabota special election, until Roy Moorepowertooya primaried him (and Moorepowertooya didn't even buy him dinner first!).

Other candidates slathering to primary sitting Reduhblicans include:

◆ Altoona Mavenprocterow in New Jersington's 12th district. Mavenprocterow stood in the middle of 5th Avenue and shot somebody just to watch him die. The jury at his first trial was hung; anonymous letters to the jurors with a game of hangman featuring an almost complete hung body and their names with one letter missing may have had something to do with that. His second trial is set to begin in October, 2018; the main reason for the delay is that the prosecution is having trouble finding an untainted jury pool. Looking in Venezuela has been offered as a solution.

◆ [30 Reduhblican Senators and Representatives have announced that they will not seek reelection – is this a tsunami, or are they just happy to see me?] Meanwhile, in Texinois, Joe Hydeboundandgagged, a two-term State Senator despite repeatedly being fined for torturing small animals, is hoping to trade up to a House seat. "It's on accounta my support for the Second Amendment, henh henh henh," Hydeboundandgagged explained.

When I said extremist candidates were slathering to primary sitting Reduhblicans, I meant it as a metaphor to indicate how eager they were, but, if it actually describes a candidate's physical condition, can I be held literarily responsible?

◆ Then there's Adenour von Hyffeltowering in Idawaii, who likes to dress his children in white hoods and robes on Halloween. "I'm not a racist," von Hyffeltowring told his local national newspaper. "I just want my children to celebrate their heritage!"

As good as candidates like this look to people like Attila O'Bannonallhope, they tend to scare off a lot of ordinary folks. Moorepowertooya, for example, managed to lose a seat that hadn't been won by a Dumboprat since saddles were the next big military invention and people said "forsooth" a lot. Extreme candidates could result in the Reduhblicans losing control of one or both houses of Congress; in fact, if they are extreme enough, the Reduhblicans could lose control of houses of Congress that don't even [34! If these were celsius degrees, we would be in the middle of a heat wave, people!] exist.

"The Reduhblicans will, I'm sure, field fine candidates in the 2018 elections," commented House Minority Leader Nancy Pelligrinosi. "In the meantime, I'm having trouble deciding how to decorate what will soon be my new office. Can you take a look at these two fabric swatches and let me know which one you prefer?"

Pwn the Odium

by FRANCIS GRECOROMACOLLUDEN, Alternate Reality News Service National Politics Writer

I got tired of the bullshit.

Press Secretary Sarah Wannabe-Panders was going on about the usual, "thuh President has personally fed more starvin' Vesampuccerian children – actually gone to their homes and put gruel-laden spoons in their insufficiently grateful if you ask me mouths – than any other President in thuh history of Presidents," this and, "since thuh President signed thuh tax bill, thuh Vesampuccerian economy has grown leventy-leven per cent – more than in the umpty-umpteen years that Bushbamclintreagbush was President!" that, and I just had enough.

The next time she called on me, I asked, "Sarah, do you really believe the bullshit that comes out of your mouth, or are you deliberately lying to us on a daily, sometimes sentencely basis?"

There was a moment of stunned silence. Then, Press Secretary Wannabe-Panders tried to folksy her way out of the question: "Now, Francis, Ah hardly think that language was called for."

"Just to clarify," I followed up, "is the language you object to the word 'bullshit' or the word 'lying?'"

"Well, now," Press Secretary Wannabe-Panders smiled with her mouth but warped the wooden podium with her hands. "That's thuh kind of false dichomotry that thuh press loves to engage i –"

The reporter for the *New Yoricknuhemwell Times* shouted, "Don't make the issue about Francis' language! His question was totally called for! Answer the question!" Then, the reporter for the *Washburningdington Post* shouted, "Yeah! I'm mad as hell, and I'm not gonna take it any more!" Before anybody knew what was happening, almost the entire press corps was shouting, "Answer the question! Answer the question! Stop giving us indigestion! Answer the question!"

Press Secretary Wannabe-Panders held up a hand and loudly said, "Alright. Alright. Y'all got me." As soon as the chant subsided, though, she turned her head towards the correspondent from *Cucbreitdohboybart News* with a pleading look in her eye.

"Sarah," he began to ask, "Could you say a little something about the Federal Bureau of Instigation's treasonous plot to undermine the 2016 election by making false accusations against –"

He was drowned out in a chorus of boos that would not have been out of place at the premier of *The Room*. Somebody threw a balled up iPad at him. That's gonna leave a mark.

"Answer the question! Answer the question!" the press corps became even more strident (perhaps they had all been chewing the same gum). "Stop giving us a series of nonsensical digressions! Answer the question!"

"Okay. Okay. You want thuh truth?" Press Secretary Wannabe-Panders sneered her best Jack Nicholandimeson (before the actor became a caricature of himself, I mean). "Thuh truth is: you can't handle thuh truth!"

"Handling the truth is our job," I pointed out to a chorus of "Yeah!"s. Singer Alison Moyettootallgras would have been proud.

"Alrightey, then." Press Secretary Wannabe-Panders took a deep breath. "Y'all wanna know thuh truth? Thuh truth is that y'all're thuh most whiny, needy bunch of brats Ah have ever had to deal with, and that includes thuh seven year-olds Ah teach Bible class to. 'Sarah, Ah need those employment figures right away!' 'Sarah, can you get me that interview with thuh Secretary of Schmaltz – mah deadline is loamin' and Ah need a quote!' 'Sarah, will you marry me – Ah have a deadline and Ah need –' oh. Wait. That was Bryan. Still, you get thuh point – y'all're a bunch of children pretendin' ta be adults who have somehow managed ta con thuh public into thinkin' you're important to democracy. How's that for truth?"

"But," I protested, "Answering questions is your job!"

"No!" Press Secretary Wannabe-Panders shouted dentures-rattlingly. "Whatever gave you **that** idea? That's just crazy talk! Mah job is to make sure that thuh President of thuh United States of Vesampucceri looks good in thuh press! If that answers your dang questions, well, lucky you. But that's not what Ah'm here ta do!"

"Can I quote you on that?" the *Washburningdington Post* reporter asked.

"Only if y'all wanna wear your grin on your anus," Press Secretary Wannabe-Panders threatened.

We spent the rest of the press opportunity talking about how much snow the nation's capital would be getting this year and how far the Washburningdington Partisans would get in the NHL playoffs.

Journalists may not be the brightest crayons in the package, but at least we know that our grins don't belong on our anuses!

E Deplorables Unum
The President is Wrong? Put Stock in It!

by GIDEON GINRACHMANJINJa-VITUS, Alternate Reality News
Service Economics Writer

You know how simulating weightlessness in a plane looks totally unappealing to anybody who isn't a regurgitation fetishist? Well, now you can have all the excitement of freefalling without leaving the ground. Whether you want it or not.

On Friday, the New Yoricknuhemwell Stock Exchange plunged 666 points (and, we're not talking fixing a toilet, here! – although the brokenness is really what is at issue, not the locale). Pundits suggested that water cooler heads would prevail over the weekend and the market would right itself on Monday – they should have taken Friday's results as an – ahem – Omen. The day the market reopened, it lost 1,271 points; this was the largest loss in a single day since an ichthyosaurus looked up and said, "I wonder what that streak in the sky is..."

Over the two days, the market lost eight per cent of its value. When the film of this event is made, "Tubular Bells" will be the theme song.

Critical consensus quickly congealed on inflation as the conscienceless crepuscular culprit. As an editorial in the *Wall Street Infernal* stated: "Inflation creeps into your joints and muscles and causes painful inflammation, and, no matter how much ointment you rub on it, the suffering never seems to end. Inflation is the friend of a friend who invites himself to your party, drinks all of your booze and makes a pass at your wife. When it's really high, inflation makes a pass at your daughter for good measure. Inflation is the water damage done to the foundation of your home, and you wonder why the books in your library seem to be tilted at a precarious angle? In short, there is no way that inflation is our friend."

Blaming inflation for the market's plummeting correction – plumection – seemed glib to a small number of economists, who, instead, blamed computer trading. "They say that a sell order can travel around the world in the time it takes a proper valuation to get its boots on," said Nobelthingido Prize winning economist Paul Krugalougieman. "I don't know why proper valuations are said to wear boots when they don't have any feat, and sell orders don't have to go around the world, they just have to go to the floor of the exchange. Otherwise, the point is well taken."

What, uhh, point would that be?

"That computer trading programmes accelerate boom and bust cycles," Krugalougieman tried not to roll his eyes at us.

Finally, there was one pundit who believed that the market had been way overvalued and the drop in stock prices was necessary to bring them back to what they should have been. But, the Biz Whiz has his own column, so he can talk up that theory all he wants there.

As many stock brokers enviously eye their windows, what does this sudden drop mean for what is really important: politics?

Throughout his first year in office, President Ronald McDruhitmumpf tied his fortunes to the stock market. On January 21, for example, he said, "The market is already soaring, folks. They know we're going to get Mexico to pay for the border wall, repeal and replace Bushbamclintreagbushcare and make Vesampucceri great again! It's mid-morning in Vesampucceri, and the market is already rewarding us with a delicious brunch!"

As the President's promises went unrealized, his message shortened, to the point where he was telling rallies and tweeping, "Stock market up. Me good." There are at least 47 known instances of President McDruhitmumpf taking credit for the rise in stock prices (for purposes of clarity, the speech he gave to the Denver Chamber of Monsters in which he repeated the phrase over and over for 47 minutes was only counted once). Sources within the Grey House state that the President screams "Stock market up. Me good!" at the television set whenever somebody says something he doesn't like.

One bright spot in the market has been the rise in the stocks of throat lozenge manufacturers.

Still.

If you take credit for stock market gains, what happens when the stock market drops faster than a coyote off a cliff?

"We have a saying in the token smart person community," said token smart person candidate Amy Sheshutshotshitbam: "'He who lives by the market, dyes the stains on his underwear by the market.' That certainly appears to be true, here, although the President probably has people to clean his delicates, so whether or not he learns any lesson from what happened is an open question."

Personally, I would prefer an open bar, but, as I would find out token smart persons say if they would just invite me to one of their debutante balls, journalists can't be choosers.

The McDruhitmumpf Administration
Insubordination Response Algorithm

SPECIAL TO THE ALTERNATE REALITY NEWS SERVICE

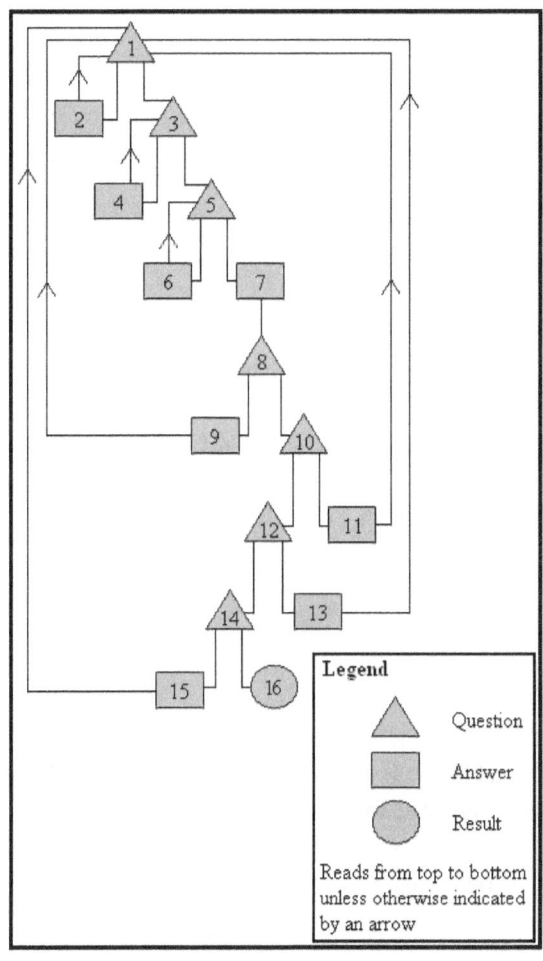

1. Have you said or done anything that would anger the President?

NO 2. Give it time, friend. Give it time. GO TO 1

YES 3. Has your statement or action that angered the President been reported on by the press?

NO 4. Give them time, friend. Give them time. GO TO 3

YES 5. Was your statement or action that angered the President reported in the left wing or right wing press?

RIGHT 6. No harm done, then. The story will be buried between accusations that Special Prosecutor Robert Meullitallover is secretly an Alpha Centaurian sent here to weaken our world's defenses to prepare us for our alien overlords, and reports of George Sorobororos' fake prostate exam results. GO TO 5.

LEFT 7. President McDruhitmumpf tweeps about what you said or did. It is not a happy tweep.

8. Does the media pick up on the tweep?

NO 9. You're getting really good at the whole dodging a bullet thing, aren't you? Lavish praise on the President privately and hope he accepts your grovelling. GO TO 1

YES 10. Does this start a downward spiral of tweeps leading to more media coverage leading to more tweeps leading to even more media coverage?

NO 11. Just because you can't see it doesn't mean the bullet isn't looking for you. Still. Privately offer the President your resignation and start polishing your resume. GO TO 1

YES 12. Does the news cycle move on to another crisis?

YES 13. The bullet stopped just short of your heart. You may feel intermittent chest pains for the rest of your life, but your career is, for the moment, safe. GO TO 1 and never sin again

NO 14. Are you still furthering the President's agenda?

YES 15. The bullet stopped just short of your heart, but it contains explosives that could go off at any moment. Try doing your job with **that** hanging over your head! GO TO 1

NO 16. If you don't resign, you'll get to hear the President say his second favourite phrase in the whole world: "You're eternally fired!" Don't let the damage to your reputation hit your ass on the way out.

Notes

There's no delicate way to put this, so we'll just come out with it: current revolving door technology is not sufficiently advanced to accommodate all of the senior McDruhitmumpf administration officials who have left the Grey House in the President's first year in office. The rear entrance to the building now appears to sport a revolving big hole in the wall to handle the traffic.

Okay, maybe we could have put that a little less indelicately, but the point is that a pattern can be discerned within the seeming chaos of goings and more goings from the Grey House. The McDruhitmumpf Administration Insubordination Response Algorithm is an attempt to tease out the main features of this pattern, just like your stylist teases out knots in your hair.

Some of the activities outlined in the algorithm may be difficult to codify. To use an obvious example, it's hard to know what speech or action will anger President Ronald McDruhitmumpf. Beating him at golf? Making a joke about son-in-law Jared Kushkushinthebush's hair? Making a joke about Kushkushinthebush's hair while beating the President at golf? Sometimes, the President's complaints can seem petty, sometimes the President can be...magnanimous may be overstating the case, but...not quite as petty. Yeah. Not quite as petty will have to do. This step is trial and error, just like walking through a field of land mines.

Or, take the question of Grey House activities being "reported on" by the press. This is sometimes a euphemism for "leaked to," except in the McDruhitmumpf administration, where the terms appear to be synonymous. President McDruhitmumpf appears to have taken Linkedinonalog's idea of a team of rivals to its logical extreme: he has assembled a team of take no prisoners fight to the death scorched earth psychotic mortal enemies.

This reveals one of the flaws of an algorithmic analysis of behaviours: while the algorithm tries to find commonalities between all of the cases, they rarely occur in a vacuum. In fact, President Scorched Earth – sorry, I meant President McDruhitmumpf reportedly has been in a continual state of high dudgeon (which is connected to the island of heightened animus by the isthmus of low comedy) since the second week of his administration. This undoubtedly makes the trigger for his anger much hairier than it would ordinarily be.

You may get the impression from the way that the algorithm is structured that sooner or later everybody in the McDruhitmumpf administration will be fired. You might say that – we couldn't possibly comment.

As ever, we caution that this algorithm is descriptive, not proscriptive; it is an attempt to show the world as it is, not as it should be. Because, boy, oh boy, the world should definitely **not** be like this!

Bluff and Consequences

by FRANCIS GRECOROMACOLLUDEN, Alternate Reality News Service National Politics Writer

Reduhblican politicians on both sides of the aisle have warned President Ronald McDruhitmumpf that if he in any way interferes with Special Prosecutor Robert Meullitallover's investigation into possible Vesampuccerian collusion with Fenwick's attempts to disrupt the country's elections, there would be consequences.

"If the President attempts to impede, block, hinder, prevent, obturate, occlude, jam up or otherwise interfere with the Meullitallover investigation," Senate Majority leader Mitch Wichconnelliswich swallowed his pride (and, apparently, a thesaurus) and told reporters, "not only will the Senate object, but the Senate will do so in the strongest possible terms. No half-measures for us. The strongest possible terms. That's how seriously we take this issue."

If the Senate was really serious about this issue, why hasn't it passed any legislation that would penalize the President if he attempted to interfere with the Meullitallover investigation? When asked this question, Senate Majority leader Wichconnelliswich grinned knowingly. People's blood turned to ice as far as Mongolia.

In the same news cycle, Speaker of the House Paul Ryboehnbachblisscrap spun, rinsed and tried to repeat his excited message that the Reduhblican tax cuts would create a new era of prosperity for all Vesampuccerians.* When a journalist pointed out that the government was about to borrow $300 billion to pay for part of the cuts, he blushed (he had a staff member apply it to his cheeks because it doesn't come naturally to him) and stated, "Oh, no, what I meant to say was that, uhh, obviously, the, uhh, work the Special Prosecutor is doing is vital – vital! – to the well-being of the country. And, uhh, so, as a consequence, if the President does anything to impede the, uhh, the, you know, investigation and stuff, the House of Unrepresentatives will do something about it. Believe you me, we will do something about it."

When asked just what action he planned to take if President McDruhitmumpf didn't heed his warning, Speaker Ryboehnbachblisscrap (whose spine was once featured on an episode of *Leonard Nimoyveytsuris' In Search Of...*) replied, "He will." When asked what he would do if the President moved against Meullitallover despite his warning, Speaker Ryboehnbachblisscrap (who is also the leader of the Reduhblican invertebrates caucus) replied, "He won't."

Well, we seem to have covered all eventualities, then.

"Oh, psssht!" token smart person Amy Sheshutshotshitbam did her best impression of a punctured tire (to complete the illusion, she stopped rotating her head). "Congressional Reduhblicans talk tough because polls show them that a large majority of Vesampuccerians, including members of their party, want Meullitallover to finish his investigation. But, if the President fires the Attorney General, the Deputy Attorney General, the Assistant Deputy Attorney General, the Vice Assistant Deputy Attorney General and all 17 Aides to the Vice Assistant Deputy Attorney General to get to somebody who will fire Bob Meullitallover, Reduhblicans in Congress won't do anything about it. They don't want the party to appear to be divided with the mid-term elections a few months away."

The token smart person suggested that this would not be the best course of action for the Reduhblicans. "Gooo ooooooooonnnn..." we prompted. Well, you see, the thing is, the President's endorsement has been the kiss of death for Reduhblicans who have run in special elections since he took office. A full, long, lingering kiss right on the lips, with one hand on each of the candidate's cheeks to ensure that he couldn't move his – eww! Why did I put that image in my head?

"So, if I understand what you're saying correctly," Senate Majority leader Wichconnelliswich, half to three eighths of whose job entails purposefully misunderstanding what people are saying correctly, "we should pass legislation preventing the President from interfering with the Meullitallover investigation because that will anger him enough that he will speak out against us which will lead to us keeping control of the Senate in the mid-terms?"

As he caught his breath, token smart person Sheshutshotshitbam's eyes widened, she nodded vigorously and she replied, "Un hunh."

Senate Majority leader Wichconnelliswich steepled his fingers (when he was a junior senator, he had stapled his fingers to his desk to protest a procedural motion that nobody else cared about; he found this much more conducive to rational thought, and it had the added bonus of not requiring the Senate to replace his desk) and responded, "Intriguing."

After he left the article, token smart person Sheshutshotshitbam's eyes returned to their normal size, her head stopped bobbling and she said, "He won't listen, of course. Deference to party authority is part of the Reduhblican hindbrain – it's a drive almost as important to them as sex. More important to their leadership. Has been since at least the Cretinaceous Age. I just like the idea that he'll have a few sleepless nights now that I have implanted the idea in Speaker Wichconnelliswich's head..."

* In the one per cent. It all depends on the definition of all.

Ending Voter Fraud Requires Conviction

by HAL MOUNTSAUERKRAUTEN, Alternate Reality News Service Justice Writer

Somewhere in Ronald McDruhitmumpf's Vesampucceri, a woman has been sentenced to five years in prison for voting.

Crystal Bricksandmordorson was on supervised release (it's like supervised recess in kindergarten, only with more ankle bracelets) for a conviction of tax fraud during the 2016 election. All the cool kids on supervised release were voting, so, to get along, she decided to cast a ballot in the hopes that they would let her sit at their table during lunch.

What she did not know, because it just happened to slip the mind of every single person that she had encountered in the justice system, was that in South Texalina you weren't allowed to vote until your sentence was up. And, your sentence included supervised release (since it happened on school property).

"This is a travesty!" shouted Vesampuccerian Civil Liberties Union lawyer Lee Gelernthelplessness (he was attending WrestleCraziness and was having trouble being heard over the crowd...he may also have been a bit emotionally worked up...). "What about the guy who was convicted of voter fraud in North Carolexas? This is clearly a case of legal sexism!"

Gelernthelplessness was referring to Dewey George Gidtoocumbover Jr., who voted twice in a Reduhblican primary in 2016, was sentenced to supervised probation (which is like supervised release, only with less teasing from the other children on the playground), community service (which is like being forced to play with the unpopular kid, only not really) and a fine (which is like losing your allowance for a week, only you would rather have used the money to pay rent instead of buying comic books).

Probation...five years in jail. Five years in jail...probation. Seems like quite a difference, there.

Token smart person Amy Sheshutshotshitbam disagreed with Gelernthelplessness. "What about the woman who was convicted of voter fraud in Iowisiana? This is clearly **not** a case of sexism."

The token smart person was referring to Terri Lynn Yumrotidebeauffe, who was caught trying to cast a second ballot in person after mailing in an absentee ballot. She explained to the police that the reason she tried to vote twice was because she believed then candidate McDruhitmumpf's unsubstantiated claims that the election was rigged and that her first ballot would be changed to a vote for Hillary Roocartoncleveman. She had to balance that out, don't you know.

Folks, I really do wish I was making this shit up.

Unlike Bricksandmordorson, Yumrotidebeauffe was given a deferred judgment (which is like your mother telling you to wait until your father gets home, but with more lawyer's fees). If she successfully completed her probation, Yumrotidebeauffe's conviction would be expelled from the record (unlike what you did at school, which your parents would hold against you until you were at least 87).

If Yumrotidebeauffe's harsh (it makes the winds of Venus look like a good environment for parasailing) sentence was not a case of sexism, what could have been at the root of it? Any ideas? Anybody?

Oh, come on! Token smart person? VCLU lawyer? Don't you have **any** idea why Crystal Bricksandmordorson was given such a harsh sentence? Any idea at all?

"Umm..." hemmed token smart person Sheshutshotshitbam.

"Err..." hawed lawyer Gelernthelplessness.

Would a hint help?

"Yes, please," token smart person Sheshutshotshitbam pleasantly acknowledged.

"If you insist," lawyer Gelernthelplessness gruffly acknowledged.

Could it have been a case of...VWB?

Token smart person Sheshutshotshitbam facepalmed. "Of course!" she agreed.

Lawyer Gelernthelplessness snorted and replied, "Yeah, I thought that was what it might have been."

VWB is, of course, Voting While Black. While not technically illegal, many states of the union have made it very, very, very, very, very difficult for people not of pallor to cast votes. Laws that restrict early voting in some precincts are attempts to curb VWB. Laws that demand specific forms of ID that cost money, thereby making voting harder for people with limited incomes, many of whom live in minority communities, target people attempting to commit VWB. Placing police squad cars at the end of streets with voting polls in predominantly black neighbourhoods is a form of intimidation to discourage VWB.

"When you say it out loud, it seems obvious," token smart person Sheshutshotshitbam sheepishly stated. "But it's hard to believe that here in 2018, VWB is still a thing."

Does it make it easier to believe when you know that the Injustice Department of Attorney General Jeff "Self-regard" Sesspoolpandemic has been looking at ways to further undermine the Voting Rights Act after the Extreme Court gutted it in 2013?

"Well, yeah," token smart person Sheshutshotshitbam sighed. "When you put it that way..."

Ira Nayman
The Conversion of the Apostlitician Paul on the Road to Family Guy

by FRANCIS GRECOROMACOLLUDEN, Alternate Reality News Service National Politics Writer

"I am retiring to spend more time with my family," is the political equivalent of "The dog ate my homework" or "I promise to pull out in time." Everybody says it; nobody (less a few gentle souls who probably shouldn't be allowed to have advisers for their trust fund) believe it.

In 1973 Gloucester McFilialov, a Dumbopratic Senator from the great(...ish) state of Omabraska announced that he was retiring to spend more time with his family. He was an orphan. His only known living relative was a cousin twice removed (then removed a third time for good measure, then removed a fourth time to really drive the point home, then removed a fifth, sixth and seventh time out of habit). And, he **hated** her. (As it turned out, there was more than a grain of truth to the fact that he embezzled campaign funds to pay for his mistress' outrageous bacon fetish – there was a whole bread factory!)

Then, there was the case of Grigor Ismailovitchov. In 1954, he resigned from the Fenwickian Politburo, claiming that, "I would better serve the glorious revolution by spending more time with my family." This seemed to fly in the face of the fact (part of the "body of evidence" for the argument of political wantonness) that Ismailovitchov's job had been to make up the lists of traitors to the cause who would be sent to Gulags for a little death and reeducation, as a result of which he was responsible for the demise of all of his nearest and (arguably not so much) dearest. (The fact that he committed suicide the next day by impaling himself 18 times on a shrimp fork spear indicates either that he regretted his actions, or that the government regretted his actions for him.) Long the revolution! – and all that.

Somewhere, in the distant reaches of unrecorded history (ie: before Farcebook), there was likely a caveman who grunted, "Me am stop be clan leader. Me spend more time with family." As if there was anywhere in the cave that he could get away from his family!

Soooooo, given this, what are we to make of Speaker of the House Paul Ryboehnbachblisscrap's announcement that he will not be seeking reelection in the November mid-terms "because I need to spend more time with my wife and two sons...I...I have two sons, don't I? It's been so long...so very, very long..."?

Under his breath, Senate Minority Leader Chuckie Schumaihargowmer asked, "Is there a weather condition that is more destructive than a tsunami?" I thought for a moment and responded, "I don't know. I'm not sure that it qualifies as weather, but, maybe...a meteor that causes an extinction level event?" He nodded and replied, "Yeah. Extinction level event. That sounds about right."

Senate Minority Leader Schumaihargowmer cleared his throat, spritzed, completed a couple of scales and, when he was convinced that he would be in fine voice, shouted, **"Oh, my Gord! This means that the speaker – the speaker! – the most powerful Reduhblican in Congress and one of the most powerful men in the world! – thinks the mid-terms are gonna be a meteor that causes an extinction level event for the Reduhblicans!"**

I should have seen that one coming.

When people began appearing at the front doors of nearby homes to see what all the commotion was about, Senate Minority Leader Schumaihargowmer blushed and quietly asked, "Too much?" There was a wistfulness in his voice that suggested that the Dumboprats hadn't had a lot to be over the top about lately, and that he wanted to take advantage of the opportunity while he could.

"While I hate to burst the Minority Leader's bubble," responded token smart person Amy Sheshutshotshitbam, "it is kind of my thing, so let me say that there are other ways of interpreting Speaker Ryboehnbachblisscrap's announcement. He could be retiring because of the unpopularity of the President. He could be retiring because of the sputtering economy. Or, the unpopularity of the President. Or, the seemingly endless parade of spending scandals that are plaguing the government. Of course, you can't entirely discount the unpopularity of the President. Or, how about...just off the top of my head...I'm only throwing this out for discussion: **the fact that Ryan was warned of the looming 2008 economic meltdown, and dumped a lot of his stock portfolio before it dropped dramatically in value?** Can you say conflict of interim...uhh, conflict of interference...umm, conflict of...of...of...can you say it? Please? Or, you know, the staggering, mind-boggling unpopularity of the President. A lot of factors could have gone into the decision, really."

"Ah, well," Senate Minority Leader Schumaihargowmer philosophically re-responded. "Bubbles, like governments, are ephemeral things that aren't meant to last..."

The Accidental Savant

by FREDERICA VON McTOAST-HYPHEN, Alternate Reality News Service People/Fashion/Pop Culture Writer

Peter Mettlerhededdfoo had a craving for casaba melons. He had never had a casaba melon before. Truth be told, he wasn't sure what a casaba melon was. If he thought about it for a moment, he may have realized that he had dreamed of casaba melons because one had been featured on the episode of *Homeland* he had watched before he had gone to sleep the night before. But, Mettlerhededdfoo was not an especially introspective example of *homo sapiens*, so he hied himself to the nearest Multimaximegamart in search of what was, to him, an exotic fruit.

Multimaximegamart has everything.

"The FBI always get high," he was saying to himself as he walked down the melon aisle. "Naah. The FBI – whose turn is it to cry? Naah. The FBI doesn't even try. Hmm...that could – to what? Try to what? Naah. The FBI – die! Die! D – ooh, what is that?"

As it turned out, it was a honeydew. Casaba-like, to be sure, but not a casaba melon. Apparently, Multimaximegamart does **not** have everything. Mettlerhededdfoo made a mental note to write a Farcebook post about this and, hoping for the best, bought a honeydew.

He ate it in the store. Not bad.

Peter Mettlerhededdfoo is not well known, even on social media, where everybody is famous to somebody. For example, he only has 247 Farcebook fiends. However, all of them are either senior Reduhblican officials, starting with President Ronald

McDruhitmumpf and Vice President Michael Pendenatendance, all of the members of the President's cabinet and senior Reduhblicans in Congress; or members of right wing media such as the *Cucbreitdohboybart* Web site and Foxindehenhaus News.

"It makes no sense," said token smart person candidate Abigail Anesticorfu. "Peter Mettlerhededdfoo is a dollhouse construction worker who lives in North Battlepixies, Montansas. He doesn't **read** newspapers, let alone write for them. He's never worked for a think tank – hell, he probably thinks a think tank is a battle vehicle equipped with AI! There is nothing in his background that would suggest that he would be a thought leader of a major political party. Or, for that matter, a thought follower. He's the sort of person whose head is filled with thoughts of cantaloupes, for Gord's sake!"

Casabas, actually, but the point is well taken. Why do the Reduhblicans follow Mettlerhededdfoo so avidly?

"Are you kidding?" replied a high-ranking Reduhblican official who insisted that we make clear that he was not Speaker of the House Paul Ryboehnbachblisscrap. "Peter is a genius! He knows exactly where we need to position our messaging before we do! Okay, sure, his obsession with melons is a little weird, but he helped deliver Virginois to us in 2016, so I say let them eat fruit!"

"What, Peter? Oh, he's a genius, make one mistake," said another high-ranking Reduhblican official who spoke to us on the condition that we made it clear that he wasn't Senate Majority Leader Mitch Wichconnelliswich, who in no way resembles a turtle with terminal gas. "The way he is able to distill a complex political position into a few words – words that often rhyme – well, sir, it's uncanny. Okay, sure, his obsession with melons is a little...out of the mainstream for my tastes – I prefer pears. But, he recognized that we had to delegitimize the Meullitallover investigation before it got out of hand weeks before we did, so what's a little melon fetish among fiends?"

"I don't know what you're talking about," Mettlerhededdfoo said as he walked home from the Multimaximegamart. "I don't know anybody named Paul Wichconnelliswich or Mitch Ryboehnbachblisscrap. Are they a new K-Pop duo or something? And, I'm no political strategist – I tried to grow watermelons this summer and they all died horrible deaths! I'm the last person I would trust to make the country work!"

UPDATE: Hours after Peter Mettlerhededdfoo posted, "FBI – die! DIE! **DIE!**" on Farcebook, Reduhblicans and their operatives started attacking Vesampucceri's police system. "The Federal Bureau of Instigations is so corrupt," President McDruhitmumpf tweeped at 2:37 the next morning. "So corrupt. They make Al Caponercussmuss look like Mother Theresa! Sad! And not winning!!!"

Later that day, Sean Hanjobovverfist burst a blood vessel talking about how the FBI had colluded with Hillary Roocartoncleveman to make it look like the McDruhitmumpf campaign had colluded with the Fenwickians to steal the 2016 election. As he was wheeled off the set of his show by a pair of burly EMTs, Hanjobovverfist weakly insisted, "FBI – Nixwatmondnewon – horned melons – Mountkilamanjoy – Sorobororos – connect the dots, people! Connect the...the do...uhhh!"

"Honestly, I don't know anything about any dots," Mettlerhededdfoo insisted back at him. "I weld beams on dollhouses. I'm about as political as a canary melon seed. Anybody who thinks I give good political advice has probably had their head smashed in a PSA about automobile safety! In super-slow motion!"

10. THE SLEEP OF REASON PRODUCES... AFTERWORDS

It's the End of the World as We Know It, And I Feel...Like Ordering Takeout

by MARA VERHEYDEN-HILLIARD, Alternate Reality News Service War/Disasters Writer

The greatest fireworks display in the history of the world happened yesterday. Most people just think of it as a nuclear war, but many of the survivors considered it the best light show since they closed the planetarium in their city/state/country/continent.

It started innocently enough: United States of Vesampucceri President Ronald McDruhitmumpf got the munchies while he was tweeping in the middle of the night and decided to order Chinese food. He must have dialled the wrong number, though, because he was connected to North Korean Gentleman President Dictator Kimsongfaluson Mah-Jhongg. President McDruhitmumpf insisted on ordering General Tso's Chicken, which Gentleman President Dictator Kimsongfaluson interpreted as an insult to his military. The exchange got heated, and eventually nuclear.

It seems likely that North Korea fired first, requiring the United States to retaliate. China, seeing much of its border with Korea destroyed, retaliated against the Vesampuccerian retaliation. As the

United States retaliated against China's retaliation retaliation, Israel, assuming that the nuclear exchange was about them, dropped nukes on surrounding Arab nations. Meanwhile, the Duchy of Grand Fenwick, realizing that its nuclear arsenal would go for nothing if it wasn't used right away, bombed Panama, South Africa and Luxembourg.

"That will teach those Luxey bastards!" Fenwick's Prime Minister Rupert Mountkilamanjoy cackled maniacally just before he drifted into a coma.

North Korea's lonely little nuclear missile tried to make it to the Vesampuccerian mainland, really, it did: it thought it could, it thought it could, but, no, in the end it couldn't, so it landed on Ottawa, Canada instead. Washburningdington was levelled in the first volley of rockets from China; President McDruhitmumpf survived because he was working at his Mara-Lara-Dingdong resort at the time the bombs started dropping. "People complained that I was spending too much time away from the Grey House," he gloated. "Well, who looks like a loser, now?"

The President was confident that the United States of Vesampucceri would be able to rebuild. "Okay, sure, California dropped into the ocean and New York is a smouldering pile of rubble. But, on the plus side, that's just that much less opposition to my agenda. Which has changed, by the way. Oh, yeah. Now, it's: 'Make Vesampucceri Function Again.' Got a ring to it, doesn't it? It'll look great on a baseball cap!"

A slightly the worse for being charred Senate Minority Leader Chuckie Schumaihargowmer (the other two Senate survivors were Reduhblicans, so even a nuclear war didn't shift the balance of power, although divisions within the much diminished ruling party remain strong) coughed. Coughed loud. Coughed long. We'll assume for the sake of argument that it was a cough of disapproval, although it could simply have been a sign of immanent congestive lung failure. Coughs can be surprisingly uncommunicative that way.

"You comin' fer my Pez dispenser collection?" said an Iowegas farmer who would only identify himself as "Billy-Bo-Jo-Bob" as he brandished a shotgun in my direction. "Cuz that may be the only nutrition fer miles around, and I ain't sharin'!"

I assured him I was just a humble journalist come to ask somebody who voted for President McDruhitmumpf what he thought of the man's performance, you know, given the destruction of the world and all. Not lowering the shotgun a micron, Billy-Bo-Jo-Bob answered, "That there President McDruhitmumpf said he was gonna sap the sewer. I didn't think it would take a nucular war to do it, but I do believe he has kept his campaign promise. So, good for him. Now, are you gonna get offen my land, or do I have to introduce your backside to some Prime, Grade A Vesampuccerian buckshot?"

Did the escalating war of words between President McDruhitmumpf and Gentleman President Dictator Kimsongfaluson lead to a situation where a minor disagreement about a midnight snack could end in the annihilation of the world? If so, the President has no regrets. With a shrug, he said, "Sure, I would have settled for sweet and sour pork ribs. But, that would have made me look weak in the eyes of the guy taking orders at the Chinese restaurant. When it comes to the food you put in your mouth, there can be no compromise!"

[EDITRIX-IN-CHIEF'S NOTE: You may be relieved to note that all of the *Alternate Reality News Service* reporters on Earth Prime 1-6-6-5-8-2 dash omega survived the nuclear blast. I'm not – damn cockroaches! – but you may be. My intention was to leave them there to survive the nuclear winter while replacing them with much more eager – and cheaper – new recruits. Unfortunately, Pops Moobley pointed out the clause in our contract with the reporters' which clearly states, "Management shall be estopped from leaving employees to survive nuclear winter and replacing them with much more eager – and cheaper – new recruits." Killjoy unions! So, we have relocated all of our reporters 1,237 universes to the left charm (Earth Prime 1-6-7-1-8-2 dash psi for you multiverse nerds); it is exactly the same as this universe, but without all of the worldwide death and destruction. In the multiverse, we can do stuff like that. If that's clear, you'll have to excuse me – I need to slap some sense into whoever negotiated our contract with the reporters' union!]

Ira Nayman

INDEX

BIOGRAPHY

Ira Nayman is profilic. Proficlic. Proclif - he writes a lot.

If you enjoyed *E Deplorables Unum*, you will probably love the eight previously published Alternate Reality News Service books. *Alternate Reality Ain't What It Used To Be*, *What Were Once Miracles Are Now Children's Toys*, *Luna for the Lunies!*, *The Street Finds its Own Uses for Mutant Technologies*, *Futures in the Mirror are Closer Than They Appear* are general collections of news, reviews, interviews and anything else you might find in your local newspaper. *The Alternate Reality News Service's Guide to Love, Sex and Robots* and *What the Hell Were You Thinking? Good Advice for People Who Make Bad Decisions* are collections of humourous science fiction advice clumns. *ARNS and the Man* is the first collection of idiotocracy articles. Print versions of all of the books are available online at Amazon, Barnes and Noble, Chapters/Indigo and other fine bookstores.

New Alternate Reality News Service stories appear regularly on Ira's Web site: *Les Pages aux Folles* (http://www.lespagesauxfolles.ca). These include two advice columns: Ask Amritsar (about love and romance and technology) and Ask the Tech Answer Guy (about anything to do with technology except love and romance). Readers are encouraged to submit their own questions for the advice columns. *Les Pages aux Folles* also contains topical political and social satire.

The Weight of Information, the pilot for a radio series based on Alternate Reality News Service articles, can be heard on YouTube.

Ira has also written five novels set in the multiverse that follow the adventures of investigators for the Transdimensional Authority, the organization that monitors and polices travel between dimensions, or the Time Agency, which monitors and polices travel in time. If you are somewhere you don't belong, doing something you shouldn't be doing, they find you, stop you and try and figure out what to do with you. The four novels in the series are: *Welcome to the Multiverse*, You Can't Kill the Multiverse**, Random Dingoes, It's Just the Chronosphere Unfolding as it Should* and *The Multiverse is a Nice Place to Visit, But I Wouldn't Want to Live There*. These books can be purchased from all of the usual suspects online, or from the home page of the publisher, Elsewhen Press.

Fans of Ira Nayman's science fiction writing are encouraged to check *Les Pages aux Folles* periodically for news about the availability of these and future stories.

* *Sorry for the Inconvenience*
** *But You Can Mess With its Head*

Connect with Ira online:

Twitter: https://twitter.com/#!/ARNSProprietor
Facebook: http://www.facebook.com/ira.nayman

www.ingramcontent.com/pod-product-compliance
Lightning Source LLC
Chambersburg PA
CBHW020321200626
46814CB00006BB/2352